The Flip Side of Money

Earl Sewell

The Flip Side of Money

sepia

**BET☆
BOOKS**

BET Publications, LLC

SEPIA BOOKS are published by

BET Publications, LLC
c/o BET BOOKS
One BET Plaza
1900 W Place NE
Washington, DC 20018-1211

ISBN 0-7394-6057-9

Printed in the United States of America

You can't raise grown people.

—Earl Sewell Sr.

1

Veronica

"Wake your trifling ass up!" Bonnie stood in the doorway of the bedroom and flipped the light on. "I said, wake your shiftless and trifling ass up!" The intolerant snarl of the words roared through the bedroom like a thunderclap. The warm blue comforter that was blanketing Veronica was viciously snatched away from her body.

"Why did you do that?" Veronica barked at Bonnie as she adjusted her eyes to the sudden brightness. "Have you lost your mind or something?"

"You know damn well why I did it. Now get your no-good ass up." Bonnie marched over to the foot of the bed, grabbed Veronica's left leg at the ankle, and flung it off the edge of the bed. "You're not staying in my house another night."

"What!" Veronica was irritated by Bonnie's intrusion and by her proclamation that she was being tossed out.

"You heard what I said!" Bonnie's bitter words were cold like an arctic wind. "Get up. I don't know where you're going, but you're getting the hell out of my house."

Veronica sat upright and glanced at the digital clock situated atop the small night table. "Bonnie." Veronica looked at her as if she was retarded. "It's one-thirty in the morning. Can't this drama wait until sunrise? I don't have time for this tonight." Veronica reached toward the foot of the mattress to retrieve the comforter.

"No. Get up!" Bonnie hissed through gritted teeth as she grabbed Veronica's arm and yanked her to her feet. "I'm not playing with you. Start packing your shit." Veronica studied Bonnie's light brown eyes, which were blazing with rage. "Let me go!" Veronica jerked her arm away. "Who the hell are you trying to manhandle? And why are you hollering at me like that?"

"My loudness is a reflection of how pissed off I am with you. Now get up so you can get out," Bonnie ordered as she retrieved from the closet the busted suitcase Veronica had arrived with a few weeks ago. Bonnie placed the suitcase in front of an open dresser drawer, then began shoveling her former friend's belongings into it.

"Come on, Bonnie. Can you at least tell me what is going on?" Veronica asked as she slipped on a pair of black cotton sweatpants and a matching top.

"I can't believe you did me like this. I've been your girl since childhood," Bonnie vented as she continued to shovel one dresser drawer filled with clothing after another into the large suitcase.

"Can you at least fold my things so they're not all balled up?" Veronica felt her anger swelling as she wiggled her bare feet inside a pair of white canvas gym shoes. "I don't like this, Bonnie. It's not right to wake me up from my sleep in the middle of the night and insist on putting me out. Where am I supposed to go? Huh? I have no place to go. What's the freakin' urgency?" Veronica asked as she purposely shoved Bonnie away from the dresser. She pushed harder than necessary, causing Bonnie to lose her balance and tumble to the floor.

"You shouldn't have done that," Bonnie huffed. Veronica had just given her the final justification to claw the side of her face with a swift swipe of her fingernails.

"Shit!" Veronica immediately placed the palm of her hand

on the side of her face, feeling the sting of the deep claw marks Bonnie had etched on her ear and cheek. "You don't put your damn hands on me!" Veronica shrieked with anger as she positioned herself to fight. "You want to fight me? Huh? Come on." Veronica encouraged Bonnie to take another swing. While Bonnie took a moment to calculate what her next move would be, Veronica lunged at her, snatched a fistful of her hair, and wrestled her down to the floor, face-first. Bonnie tried to jerk free from Veronica's clutch, but Veronica quickly maneuvered around her and placed the weight of her body on Bonnie's back.

"Let me go, Veronica!" Bonnie said, more as a threat than as a concession.

"No, bitch. First you tell me what the hell is going on." Veronica pulled back on Bonnie's hair, causing her neck to shift to an awkward position. Bonnie once again attempted to wrestle herself free from Veronica's clutch. For a brief moment, she tossed Veronica off of her back, but Veronica repeatedly slapped her with an open hand on the back of her head until she gave in.

"I don't want to fight you, Bonnie. You know you can't fight. You never could. Why are you doing this?" Veronica pleaded for the reason behind Bonnie's attack.

"Let me up." Bonnie's voice quivered. Veronica could tell she was losing command over her emotions. "Just pack your shit. I'll be waiting for you at the back door."

"Can't we talk about this?" Veronica asked, releasing her clutch and allowing Bonnie to return to her feet.

"No," Bonnie answered. "Not after what you did."

"What, Bonnie? What did I do that was so horrible?"

Bonnie glared at Veronica with contempt. "You certainly know how to play the role of innocent victim. Your ass just got off parole, and you're already back to doing the same dumb shit that got you locked up in the first place. I knew you were a thief, but I never thought you'd go this far. If you're not at the back door in fifteen minutes with all of your belongings, I'm calling the police." Bonnie paused in thought. "If my kids weren't in this house, Veronica, I'd knock your head through one of these walls."

"Don't let the kids stop you. Come on. I'm waiting for you. I want to see you try and do that." Veronica curled her fingers into fists and took the stance of a prizefighter ready for battle.

Bonnie backed away from her. "I've already taken your copy of the door key. Hurry up. I just want to get this over with," Bonnie said as she left the bedroom.

"Bonnie!" Veronica called to her now that she realized their physical scuffle had concluded. "It's December. It's cold outside. Don't do me like this." Veronica was now pleading for mercy. She caught up with Bonnie in the kitchen and studied her as Bonnie took a drag off a cigarette. A tin ashtray sat next to a butcher-block that sheathed an assortment of cooking knives. "I know you're not going to put me out on a winter night like this. That would be cold-blooded. Besides, who is going to watch your kids while you work the night shift? You can't just leave them with anyone."

"You know what? I'd rather bring my kids with me and have them sleep in the break room than leave them here with the likes of your thieving soul."

Veronica studied Bonnie's eyes and could see she was calculating something.

"I think the cold December air, the frozen blood pumping through your veins, and your cold-blooded heart won't have an issue getting acquainted."

"You're stressed, Bonnie. You only smoke when you're stressed or when something has upset you. What is it, girl? What happened? Don't do this to me. We go back too far."

"Veronica," Bonnie huffed with disbelief, "I can't believe you're standing here looking at me like you don't have a fucking clue as to what is going on. When I agreed to allow you to stay here, I gave you some rules to follow. I told you that if you ever broke one, or did something to my kids, I'd make you regret it. As usual, Veronica, you've fucked up."

"How, Bonnie? What did I do?" Veronica spoke softly, attempting to take a more understanding approach. She kept a close eye on Bonnie as she smashed her cigarette.

"Veronica, don't mistake my calmness for weakness. I'm using all of the restraint that I can muster up to keep myself from going ballistic on you. You're a fuckup, and I'm not going to put up with your shit any longer." Bonnie paused, and Veronica could feel the tension hovering in the air.

"The longer you stand there, the more I want to put an end to your shiftless existence." Bonnie unsheathed the largest knife from the butcher-block and pointed it at Veronica.

"Bonnie, put that knife down. Don't point it at me like that." Veronica eased away.

"I've tried to be a supportive friend to you. I let you into my home with my children where it's warm and safe. I've tried to give you time to get your shit in order. I was praying that you'd turn your life around this time. Instead, you've fallen into the same damn rut, and now you're stealing from me."

"Bonnie, please," Veronica interrupted her.

"Bonnie my ass!" Bonnie barked. "It's one week before Christmas, and you went into my bedroom and stole the money I'd saved up all year to give my kids a decent Christmas! You bitch!"

Veronica feared the murderous rage in Bonnie's eyes and the tremors of hate she was losing control over. Veronica's pulse quickened as the threat of a fatal confrontation seemed inevitable. This time Veronica didn't think she'd be able to talk her way out of harm or defend herself against Bonnie's unbridled fury.

"Stealing money from a friend is awful. But to steal Christmas from children! That's beyond words, Veronica."

"Look, Bonnie. I don't know what you're talking about." Veronica held her words for a moment as she shifted her eyes to the left. "I didn't steal anything. You know I wouldn't steal from you."

"Now you're going to insult me by acting like you're inno-cent." Bonnie moved swiftly toward Veronica but somehow re-sisted the temptation to plunge the blade into her abdomen. Veronica didn't like the point of a blade aimed at her abdomen, so she once again backed away.

"You need to slow down, Bonnie, before you do something that can't be undone."

"Right now I wouldn't feel any remorse if I gutted you like a hog and watched as you bled to death on the floor."

"I'll get out," Veronica conceded. "Just give me a minute. You're not in your right frame of mind. I'm going to get my suitcase. I'll be right back, okay?"

"You'd better hurry," Bonnie growled.

Fifteen minutes later, Veronica walked through the kitchen to the back door where Bonnie was standing. Bonnie opened the door wide so that Veronica wouldn't have any trouble ma-neuvering her bulky suitcase through it.

"Bonnie, it's fucking snowing outside. Look at it out there. There has to be at least six or seven inches of snow already on the ground," Veronica said as a gust of wind blew heavy snow-flakes inside. Veronica concentrated on the silhouette of an alley lamppost. She cringed at the sight of snowflakes falling rapidly through the beam of light.

"Bonnie, come on now. Let me stay here until the morning. People wouldn't do a dog like this."

"No, they wouldn't," Bonnie replied. "But with a snake like you, people would rather chop its head off than give it another chance to bite them. You're a snake, Veronica. I hope some day you'll change your ways."

"Well, it takes a snake to know a snake, now, doesn't it?"

"I suppose so. Do you have any of my money left?" Bonnie asked.

"I told you. I didn't take your damn money," Veronica an-swered defiantly.

"Okay. Have it your way, Miss Betty Badass. Speaking of badasses. Big Money Chuck was released recently, and I heard through the grapevine that he's searching for you. I'm praying that you were stupid enough to steal from him, because you know that people who cross Big Money Chuck pay one way or another."

"Don't go around wishing that harm will come to me. You'd better be careful of what you wish for, because it might turn around on you," Veronica warned, unwilling to allow Bonnie to direct bad karma in her direction. Veronica both feared and loved Big Money Chuck. At the present time, she feared him more than she loved him. She had her reasons for fearing him, but Bonnie didn't need to know why.

"What's the matter? Can't sleep in the bed you've made?"

"Screw you, Bonnie!" Veronica snapped back as she wheeled her suitcase toward the back door. She lifted her suitcase and set it in the deep snow on the back porch. Veronica stood in the doorway and began to button her flimsy winter coat as if she had an unlimited amount of time to ponder her predicament.

"You could have at least said that you were sorry for stealing Christmas away from my kids, wench," Veronica heard Bonnie snap at her; then she felt the powerful force of Bonnie shoving her out into the winter storm. The shove was so hard that she lost her footing, toppled over her suitcase, and fell face-first into the snow. By the time Veronica got to her feet, Bonnie had slammed the door, bolted it shut, and turned out the kitchen lights.

"Bring your ass out here, Bonnie." Veronica began kicking at the back door. "Come on. Bring your ass back out here! I know you hear me." Veronica continued to pound on the wooden door but concluded that it was useless to waste her time, breath, and energy.

"Shit," Veronica hissed. She picked up her suitcase and dragged it over to the stairway that led to the sidewalk. "Damn,"

Veronica bitched at the sight of the snow-covered steps. She carefully lifted and guided her suitcase down the porch steps to the bottom.

"My toes are already cold and getting wet," Veronica said once she reached the bottom of the staircase. She stooped down to finger a clump of cold snow out of her thin canvas gym shoes. She then searched her coat pocket for her knit hat but didn't find it.

"What the hell happened to my hat?" Veronica was irritable beyond words. "This situation is a major pain in my ass. Now I have to deal with my hair getting wet, my ears freezing, and the possibility of catching a cold," she said as she towed the suitcase along behind her as best she could. She trudged through a gangway that led out to the alley. She made a left turn and was greeted by blustering wind as she walked up to a side street, which she took to Madison Street, a main thoroughfare in Chicago. Traffic on Madison Street was creeping along at a turtle's pace because the city's snow plows hadn't plowed it yet. The sidewalks were barely passable on foot and would be even more difficult to travel while towing her large suitcase, which had a busted zipper and a bad wheel.

"Man, Veronica," she said to herself. "What are you going to do now?" Veronica glanced to her right in the direction of Austin Boulevard and the city of Oak Park, Illinois.

"I better not take my behind out of Chicago city limits and into Oak Park. The Oak Park police will most certainly view me as suspicious and will pester me." Veronica glanced to her left, back toward Central Boulevard, and decided it was best to head in that direction.

"That's one thing I don't like about this stretch of Madison Street," she complained as she slogged down the sidewalk. "The sidewalk is all ripped to hell." Veronica made it to the corner of Central Street and Madison where she decided to stop and regroup inside an all-night fast-food restaurant. She pushed open the door, maneuvered her way inside, and took a seat at a small table. She scrunched and released her frozen toes inside of her shoes to make sure they were still functional.

"My toes feel like they're about to fall off. The Hawk isn't playing tonight," Veronica whispered to herself as she considered why Chicagoans referred to bitterly cold Chicago nights like this one as "the Hawk."

The fast-food joint was warm and seemed like heaven for the moment. Veronica surveyed the dingy establishment, which had wet and grimy cardboard boxes blanketing the floor so that the owner wouldn't have to continually mop. The place was notorious for its rude service, but that didn't deter people from stopping in throughout the night for artery-clogging food.

"What happened, baby?" asked a shabby hobo, who was wearing a Santa Claus cap and was seated on the opposite side of the restaurant. "Did your old man kick you out of the house tonight?" He chuckled. He was apparently amused with his deduction. Veronica ignored the buffoon. She focused her gaze through the large window and began to think.

"Yeah, I am a snake," Veronica admitted as she replayed in her mind how she'd entered Bonnie's bedroom while she was at work and searched her closet for a spare pair of winter boots she could use. As she snooped around, she came across a white envelope marked CHRISTMAS FUND. It was resting at the back of the closet behind a small pile of gifts for Bonnie's children. When she opened it, she found one thousand dollars and a note to Bonnie from the father of her children. The note read:

Bonnie,
I know this isn't much. But here is five hundred dollars to put with the other five hundred you saved up. I'll call you and the kids on Christmas Day.

Veronica knew that stealing the money would risk ending a long friendship. "I wanted the money," Veronica mumbled as she tucked her fingers underneath her arms to warm them up.

"I didn't care about what was right or wrong, good or bad, or just plain old low-down. Besides, she spoils those damn kids rotten. Handing them a bad Christmas will make them stronger people. They'll learn to appreciate things. It will teach them that life isn't so damn rosy and that in the blink of an eye, your whole world can be turned upside down." Veronica didn't care much for Bonnie's children or for children in general unless there was some benefit they were providing her. "Hell, I don't have any regrets about taking the money, being threatened at knifepoint, or being tossed out."

"Do you need to send a Christmas wish to Santa Claus, baby?" The hobo continued to taunt her. "Here I am, darling. Come sit on my lap, and we'll talk about the first thing that pops up."

"Fuck you," Veronica said, and gave him her middle finger.

"I'm trying to, baby. Don't you want to help a good man out?"

Veronica decided it was best not to encourage the fool with conversation, so she kept her comments to herself.

I'll head down to the Austin YMCA. Veronica began to organize her thoughts. *I can get a room there for the night. At daybreak, I'll head over to my godmother Lenny's house.*

"I've got a room at the YMCA, baby," the hobo said as if reading her thoughts. "We could go down there and make Christmas cookies." He laughed to himself again.

"No way." Veronica suddenly made a change of plans and decided to take a city bus farther down Madison Street and get a motel room. "I'll get through this setback," Veronica comforted herself. "I've been on this road before, and I know how to protect myself as well as endure." Veronica's thoughts on survival were interrupted by a bad vibe. "Big Money Chuck." She spoke the source of her bad vibe, and a sense of danger caused a chill to rush down her spine as if someone had poured a pail of ice water down her back. Veronica's bad vibe consumed her and paralyzed her thoughts for a moment. She forced the thought of Big Money Chuck out of her mind.

"The last thing I want to do is talk him up." Veronica prepared herself once again to go out and brave the snowstorm. She stood up and wheeled her suitcase over to the glass door of the restaurant. She kept a sharp eye out for the marquee lights of a Madison Street bus. When she spotted a bus approaching, she wrestled her suitcase out of the door and hustled over to the bus stop.

2

Tabetha

Tabetha selected a single seat near a window on the El train and peered out of it at the traffic congestion on Chicago's Dan Ryan Expressway. She loathed riding the Dan Ryan El train, which many black Chicagoans nicknamed the "Soul Train" because ninety-five percent of the time, something unique and interesting was going on. It wasn't uncommon for a passenger to sell diverted merchandise or to start bellowing out songs in the hopes of making a quick dollar from commuters. The reason she was riding the El train this particular morning was because the Metra Electric Train Authorities announced through the media that the previous night's snowstorm, which had high winds, caused power lines to go down. The spokesperson for the transit system encouraged commuters to find alternate transportation into downtown Chicago. So Tabetha drove to Ninety-Fifth Street from the southern suburbs and parked her car in front of her girlfriend Lynise's house. She then walked a few blocks to catch the El train into the city.

Tabetha's El-train ride was uneventful until it stopped and loaded passengers at Fifty-Fifth Street. A colossal man got on the train with an equally massive brown-and-white cat perched on his shoulders. The man began asking commuters for money to feed himself and his fat cat.

"Oh Lord." Tabetha stared disapprovingly. "How ridiculous and trifling can one person be?" Tabetha said aloud in judgment of the man. "People will do anything," she whispered under her breath. Tabetha waved the burly man and his fat cat away when he asked for money to support their needs. By her estimation, neither one of them seemed to be starving or fit the criteria of someone who didn't eat on a regular basis. A lazy person was someone Tabetha refused to support or tolerate. "It's outrageous that his grown ass is out here begging."

After a few more stops, the train became overcrowded with people. Soon there was standing room only. A short man who was standing near her seat had a stale odor that was choking away the fresh breathable air.

"Goodness!" Tabetha coughed as she gazed at the man, who appeared to be in his late forties. The scent of hard booze and stale cigarette smoke was emitting from his direction.

"Hey, Miss Lady," he said to her with a meek smile. Tabetha grimaced. *Now this man wants to have a damn conversation.* She decided to be polite to the man and acknowledge his greeting, but at the same time, she turned her shoulder and showed him her back so that he'd leave her alone.

"You're a pretty woman." The short man couldn't take a hint and apparently had no understanding of body language. Tabetha wanted to get up and move, but the train was just too jam-packed to even consider it.

"If I had a woman like you taking care of me, I wouldn't have to be out here in these streets doing my thing."

Here goes another trifling idiot, Tabetha thought. *What is it, Moochers Day or something?*

"Yeah, whatever that is," Tabetha muttered in a low voice as she continued to ignore him and wrinkle her nose at his polluted stench.

"You're one of those downtown office sisters, aren't you? I'll bet that you have a nice job, and you make good money, don't you? I'll bet that you get lonely at night and need a man like me to keep you company."

Tabetha responded by displaying the wedding ring on her finger.

"Oh, I'm sorry, baby." The short man was suddenly apologetic. "No disrespect. I didn't mean you no harm." He was silent for a moment. "I'm going to leave you alone, okay," he uttered. "I used to have a wife, but it didn't work out. You know how it is." He paused. "She didn't know how to take care of me. She didn't understand that I needed to lean on her for a while when things didn't go right."

"Whatever," Tabetha mumbled; she didn't care to hear his life story. The man kept his word and remained silent. When the train stopped at Twenty-Second Street, he maneuvered his way through the cluster of passengers and exited the train.

It gives me a headache when I hear grown ass able-bodied men complain about how they want a woman to take care of them. Why are some men like that? Tabetha wondered. As the train continued its journey into downtown Chicago, her thoughts became fixed on her strained marriage. She and her husband, Gilbert, were bickering about money and other unresolved conflicts.

"Don't do that, Gilbert." Tabetha recalled how she'd snapped at him the previous night when they were grocery shopping. "It's embarrassing to have you walking around with a calculator adding up every cent."

"What do you mean embarrassing?" Gilbert frowned. "I need to know how much money I'm spending so that I know when to stop. Besides, I need to keep a closer eye on what I spend so that I can save up enough to have my car repaired."

"I told you that I'd take care of that." Tabetha snatched the calculator from him and flung it in her purse. She felt as if Gilbert was purposely trying to embarrass her out in public.

"And I told you that I didn't want you bailing your son Rick out every time he messes up. He has to learn how to take responsibility for his actions," Gilbert fired back.

"Gilbert, just let me handle the repair bill on your precious little car so that we can move past this."

"No." Gilbert was unyielding about his position. "If we don't teach him how to take ownership of his behavior, he'll grow into a man who will expect his mama or some other woman to take care of him. You're grooming him to be the type of person you loathe."

"Gilbert, that's fine, and I agree with you, but what does that have to do with you irritating me with a calculator? I don't like the image of it. It makes me feel as if we're on welfare or something."

"Welfare. Get a grip, Tabetha. Families set up budgets all the time. I'm just making sure that I don't go over the limit I set."

"Gilbert, I have enough money if we go over." Tabetha wanted Gilbert to drop the issue.

"What good is having money if you have poor spending habits, hmm?" Gilbert raised his eyebrow and judged her with his eyes.

Tabetha exhaled hard as she pushed the cart toward the produce section. "Why is everything always about money with you?" Tabetha griped as she inspected a bin of red seedless grapes. "You know, sometimes you're really impossible to deal with."

"I'm not impossible; I'm practical. I just don't see the need for frivolous spending."

"Is that another way of saying you're cheap?"

"I'm not cheap. I'm realistic."

"No. You're cheap, Gilbert," Tabetha corrected him, and walked away in the direction of the deli counter. She was done speaking with him about his frugal ways.

When the El train reached the State and Lake Street station downtown, she got off and hustled down the platform steps, which placed her in front of the Chicago Theater on State Street. She glanced up at the marquee, which said that tickets were still available for the holiday concert on Friday evening. She made a mental note to contact the box office and get tickets for her and Gilbert, even though she was still harboring sour feelings about his cheapness.

On second thought, I'll get tickets for my girlfriend Lynise and me. Gilbert would gripe about the fact that I spent extra money on the purchase of the tickets, Tabetha concluded. *I just hope Lynise is able to go, but knowing her busy schedule she may not be able to.*

Tabetha headed south toward Marshall Field's department store on State Street. She'd taken the remaining two weeks of the year off as vacation from work to celebrate the holiday season. She was spending most of her day taking care of some Christmas errands. Afterward she would meet up for dinner with Marlon, the father of her son. She was meeting him to ask that he reimburse Gilbert for the damage Rick had done to his car. Tabetha had taken a little extra time to get ready that morning because it had been almost a year since she'd physically seen Marlon. A spiteful chamber in her heart wanted to make sure she looked her absolute best when she saw him. After all the years that had come to pass, she still wanted Marlon to regret the day they split up. She didn't understand why she felt that way; she just did.

At 4:55 PM, Tabetha entered an office building on West Wacker Drive, which was where they'd agreed to meet. She waited for Marlon in the crowed lobby, which was filled with employees exiting the building for the evening. After waiting for what she considered to be too long, she flipped her wrist to check the time on her watch.

5:08 PM. Just as she was about to cop an attitude about him being tardy, she saw him exiting an elevator. Tabetha believed that some men and women are born with a special type of karma. They possessed a special type of vibe people are drawn to. Even as infants, people are drawn to these individuals like bees to honey. There is something extra special about them. Perhaps the attraction rested with the fact that they didn't cry as much, or they caught on to things quicker or seemed more mature than their years. Whatever this uniqueness was, Marlon had it. He had a special type of sexy and self-assured karma that changed the way a person felt in his presence.

Marlon spotted her in the lobby and approached her. Tabetha's adrenaline spike caught her off guard, and she had to restrain her unwanted thoughts of desire as she studied him. Marlon was just over six feet tall. His skin was brown and even-toned. His complexion appeared darker than she remembered; he appeared to have a tan. *He must have just returned from somewhere warm,* she thought to herself. It was clear that the sun had been kissing his brown skin. Marlon had a strong jaw, full lips that were manufactured for kissing, and hypnotic eyes that had the ability to seduce at will. Marlon was a muscular well-built man with a mighty chest, bulging biceps, and strong shoulders. Even though he had on his winter coat, she could still see the outlined details of what was beneath. "He still has that sexy and confident stride," she whispered to herself. "Damn, I hate the fact that he still looks so good."

Two women came and stood next to her. They began discussing their day as they bundled up to leave the building. The flow of their conversation was cut short by the presence of Marlon. Tabetha overheard them gossiping about how handsome and wealthy he was.

"He isn't all that, ladies. You can trust me on that one," Tabetha blurted out, making sure they heard her clearly.

One woman gave her a distasteful glare. "Who asked you for your thoughts?" The woman got catty with Tabetha. "I can't stand a woman who is full of insecurities." The woman snickered as she and her girlfriend continued on their way.

"Well Merry Christmas to you too," Tabetha mumbled under her breath. She wasn't about to allow the woman's comment to change the mood of her holiday spirit.

Marlon's handsomeness and meticulous grooming habits had gotten on her nerves when they were together, because no matter where he went, women always noticed him. He had the ability to captivate an audience even when he wasn't trying. Any decent single woman could take one glance at him and add him up from his fresh haircut all the way down to his expensive handmade shoes and know he had great potential.

"Tabetha." Marlon embraced her. Tabetha stepped into his full embrace and wrapped her arms completely around him. The soft scent of Marlon's cologne made her inhale the air surrounding them a bit deeper.

"You look spectacular."

Tabetha wasn't ready for the compliment but was glad to receive it. "Thank you. You look okay too," she stated, not willing to expose the truth, which was that after all this time, he still had the ability to stir some sort of passion in her. Tabetha hated to admit it to herself. Marlon was as much a part of her as her fingers were to her hand.

"You look as if you've been someplace warm. You have a tan," said Tabetha.

"Yeah, I have some property in Florida. I returned from there the other day but will be heading back to spend New Year's Eve."

"It must be nice to have the ability to jet away anytime you wish," Tabetha said sarcastically. Before Marlon could respond to her sarcasm, she asked another question. "What kind of cologne do you have on?"

"It's Michael Jordan's cologne. Do you like it?"

"It's not all that." She wanted her comment to give him a confidence complex but realized it didn't work when Marlon didn't react. *He can probably see right through me,* she thought as she fought back the sudden urge to bury her nose in the side of his neck. *It doesn't make any sense that my ass is still hot for him like this.* Tabetha scolded herself for having sensual thoughts.

"Well, I see you've had some cosmetic work done on your teeth. They're not sunshine yellow." Tabetha knew that she should have just complimented him nicely instead of adding a back-handed slap to it. But she couldn't help herself. She and Marlon had been officially separated for years, and although she had moved on and remarried, both resentment and unyielding passion for him were still lingering in her heart. *I wish there was a way to make my heart stop caring for him,* Tabetha admitted.

"I haven't been here two seconds and already you're starting in on me," Marlon finally responded to her negative energy toward him. "If you came here to fight with me, you've picked the wrong day. I'm not going to let you mess up my holiday spirit, Tabetha. You have a nice afternoon." Marlon began walking out the door.

Tabetha folded her arms across her chest like a defiant child as she watched him exit the building and hail a cab. When she realized that Marlon meant what he said, she exhaled away her animosity, picked up her shopping bags, and joined him outside.

"Okay, so where do you want to go for dinner?" Tabetha huffed without apologizing for her behavior.

"Do you have your attitude in order? Have you calmed down enough to have a mature conversation?"

"Excuse me. I don't have an attitude, Marlon," she quickly lashed back.

"So you just enjoy insulting me, right? No matter how much I try to be cordial to you, you still insist on insulting me."

"You shouldn't wear your feelings on your shoulder, Marlon." Tabetha grinned at him, because she actually did succeed in giving him a complex. "Besides, I didn't insult you."

"Then what was all that back there?" Marlon pointed in the direction from which they had come.

"I was just being spunky," she answered. "Now, where are we going? We have business to take care of."

"The Plaza Club," he answered. "And I'd prefer it if you toned down your spunk a bit."

"Whatever," Tabetha answered, unconcerned with his request. "Why are we going there? That's an expensive place."

"Because, in spite of all your spunk, I think you deserve to be pampered and treated to a nice meal. Besides, I know that your husband can't afford dinner at the Plaza Club. I mean, given his occupation and all." Marlon chopped down Gilbert and his occupation as a bus driver.

"Don't go there, Marlon." Tabetha got defensive. "Leave Gilbert out of our conversation." At that moment, a black town car pulled up to the curb.

"Good evening, sir," the driver greeted Marlon as he got out of the car.

"Wait, I thought you were hailing a cab?" Tabetha asked, confused.

"No," Marlon answered, "I can afford to travel luxuriously."

The driver approached Tabetha, picked up her bags, and placed them in the trunk of the vehicle. He then held the rear door open for them and dutifully whisked them off to the Plaza Club.

Tabetha and Marlon took their seat at a candlelit table at the Plaza Club. Tabetha studied the spectacular view of Lake Michigan and Michigan Avenue.

"You should order anything you want," Marlon said as he picked up the dinner menu.

"So this is what wealth will do for you," Tabetha said as she surveyed the room, noticing what appeared to be well-educated and wealthy members of the club networking. "This is what you've always wanted. To be a member of some elite club."

"Membership has its privileges," Marlon stated. "As a member, I have access to private clubs just like this one all around the country. Clubs like this are great places to seal business deals or entertain clients," Marlon explained.

"I know what the clubs are for, Marlon. I'm not some ghetto girl from around the way who has never been outside of her own neighborhood."

"Tabetha, I wasn't suggesting that you were," Marlon said with a soft voice. "I'm going to have the grilled prosciutto-wrapped shrimp served over linguini. What are you going to have?"

"Doesn't look like they serve fried chicken in here," Tabetha playfully joked as she allowed herself to relax a little. "I'll have the salmon. After all, it is Friday, and according to folklore, it's the best day of the week to eat fish."

When the waiter arrived, Marlon gave the server both of their orders.

"You still like jazz music, don't you?" Marlon asked.

"Of course I do. I haven't changed that much," Tabetha answered.

"There is this great jazz band that will be performing here this evening. After dinner you should hang around and listen."

"Marlon, you and I are going to have dinner and discuss getting Rick through the remainder of his junior year of high school without me or Gilbert killing him. Gilbert went ballistic when he discovered that his custom Excalibur car, which he'd been restoring for years, was taken without his permission. That was bad enough, but then Rick returned it with one side smashed up. He got into an accident with a damn tree while trying to look cool. Thank goodness he didn't hit somebody."

"Gilbert didn't put his hands on my son, did he?" Marlon wanted to know.

"No, I didn't let him, but it wasn't easy. Gilbert was ready to send him to the underground motel for smashing up his car."

"Why did Rick take Gilbert's car?" Marlon asked as he tried to understand his son's inexcusable behavior.

"He wanted to impress some girl named Marcia who was

going to be at the school basketball game. Apparently she's all that." Tabetha wanted to pop her fingers for added emphasis but didn't want to draw attention to herself. "Apparently Miss Marcia will only be seen with a guy who has a car. Not just any car, now. According to Rick, any man who wants to be with her must drive a Lexus, a Mercedes Benz, or a BMW. She can't be seen in any other type of car."

"Who is this girl? What is her family like?" Marlon asked.

"Some young girl with unrealistic expectations of a seventeen-year-old boy. She probably inherited her expectations from either a deranged mama or from watching too many hip-hop videos."

"What are Rick's grades looking like this quarter?"

"He's slipping, Marlon. Between the mature-rated video games, the slut music videos, and a sudden desire to be a thug with something to prove, he's been distracted. He's changed on me. He wants to be a man but doesn't know the first thing about being one." Tabetha paused and then reached into her purse and removed a white envelope. "The damage to Gilbert's car is forty-six hundred dollars." Tabetha took out a repair estimate to show Marlon. He glanced down at the bill, then back at Tabetha.

"I told you when Rick turned thirteen to let me take him. I pleaded with you to let him move in with me so that I could get him through his teenage years. But no. You insisted that I was trying to take him away from you and turn him into some irresponsible menace who you would loathe."

"Why are you bringing up old shit, Marlon?" Tabetha didn't like that Marlon was trying to make her see an error in judgment.

"Because it's relevant!" Marlon snapped at her. "You argued with me so hard that you lost your voice and raised your blood pressure so high that you had to be hospitalized for a night. At the time, you were quick to tell me your husband was the best man for the job." Marlon glared at her.

"Marlon, you really shouldn't go there," Tabetha warned.

"No," Marlon said, unafraid of her threat. "You need to hear this. In my mind, the fact that Rick took property that didn't belong to him suggests to me that he doesn't respect Gilbert. And if he doesn't respect Gilbert, and he's living in the man's house, something is going to happen. And let me tell you right now, if Gilbert harms my son, I'm holding you accountable for it."

"Don't you dare try and lay a guilt trip on me, Marlon." Tabetha raised her voice at him, suddenly not caring about creating an ugly scene at the exclusive club. "You left us because you wanted your freedom. I was the one who had to explain to him why his daddy left. I was the one who made sure that he made it to all of the peewee football games, and I was the one who comforted him while you were off gallivanting around."

"I wasn't gallivanting around, and you know it. I pulled myself up by my damn bootstraps and made something of myself. That should be every man's goal. I sent you what I could at the time to support him, and it's not like I've never been around during that time. So stop talking to me as if I was a deadbeat father."

"Whatever, Marlon. There is a difference between being around and being a father."

"Oh, so you want to go there."

Tabetha could tell that Marlon was sharpening his tongue to lash out at her. "Who was the man who purchased his football equipment? Huh? Who was the man who paid all of his activity fees, huh? Who was the man who took care of his medical bills when he hurt himself?"

"Marlon, let's not get into it, okay? It's the holiday, and I really don't want it ruined by having a nasty spat." Tabetha studied Marlon's eyes as he leaned back in his seat to consider taking up their argument at a later time. Marlon once again glanced down at the repair bill. He shook his head disapprovingly.

"I take it that your wonderful husband wants me to pay the repair bill for his car," Marlon said with a displeased tone.

"That's where you're wrong," Tabetha said, meeting his gaze. "Your son told Gilbert that his real daddy would pay for the repairs. You see, Marlon, your son views you as daddy big bucks who can fix everything with money," Tabetha said, satisfied that she'd gotten in the last word.

Tabetha arrived home at eight-thirty in the evening. When she entered through the front door, she became instantly irritated by the sight of footprints tracking through the house.

"Rick!" she yelled. She didn't hear a response from him, so she stepped forward, walked halfway up the staircase, and yelled out his name again.

"Rick!" A second later she heard his bedroom door squeak open and the sounds of loud music engulfed the house.

"What?" Rick hollered back.

Tabetha marched up the stairs to confront him and his attitude. "Turn that music down," she ordered him.

"Hang on," he said, then went into his room to turn his stereo down.

Tabetha went toward his room but stopped at the doorway. The sight of Rick's unorganized room disgusted her. "Rick, I don't want to have to tell you again about tracking melted snow through the damn house. My floor downstairs looks nasty."

Rick plopped down on the side of his cluttered mattress. Tabetha could tell by his body language that he wasn't in the mood for one of her lectures.

"My bad," Rick answered.

"My bad, my ass!" Tabetha had grown tired of his casual comments. "Go grab a mop to clean my floors."

"Okay, in a minute," Rick said as he stood up to turn his music back up.

"Now, Rick! I'm not playing with you." Tabetha raised her voice at him.

"Jeez, you act as if the house is on fire or something," Rick mumbled under his breath as he moved past her.

"What did you say?" Tabetha asked. "If you have something to say, say it."

"Nothing," Rick answered as he rushed down the stairs.

Tabetha walked to the end of the corridor and entered her bedroom. When she flipped on the light switch, she grumbled. "Gilbert," she said aloud to the empty room, "how many times do I have to tell you not to leave your clothes piled up on the floor? If they're dirty, toss them in the laundry chute so they can be washed. These men act as if I'm their maid." Tabetha slipped off her shoes, crawled into her bed without removing her street clothes, and turned on the television. She began to channel surf, hoping to find a program that would help her unwind. She decided to watch a family network presentation of *The Wizard of Oz*. Just as the tornado swept Dorothy and Toto away, she heard the doorbell chime.

"I bet Gilbert forgot his key again!" she whispered to herself.

"Mom," she heard Rick call up to her.

"What!" she hollered back, still irritated with him.

"Lynise is here to see you," Rick shouted out.

"Lynise. Why is she dropping by so late?" Tabetha wondered as she got up and headed downstairs.

"Where in the world has your ass been?" Lynise asked with jovial cattiness as Tabetha entered the family room where Lynise was waiting on the sofa. Lynise had been her best friend since college. She was an attractive woman with a round face, caramel skin, and who loved wearing her hair in short styles.

"You've cut your hair again," Tabetha scolded her. "Sisters would give a kidney to have strong healthy hair like yours that grows. Not you, though; you chop it off every chance you get."

"Girl, please. Long hair is overrated." Lynise discounted Tabetha's belief.

"Turn around, let me see," Tabetha requested as she inspected her friend's hair.

"You need to tell your stylist to be careful when dealing with the back of your neck. Your skin is all red and irritated from the hair clippers."

"Really?" Lynise reached to touch the back of her neck with her fingertips.

"Stop. Get your fingers away from there. You'll irritate it more by touching it. Make sure you wash your neck with a real good skin cleanser so that it doesn't get all bumpy."

"See, you are going to make me call my stylist back and ask for a refund," Lynise said, concerned.

"There is no need for that. Your hair looks fine; it's your skin that's a little irritated. Anyway, what do you mean, where have I been?" Tabetha asked.

"I've been trying to call you this evening," Lynise said. "You know Duane doesn't live far from you so I was killing time at his place until he began hinting around that he was ready for me to leave. Apparently I was preventing him from doing something. I swear, I'm not going to keep giving up all of this good love to brothers who don't appreciate it. I'm seriously thinking about dating white guys. Anyway, I'm done venting about my love fustrations, where have you been?"

"I had dinner with Marlon today," said Tabetha. "As usual we got into an argument."

"Again? I don't know how you guys stayed cordial with each other long enough to make Rick," Lynise joked.

"Well, we didn't argue the entire time," Tabetha admitted. "Marlon did something strange, though."

"What?" Lynise asked as she raised her eyebrow.

"He listened. For the first time, I think he's actually listening to me instead of just hearing words of criticism fly out of my mouth."

"Well, that's a good thing," Lynise said as she brushed her fingers across the base of her neck.

"Stop fumbling with your neck!" Tabetha scolded her like a child.

"Wow, I can feel how irritated my skin is. She must not be

cleaning those clippers of hers." Tabetha saw an angry expression form on Lynise's face. "I might call her back and give her a good piece of my mind."

"Lynise. Relax, you'll be fine," Tabetha said, trying to defuse her before she overreacted.

"Okay." Lynise opened her purse and searched for a breath mint. "What else did you and Marlon talk about?"

"After all the fussing we did, he gave me a Christmas gift," said Tabetha.

"Well that was nice of him. I don't see anything wrong with that," said Lynise. "What did he give you? Some small trinket?"

"Money," Tabetha answered.

"Oh, so he's going to pay to have Gilbert's car fixed?" Lynise assumed.

"Yes, he gave me the money for that, but he also wrote me a check for two thousand dollars and said that it was a gift."

"Girl, you bullshitting, right?"

Tabetha noticed the excitement in Lynise's voice. "No," Tabetha answered. "What do you think this means?"

"Who gives a damn? All I want to know is did you take the money?"

"I wasn't going to at first, but he insisted. He said it would be insulting to give it back. I felt guilty about taking it, and I don't know why," admitted Tabetha.

"Girl, I wouldn't feel guilty about shit." Lynise laughed loudly. "But look here, if you feel that bad about taking the money, give it to me. I know just what to do with it."

Tabetha laughed. "I'll bet you do."

"You're not going to tell Gilbert about it, are you?" Lynise asked.

"Of course I am. Gilbert and I don't keep secrets. Why would you ask that?"

"Hey, you know how men are. A brother might feel threatened by a man who can hand a woman money like that and not miss it. Men are territorial."

"Gilbert is not like that." Tabetha discounted Lynise's assumption. "Gilbert is a very reserved and mild-mannered man. Stuff like that doesn't bother him."

"Then why do you have that strange look on your face, Tabetha?" Lynise asked.

"It's nothing," Tabetha said, not wanting Lynise to know that her thoughts were still analyzing Marlon. Tabetha needed to know why he'd changed. She wanted to know what made him change.

"So what are you going to do with the money?" Lynise asked, interrupting her thoughts.

"The money?" Tabetha said as if she wasn't sure what Lynise was speaking of. "Oh." She laughed a little. "I'll put it to good use. I'll do like Marlon suggested. I'll buy myself something nice for Christmas," Tabetha mumbled.

"Tabetha, stop mumbling. I hate it when you do that."

"I'm sorry. I'm just overanalyzing Marlon's gift. For some reason he gave me the impression that . . . never mind." Tabetha stopped.

"Lord, you're sitting there daydreaming about Marlon, aren't you?"

"He's up to something, Lynise. I don't know what it is, but I can feel it."

"Well, just make sure you don't tread old water. It took a long time for you to get him out of your system."

"Lynise, please. What Marlon and I had is over."

"It had better be," Lynise said seriously. "When you guys broke up, I thought for sure you were going to kill yourself."

"Stop lying to me, Lynise. I wasn't that bad."

"Yes, you were." Lynise stood her ground. "I don't want to see you go through anything like that again."

3

Gilbert

Gilbert pulled his sedan into his driveway. He turned off the ignition and sat in his car for a moment, relaxing his head on the seat's headrest and closing his eyes. He was returning home, exhausted after a long day at work as a bus driver for the Chicago Transit Authority.

"Damn," he said aloud. "Why don't my plans ever develop the way I want them to?" Gilbert spoke to the empty space around him as if it were going to respond. "I can't stand it when shit doesn't work out the way I intend it to." Gilbert groaned as he wrestled with his frustration. He heard the faint sound of giggling and opened his eyes. He glanced out of the driver's side window and saw his newlywed neighbors laughing and kissing each other as they entered their home and slammed the door shut. Watching his neighbors openly display their affection for each other caused Gilbert's memory to drift. He thought about a fall day a few months ago that he and Tabetha had spent at the mall. They'd wandered into an expensive and chic boutique because of the fur coats in the display window that caught Tabetha's eye.

"Oh, Gilbert, look at this one." Tabetha walked over to a mannequin modeling a full-length fur coat at the rear of the store. "This is what I'm talking about, babe." Tabetha smiled as she studied the brown, full-length, dyed directional, female mink coat. "This would look so good on me," Tabetha said, fantasizing about how she'd look. Gilbert noticed the longing glint in her eyes.

"Ever since I was a little girl, I've always wanted a full-length mink coat."

"Would you like to try it on?" asked a saleswoman who had come over to offer her assistance.

"Yes, I'd like her to try it on," Gilbert told the saleswoman. He wanted to make her dream come true. He wanted her to have the coat. The saleswoman removed it from the mannequin.

"Follow me," instructed the saleswoman as she walked over to a full-length mirror. She assisted Tabetha with the coat, and then stepped back so that Tabetha could see how she looked in it.

"Oh, this one even fits me perfectly." Tabetha smiled as she pivoted from left to right, studying how she looked from different points of view.

"You look spectacular," complimented the saleswoman.

"I have to agree with her, babe," Gilbert said. "You look fabulous." Gilbert had calculated in his mind that the coat couldn't be more than fifteen hundred dollars. He was all set to drain his savings account so that Tabetha could have the coat.

"Do you want me to get it for you, baby?" Gilbert asked as he stood behind her, smiling. Tabetha twirled around and gave Gilbert a funny look.

"What?" Gilbert asked. "If you want it, babe, I'll get it for you." Gilbert's heart was much bigger than his finances.

"I could ring it up for you," said the saleswoman. "We even offer storage. We could store it for you, and you could return to pick it up once the weather turns cold."

"How much is the coat?" Gilbert was set to reach for his wallet.

"Eight thousand, five hundred dollars," informed the saleswoman.

"How much?" Gilbert almost choked on his own saliva. He honestly had no clue as to how expensive a mink coat was.

"Eight thousand, five hundred dollars," repeated the saleswoman.

Gilbert looked at Tabetha, who was still caught up in the fantasy of owning the coat. She hadn't even heard the price.

"I can't believe that you're actually going to buy this for me, babe." Tabetha glanced at Gilbert through the mirror and didn't notice that his expression had gone sour. He was suddenly ready to make an abrupt exit.

"This coat feels so good on my skin," Tabetha continued on, oblivious to his mood change.

"Do you have a layaway plan?" Gilbert asked the saleswoman.

"Yes," she answered. "If you give me a moment, I'll pull up the paperwork so that I can go over the terms of layaway with you. We also have financing options if you want to go that route."

"No," said Gilbert. "The last thing I need is another credit card bill."

"Okay, give me a moment to retrieve the paperwork," said the saleswoman before she stepped away.

"Gilbert, honey, are you serious?" Tabetha asked. "You're just going to walk up in here and buy me a fur coat, just like that?" Tabetha was buzzing. She felt so cared for and appreciated.

"If you want it, babe, I'm going to get it for you," Gilbert said, not believing the words coming out of his own mouth. He knew he couldn't afford the coat or her expensive tastes, but he was going to break his neck trying. It didn't matter to him that a lot of the material things she longed for were out of his financial range. He didn't want to disappoint Tabetha. He hated it when he disappointed her. For a brief moment he considered sharing the cost of the coat with Tabetha, but his pride got in the way of saying it.

Gilbert's plan was to get Tabetha's mink coat out of layaway for a Christmas gift. He intended to work overtime to come up with the payments. But the job had cut back on any extra hours and he was unable to find a suitable part-time job. So Gilbert had to return to the store, cancel the layaway plan, and lose some of the money he'd put down on the coat.

Gilbert exhaled as he opened up his car door, stepped out, and walked to his front door. Once inside, he removed his shoes without untying them. He walked down a narrow corridor, entered the family room, and plopped down on the tan leather sofa. He reached forward, picked up the black television remote, and turned on the set, which was situated kitty-corner on an opposite wall. He slumped back into the sofa and watched a program about an exercise machine that claimed to burn away stubborn stomach fat. Gilbert unconsciously rested his hand on his plump belly and wished for a flatter, sexier stomach.

"When did you get home?" Tabetha asked as she entered the family room.

"Just a minute ago," Gilbert answered as he clicked the channel.

"You just missed Lynise," Tabetha informed him.

"Oh yeah, how is she doing? What's the love bunny into these days?" Gilbert asked sarcastically.

"Lynise is Lynise. Same old stuff, just a new day. She's still searching for Mr. Right but keeps running up on Mr. Wrong. She says that she's thinking about dating white guys."

Gilbert chuckled. "No white dude is going to be bothered with Lynise and her high-strung attitude."

"What do you mean high-strung? Lynise is not high-strung. I'll admit she's carefree, but not high-strung."

"Call it whatever you want to, but your girl may be a bit too much for a white guy."

"So what type of man do you think would be good for her?" Tabetha asked curiously, wanting to hear Gilbert's thoughts.

"I don't know if such a man exists." Gilbert laughed. He was enjoying the distraction, because it kept him from thinking about how he couldn't afford to get Tabetha's mink coat.

"That's not nice." Tabetha walked over to the sofa and shoved his shoulder. "Scoot over and let me sit down." Gilbert scooted over so that Tabetha could sit next to him.

"Okay. I think that she needs someone who is ready to settle down." Gilbert continued to channel surf.

"Well, according to Lynise, the men out there aren't willing to settle down."

"Speaking of settling down, how did your meeting with Marlon go today?"

Tabetha paused before she spoke. "It went okay."

"Just okay?" Gilbert pivoted his head and glanced at her. "He didn't upset you again, did he?"

"No. We actually had a very cordial meeting. And he, um"—Tabetha paused again so she could select her words carefully—"he gave me the money needed to repair your car."

"Tabetha. We agreed not to involve him in that. We agreed that Rick would work off his debt to me. You and Marlon were supposed to meet to discuss additional financial support for Rick's college fund and that was it. Why did you even bring the car issue up?"

Tabetha could tell that Gilbert was clearly irritated by what she'd done. "What's gotten into you?" Tabetha got defensive. "If anything, I thought you'd be happy about it. Besides, I know how you are about that car. Every time you look at it, you hiss and huff. I just want you to get it fixed so that you're not walking around here irritated."

"I don't like you going behind my back and asking him for money." Gilbert clicked off the television.

"I don't like the way you said that. I didn't go behind your back. I was just trying to get your car fixed for you." Tabetha folded her arms across her chest.

"Look, Rick is going to work off his debt to me. End of story, understood?"

"Why are you being so ungrateful?" Tabetha glared at him with a puzzled expression.

"I'm not being ungrateful. I'm saying that we are going to stick to what we agreed to." Gilbert clicked the television set back on, signaling that he had said all that he was going to say on the matter.

"All right"—Tabetha stood up—"then I'll keep the sixty-six hundred dollars he gave me for myself." Tabetha was about to walk away, but Gilbert grabbed her arm and halted her exit.

"What do you mean, sixty-six hundred dollars? The repair estimate was only forty-six hundred dollars."

"He gave me two thousand dollars as a gift," Tabetha answered with a slight smirk on her face. She didn't want the smirk to appear, it just did.

"Oh no. Hell no!" Gilbert raised his voice. "You're giving all of that money back to him."

"What?" Tabetha chuckled at the ridiculousness of Gilbert's suggestion. "No, I'm not."

"Yes, you are," Gilbert countered.

"Why?" Tabetha wasn't about to return any of the money. *Hell, I could put it to good use,* she reasoned to herself.

"Why is he giving you such a large amount of money? No man gives up that type of money unless he wants something for it."

"Are you trying to make accusations?" Tabetha felt insulted.

"Hey, if the shoe fits," Gilbert accused her.

"See there. You shouldn't say that shit to me." Tabetha's feelings were bruised. She walked away from Gilbert before she said something that would really stir up more of his insecurities.

"Damn it," Gilbert hissed. "Look, I didn't mean it that way." Gilbert chased after Tabetha, who was heading to the basement to check her laundry. She entered the laundry room and began slinging clothes from the washer into the dryer.

"Tabetha, I don't want any man handing you large sums of money."

"What if the money came from my father? Would you think that he was after something as well?" Tabetha's tone was sharp. She was still managing her feelings of being accused of sneaking around with Marlon.

"Tabetha, that's different and you know it." Gilbert was unwilling to let go of her reasoning for keeping the money.

Tabetha shut the dryer door and pressed the start button. She turned around, rested her behind against the dryer, and fixed her gaze on Gilbert.

"Look, Marlon and I have known each other since we were in fourth grade. I know him, and I know him well. Marlon is not after anything. That part of our relationship is over and dead. I don't appreciate you accusing him or me of roaming around together. He gave it to me because that's the way he is. He has always been that way, and I've told you that a thousand times."

"I don't care," Gilbert countered. He sensed a nasty argument on the horizon.

"Oh, come off of it, Gilbert." Tabetha laughed at his selective memory.

"Come off of what?" Gilbert's voice was explosive.

"Okay, you want me to spell it out for you?" Tabetha paused in thought and selected what she thought would be the right choice of words. "Marlon has always given gifts to Rick and me. He wants me to be happy and feels that a little extra money in my pocket wouldn't hurt. That's all it is, Gilbert, nothing more, okay? What's the big deal?"

"It feels sneaky to me. That's what the big deal is. In my mind, that's not normal. That man is after something."

"You know what, you're so stubborn at times, Gilbert." Tabetha knew that what she was about to say would shoot an arrow right through the center of Gilbert's insecurities. She hesitated for a moment before she fired off her words. "Gilbert, when you and I first got married, you were walking around here talking about how Marlon doesn't need to keep sending the child support because you were his father now, but the minute you realized how much money we'd be turning our backs on, you changed your tune. The extra money benefited not only Rick, but you and me as well. You weren't so quick with your demands then, so what's the big deal now?" Tabetha saw the sting of her words change his entire expression. Gilbert began scratching his neck, just behind his right ear. Tabetha was familiar with the neck-scratching routine. It meant that she had made him think about an issue he didn't particularly want to reflect on. It was also a sign of stress and uneasiness.

"Look, it's not his job to make you happy; it's mine. And the last time I checked, I still had the job." Gilbert placed his hands on her shoulders and rubbed up and down on them to defuse the tension between them. "Give the money back to him," he said with a softer tone. "I'm the only man around here who gives you gifts like that, okay?"

"Do you want me to tell him to stop sending the child support payment too?" Tabetha said sarcastically.

"Tabetha, you're skating on thin ice," Gilbert threatened her with the promise of an enormous argument.

"What if I put the money into Rick's college-fund account? That would be a good place for it, don't you think?" Tabetha asked.

"Tabetha, return the money to him. I want Marlon to get a clear message. I want him to know that his gifts aren't wanted, no matter how they're packaged."

"But—" Tabetha was about to continue her argument but was interrupted by Rick's voice.

"Yo, Gilbert," Rick yelled down the basement stairs.

"What?" Gilbert shouted back.

"You have a collect phone call. Do you want me to accept it?"

"Who is the call from?" Gilbert hollered up to him.

"It's your sister, Veronica."

"Veronica." Gilbert and Tabetha's eyes met. "Yeah, accept the call. I'll be right up."

"I mean it, Tabetha. Give it back to him."

"Yeah, whatever," Tabetha grumbled with discontentment as she tossed another load of clothes into the washer. "Go take your phone call. I'm sure that the drama queen has some incredibly spectacular story to tell you. If she begs you for money, which I'm sure she will, don't even think about coming back down here to ask me about the money I'm returning to Marlon."

"Veronica is my sister, not yours," Gilbert quickly responded to her sarcastic comment. "She's just going through a phase right now. I have faith in her. You never know, she could be calling to tell me that she has turned her life around," Gilbert said as he walked over to the stairs.

"Gilbert, please! Pigs will fly before Veronica gets her shit together, and you know it."

"No, I don't know it," Gilbert snapped at her. "If you don't have anything nice to say about my sister, then keep your damn mouth shut. I'm getting tired of telling you that, Tabetha." Gilbert raised his eyebrows up high and pointed his index finger at her. After a brief pause, he went upstairs to take his phone call.

"Yeah, whatever," Tabetha said. "All I know is that come Christmas morning, you'd better have my fur coat and not some sob story about how Veronica desperately needed money and you had to delay getting my gift." Tabetha thought about how she'd react if Gilbert didn't have her fur coat. "There will be hell to pay," Tabetha whispered as she poured a cap-full of laundry detergent into the washer.

4

Veronica

"Gilbert, what's taking you so long to come to the phone?" Veronica grew impatient. She had slogged through the snow-covered motel parking lot the evening after the snowstorm and out onto Madison Street where there was a pay phone. She'd tried to use the phone in the motel room, but it wasn't functioning. She stood at the pay phone shivering, trying to fight the bitterly cold winter air that had followed the previous night's snowstorm.

"Hello," Gilbert said into the receiver.

"I'm going to find me a new brother who cares about me." Veronica didn't waste any time giving Gilbert a guilt complex. "I can't believe that my own brother wouldn't even make time to come and see about me. I swear, for someone who says that he cares and worries about me so much, you certainly don't act like it. I could be somewhere dead on the street, and you wouldn't even know about it."

"Veronica, you know that I was going to stop by and see you. I just haven't had a chance. Why are you trying to make me feel bad?"

"Because you should, that's why," Veronica snapped at him as she shivered uncontrollably. "You had no intentions of coming around to see about your baby sister, did you? I must embarrass you or something."

"Veronica, you know that's not true."

"Then why haven't you been around to see about me? Now that Mama is gone, all we have is each other."

"Don't drag Mama's memory into this, Veronica. I care. You know that. I'd do just about anything for you."

"Yeah, right. I feel like you've disowned me. Especially since you went off and married that superficial woman you call a wife. I'll bet that you didn't get me a Christmas present or plan to invite me over for Christmas dinner, did you?"

"Veronica, Tabetha is not superficial."

"She could have fooled me." Veronica was filled with misguided jealousy.

"You know that you're always welcome at my home. You've always got a place to stay here with me. When you got released, who was the first person who offered you a place to stay?"

"You were," Veronica conceded. "But I didn't want to be way out there in the suburbs. I wanted to be in the city, which is why I stayed with Bonnie. You know I'm a city girl and would be bored out of my mind if I lived out in the suburbs with you."

"This is exactly why you need to come. I think the city life is a little too strong for you. There are too many things for you to get into."

"What are you talking about?" Veronica got defensive.

"Veronica, you're thirty-five years old, and you're not where you should be in life. By now I expected you and me to be raising children and planning family reunions. You wanted to be an anchorwoman with the perfect career and a wonderful husband. You just got sidetracked, that's all. It's not too late, you know. You can still make your dream come true. Why don't you let me help you start over?"

Veronica closed her eyes as a blast of wind penetrated her

clothing and went straight through to her bones. "Look, Gilbert. I was calling to tell you that I'm no longer staying with Bonnie. I'm going to stay with our godmother, Lenny Gray, for a while."

"What happened with Bonnie? And why are you going to stay with Lenny Gray? Doesn't she live near that criminal you got caught up with and helped the police—"

"Big Money Chuck is still in jail," Veronica lied. "I'm just going to stay with Lenny Gray until I get things together. I just wanted you to know where I was."

"Veronica, come stay with me. I have plenty of room here. It wouldn't be a problem. I don't want you getting caught up in any more of your madness."

"Man, please, madness can't catch me. I'm way too good to get caught up, Gilbert." Veronica paused in thought. "Look here, I'm going to have to call you back later, okay? We'll talk then."

Before Gilbert could ask additional questions that she didn't want to answer, Veronica hung up. Feeling as if her toes and fingers would freeze off if she didn't get inside, she slogged through the snow back to her motel room. Veronica closed the door of her room and immediately removed her cold wet feet from her thin sneakers. She sat in a small wooden chair that was near the tiny bathroom. The room was silent with the exception of the howling wind rattling the motel door.

Man it's cold in here," she condemned the drafty motel room as she shivered violently. *I can't wait to get to Lenny's house. Hopefully she'll let me in. Well, no. I know she'll let me in.* Veronica nixed the thought of Lenny Gray turning her back on her. *Old people like her love it when they have visitors. Hell, if I play my cards right, I may be able to get a little money out of her. I know that it's not right to take advantage of old people, but if I can swindle her out of a little money, I will.* Veronica smiled at her wicked thoughts. *I'm sure Lenny Gray has to be damn near senile by now.*

5

Tabetha

On Christmas morning, Tabetha woke from her sleep feeling vibrant and energetic. She was thrilled with the anticipation of receiving her fur coat. She'd been fantasizing about how people would take notice of her in such a beautiful full-length mink coat. Tabetha hadn't been so excited about Christmas morning since she was a young girl. She was going to make sure that Gilbert understood just how appreciative she was that he'd purchased such a priceless gift for her. She was careful not to wake Gilbert as she crept out of bed. She slid her feet over the edge and slipped them into her black house shoes. She walked over to the wooden rocking chair and picked up her robe, which hung neatly over one of its arms. Tabetha then entered her small walk-in closet and retrieved a box that contained her special Christmas lingerie. She came out of the closet, quietly entered the master bathroom, and shut the door. She took a rejuvenating shower, and then placed a scented moisturizer on her skin. She opened up her special box and removed the bright red lace-trim satin slip that had adjustable straps and a side slit. Tabetha caressed the silky fabric. She removed the matching bright red thong, then slipped on the entire ensemble.

"Gilbert is going to be on me like a hound dog on a bone when he sees this," Tabetha said softly. "I can't wait to put my mink coat on over this and get freaky." Tabetha giggled to herself. She exited the bathroom and noticed that Gilbert hadn't moved. *That's all right,* she reasoned. *Once I start cooking, he'll get up.* Tabetha put on her house robe and tied it so that Gilbert wouldn't be able to see her hot number, and she exited the room. She walked down the short hallway and knocked on Rick's bedroom door before she opened it.

"What are you doing in here, boy?" Tabetha asked as she entered his room. Rick was sitting at his computer, typing.

"Hey, Mom. Merry Christmas."

"Merry Christmas to you too," Tabetha said.

"I'm working on my history paper that is due when I go back to school. I know that my grades have been slipping, so I want to do a good job on this."

"Who are you, and what did you do to my son?" Tabetha asked.

"Mom." Rick caught her gaze. She noticed a twinkle of a smile in his eyes.

"What is your paper on?" she asked, approaching him at his desk.

"The Reconstruction period after the Civil War. I'm doing some research online about it. Did you know that you could go to americaslibrary.gov and find articles and facts on every aspect of American history? Look at this." Rick clicked on one of the links. "They even have photos and audio of former slaves. This one guy talks about his memories of being a slave as a young boy."

Tabetha studied the historical photo and tried to imagine how difficult it must have been to live during the 1800s.

"Let me read your paper when you're done. You know it's difficult to proofread your own work. Besides, I'm interested in reading your viewpoints." Tabetha paused and then switched the topic. "I take it you've already been downstairs and opened your presents."

"Yeah, I was down there first thing this morning," Rick answered. "The clothes you bought were tight." Rick nodded his head as he agreed with his own statement. "The gift certificates are going to come in handy as well. Oh, and the MP3 player that Gilbert got me was nice too."

"Well, you make sure you let him know that." Tabetha paused and trapped his gaze in her own. "Do you hear me? Because Gilbert didn't have to get you anything, especially after the stunt you pulled with his car."

"Will you guys just let that go? It was a mistake, okay?"

Tabetha knew Rick didn't like having to hear about his error in judgment again. "A woman can drive a man crazy if he doesn't know how to handle himself, Rick."

"Mom, I hear you. Please don't give me another lecture this morning. It's Christmas. Can you cut me a little slack?"

"Rick." Tabetha paused for a moment. "Are you having sex?"

"No," Rick answered with a bewildered look on his face.

"Do you want to have sex with this girl?"

"Mom. Can we not have this conversation?"

"Just answer the question for me."

"Yes. I wanted to have sex with her. Everyone I know is getting some action but me. Even Kevin has made it to third base."

"What's third base these days?"

"God, this is embarrassing. You know. Third base," Rick said.

"No. I don't know."

"See. Now you're getting mad. I can tell by your expression."

"I'm not getting mad, Rick."

"He was inside her panties with his fingers, okay?"

"Oh. That's what third base is. Well, look. There is more to having sex than just the physical part," Tabetha tried to explain.

"I don't want to hear about that part. I just want to know how to satisfy the urges so that I don't go out of my mind. It's a trip waking up with a boner every morning."

"A boner?" Tabetha was puzzled.

"Oh God. Never mind," Rick said, and Tabetha could tell he was embarrassed.

"Tell me. What is it?"

"A woody, Mom. A stiff one."

"You mean an erection?"

"Yeah."

Tabetha could tell that Rick was truly ready to end this conversation. Tabetha smiled and then laughed.

"What's so funny?"

"Honey, there may come a day when you'll want a woody and can't get one to save your life."

"Okay. Can we please stop now?"

"Okay," Tabetha agreed. "But if you ever have questions, you can always come to me for the answer."

"Fine. I'll do that," Rick said. "Can we change the subject?"

"Did you talk to your father?" asked Tabetha.

"Yeah, we talked. I was all set to ask him to buy me a car. But he went on this tangent about my grades and how he wasn't going to reward me for doing poorly in school. After his lecture, he said he'd consider getting me a set of wheels if I got my act together. I wanted to be like, yeah, whatever, but I understood where he was coming from. We talked about the upcoming indoor track-and-field season and how he was going to make an effort to come and watch me compete. He tried to give me a few pointers, as usual, but I'd heard them all before. You know I had to hear the tale of how good of a sprinter he was at my age. Anyway, he deposited more money into my college-fund account and sent me a check. I think I'm going to use the money to buy myself gold track spikes and some music."

"What about that girl you were trying to impress? What's her name again?"

"Marcia. She's like last week's newspaper. Old news. To be honest with you, I'm not even feeling her anymore." Rick gazed at his mother and smiled.

"You're so silly. Well, I'll let you finish your paper. Did you fix yourself something to eat? Because I'm about to go cook breakfast."

"No, hook up something good."

"I'll call you down when it's ready." Tabetha left Rick to work on his paper. When she closed his bedroom door, she smiled.

"Thank you, Lord," Tabetha said. "Thank you for giving me a son who doesn't give me too much trouble." Tabetha went into the cupboard and pulled her favorite mug down. She opened up another cabinet and removed a box of assorted teas from the shelf. She ran water in her mug, placed it in the microwave, and heated it up. When the microwave bell chimed, she took out the hot mug and placed her Earl Grey tea bag inside of it.

"I need some lemons," she said. She reached over and pulled open the refrigerator door. She removed the green bottle of lemon juice from the shelf and set it on the counter. "It's going to be a long day," Tabetha whispered. "I still have to make dinner. Let's see," she said as she searched the shelf for items to cook. She pulled out the eggs and turkey bacon along with a fresh bell pepper. She removed a can of biscuits and then closed the door. She studied the rice container and tried to determine if she wanted rice or corned beef hash. "Corned beef hash," she concluded.

Tabetha entered the family room and flipped the switch for the gas fireplace. "It's cold in here," she said as she stood in front of the fireplace, warming up. She glanced over at the Christmas tree, which was situated in front of the sliding glass patio door within the family room. She couldn't wait for Gilbert to arise so that he could unwrap the state-of-the art home theater system she'd purchased for him.

The scent of breakfast food wafting through the house tickled Gilbert's nose, causing his stomach to beg him to wake up. Gilbert opened his eyes and studied the ceiling for a moment.

"Damn, damn, damn." He cursed the sight of daylight as well as the delicious scents wafting through the house. "I know she's in there cooking up a big breakfast just for me." Gilbert groaned. "I should have told her that I didn't have the mink coat a few days ago. Doggone it, why didn't I tell her?" Gilbert hated himself. "She should like the bracelet I got for her, though," Gilbert reasoned as he got up and entered the master bathroom to freshen up.

Tabetha couldn't contain her excitement. While the food cooked, she searched beneath the tree for the box that contained her mink coat, but she didn't find it. "Oh, he must have hidden it," she determined, and then began a quick search of the closets. When she couldn't locate his hiding spot, she decided to march up the stairs and wake him up in a sexual way. As she was about to enter the bedroom, she heard the sound of the master bathroom door closing and realized that he was awake.

"I can wait a few more minutes." She contained her excitement and went back to preparing breakfast.

"Merry Christmas, baby," Gilbert greeted her as he entered the kitchen.

"Merry Christmas to you too, Daddy," Tabetha answered flirtatiously as she turned around to hug him.

"Did you brush your teeth?" she asked.

"Of course I did," answered Gilbert.

Tabetha kissed him softly on the lips. She brushed the tip of her tongue across his soft lips.

"Baby, don't let the food burn," Gilbert said as he heard the sizzle of the corned beef hash getting louder. Tabetha checked on their meal while Gilbert took a seat at a small kitchen table. He reached into his robe pocket and pulled out the neatly gift-wrapped jewelry box, which contained her bracelet.

"Tabetha, there is something I need to tell you." Gilbert exhaled as he searched for the right words that wouldn't cause her to erupt.

Tabetha turned around and saw the small jewelry box on the table. "Oh, Gilbert, how thoughtful of you. You got me some jewelry to go with my mink coat as well?" Tabetha walked over to the table and picked up the package.

"Your gift is over there." Tabetha pointed with excitement. "Okay, I can't take it anymore. Go open your present. I want to see your face when you see what I got for you."

"Tabetha, before I do that, I need—"

"Come on, Gilbert," Tabetha cut him off as she rushed over to the Christmas tree. "Open these boxes right here," she said as she watched him rip open the first box.

"You got the home theater system that I've been wanting," Gilbert blurted out with surprise.

"Now, come over here and open up this one," Tabetha said, pointing to yet another large box. She watched as Gilbert eagerly unwrapped a package that contained a new flat-screen plasma television.

"Tabetha, you shouldn't have. This must have cost—"

"Don't you go there, Gilbert." Tabetha warned him not to ruin the moment. Gilbert moved away from the Christmas tree and the presents and plopped down on the family room sofa. He suddenly felt like a jackass.

"Okay, baby, where did you hide my mink coat?" Tabetha asked, buzzing with anticipation. "Look at this." She untied her robe and displayed her hot and sexy lingerie. "I have plans for you and my coat. Get up, Gilbert, and go get it. I want to put it on," Tabetha insisted as she went to check on the biscuits in the oven.

"Baby." Gilbert walked back into the kitchen, approached her from behind, and wrapped his arms around her waist. "I didn't have enough money to get your mink coat, so I had to tell them to put it back. I got you this really nice bracelet, though."

Tabetha released herself from his hug and pushed him off of her behind.

"Stop playing with me, Gilbert."

"Tabetha, don't get mad. I just couldn't afford it, okay? I mean, that coat cost a lot of money."

Tabetha stopped the business of her cooking. "You're serious, aren't you?" Tabetha searched his eyes and found the truth. "You don't have my damn mink coat. Don't say that you waited until today to tell me that you don't have it."

"Baby, I wanted to tell you, but I didn't know how. I mean, I didn't want to disappoint you and—"

"That's low-down, Gilbert!" Tabetha felt her anger swelling. "I made sure that I came up with the gift that you wanted." Tabetha's emotions were caught somewhere between disbelief and rage.

"You know what!" Tabetha was suddenly extremely upset. "Fuck you, Gilbert." At that point, she no longer cared about preparing breakfast or Christmas dinner because Gilbert had ruined her holiday.

"Tabetha, that's not necessary. Don't you talk to me like that."

"Fuck you, you bastard!" Tabetha shouted as she moved away from him and went toward her bedroom. As she walked past Rick's bedroom, he opened the door.

"Are you okay, Mom?" he asked.

"No," Tabetha said, holding her tears inside until she reached her bedroom and slammed the door shut.

Gilbert turned off the stove and sat down at the kitchen table. He suddenly developed a massive headache. He put his face in his hands and tried to figure out how he was going to make things right with Tabetha. He didn't notice that Rick had come into the kitchen.

"Yo," Rick said to get Gilbert's attention. "Do you want me to finish cooking this?"

"It doesn't matter now," Gilbert answered. "Eat it all if you want to. I'm not hungry."

"What did you do?" Rick asked.

"Don't worry about it, Rick. It has nothing to do with you."

The following afternoon, Tabetha phoned Lynise and convinced her to hang out at the mall with her to catch a few after-Christmas bargains.

"Tabetha, slow down, girl. You're walking like you're running a race," Lynise complained about the pace at which Tabetha was marching.

"I'm sorry, I'm just so pissed off," Tabetha admitted as she and Lynise moved past one of her bank branches located inside the mall.

"I would be, too, but if you don't let that shit go, you're going to pop a blood vessel."

"I mean, can you believe that retarded motherfucker waited until Christmas morning to tell me? He could have told me beforehand, and I could have made another payment or something to keep the coat in layaway. His dumb ass told them to put my coat back on the rack."

"Tabetha, he did get you a nice bracelet, didn't he? Give the man some credit. It's not easy for anyone to buy a mink coat," Lynise said, attempting to remind Tabetha of Gilbert's redeeming qualities.

"Yeah, whatever," Tabetha said as she stopped in front of a pretzel stand and stood in a long line.

"So what are you out here looking for, anyway?" asked Lynise.

"Nothing really. I just didn't want to be in the house."

"Well, let's head on down to the shoe store. I want to see if they've marked down some leather boots I've had my eye on for some time."

"That's fine. We can head that way once I get me a pretzel."

Lynise and Tabetha headed toward the shoe store at the other end of the mall. On their way there, they passed by the boutique where Gilbert was supposed to have purchased her coat.

"Lynise." Tabetha grabbed her arm tightly, forcing her to stop. "Come on, follow me." Tabetha rushed off toward the boutique. When she got there, she stopped in front of the display window and saw one of the sales representatives dressing up a window mannequin with her mink coat.

"Lynise," Tabetha cried out. "That's my coat."

"Oooh, it's beautiful," Lynise commented. "Okay, I'd be pissed off, too, if I thought I had that coming for Christmas and didn't get it."

"Come on," Tabetha said, and rushed inside the store. She got the attention of the saleswoman who was dressing the mannequin.

"Excuse me, miss. This is going to sound like a strange question, but did that particular mink coat just come out of layaway?"

"Actually, yes, it did. It's the only one left, and the price has been reduced to make room for a new supply of coats that are coming in."

"What's the price of it now?"

"Um"—the saleswoman flipped the tag over and read the price—"it's down to eight-thousand dollars. The regular price is eight thousand five hundred."

Tabetha began to think.

"Tabetha, why are looking like that?" Lynise asked. "Girl, you're calculating something. It's written all over your face."

"Come here." Tabetha pulled Lynise out of the saleswoman's hearing range. "I'm going to get my coat, Lynise. And I'm going to get it today."

"Can you afford to?" Lynise asked.

"Yes, I still have the money that Marlon gave me. I still have the check in my purse. I was supposed to give it back, but I didn't.

I can afford the coat comfortably if I use the money he gave me. What do you think?"

"I can't tell you what to do, Tabetha."

"Okay, if you were in my situation, would you get the coat?"

"If it were me, and I had the money, shit, I'd be strutting my ass off in my new coat." Lynise chuckled.

"That's what I thought." Tabetha was about to head back to the saleswoman to purchase the coat.

"Wait a minute. How are you going to explain the coat to Gilbert?" Lynise asked.

"Look, this is my money I'm spending. It's not coming out of our joint account."

"Yeah, but he's no fool either, Tabetha. He's going to know that you used the money Marlon gave you."

"And!" Tabetha said defiantly. "A sister has to do what a sister has to do. Come on. I'm going to purchase my mink coat and deposit Marlon's money in my bank account." Tabetha got the attention of the saleswoman. "That's my coat. You can take it out of the display window and box it up."

"Would you like to try it on first?" asked the saleswoman.

"Oh, I know it fits. I've tried it on before. In fact, you know what? Change of plans. I'm going to wear it out of here. Do you still have the matching headband, scarf, and gloves that go with it?"

The saleswoman smiled at Tabetha. "Of course we do," she answered, and escorted her over to the checkout register.

"Good, because I want those items as well. If I'm going to do this, I might as well do it right," Tabetha proclaimed.

6

Gilbert

"Leave me alone, Gilbert!" Tabetha shouted through the locked bedroom door when he tried to come to bed. She'd spent the following day ignoring and avoiding him.

"Tabetha, can we talk about this? I messed up, okay. Can you forgive me?" Gilbert asked, but Tabetha didn't respond. "Can I at least come in and get my pajamas?"

"They're in the dryer down in the basement," Tabetha answered through the locked door.

"Come on, Tabetha. We can straighten this out. Just let me in?" Gilbert pleaded as he once again tried to turn the bedroom doorknob. He heard the sound of the television grow louder, which meant that Tabetha wasn't in the mood for talking at all.

When Gilbert woke up the next day, he had a bad catch in his neck from sleeping on the basement sofa all night long.

"Damn, what a night," Gilbert grumbled aloud as he sat up, tossed his feet onto the floor, and greeted the day. He walked over to a small basement window and drew back the curtain to see what the weather was like outside. The brightness of the day made him squint his eyes. Once they adjusted, he saw Tabetha back her car out of the driveway and head off somewhere.

"Oh, Gilbert, you've really screwed up this time." Gilbert walked up the basement stairs and entered the kitchen. He called out Rick's name to see if he knew where Tabetha was off to.

"Rick!" he shouted out, but got no answer. "Rick!" he called out again, but still got no answer. He walked toward the front of the house and walked upstairs. When he reached Rick's door, he knocked a few times before he opened it.

"Rick?" Gilbert glanced around Rick's room, which, to his surprise, was tidied up. However, it was clear that Rick wasn't there. *He's probably gone with Mom,* Gilbert concluded, and shut the door.

"Man," Gilbert began talking to himself as he went down the hall and into his bedroom. "I'm going to head on down to that boutique and just get the coat on credit like I should have done from jumpstreet. At least Tabetha will know at that point that I wasn't trying to ruin her holiday." Gilbert went back down into the kitchen and picked up the phone. He dialed Tabetha's cell phone, but she didn't pick up.

"Shit," Gilbert hissed with frustration. He then dialed Rick's cell number.

"Yo, this is Rick. Spit it out," Rick answered his phone.

"Rick, this is Gilbert. Are you with your mother?"

"No, I'm across the street at Kevin's house. I saw her leave a few moments ago, though."

"Do you know where she went?"

"No," Rick answered.

Gilbert could tell that he seemed to have an attitude toward him.

"How long are you going to be over at Kevin's?" Gilbert asked.

"I don't know. For a while. My mother said it was cool if I wanted to hang out today."

"Well, just remember that you still have some business to take care of with me. You owe me time for the damage done to my car." Gilbert got stern with Rick.

"That's not the information that I got, homey. Mom said that she got you the money to pay for the damages. So I don't know what you're talking about."

Gilbert didn't like Rick's tone of voice at all. "You know, when you and your mother get home, both of you are going to step into my office and straighten out a lot of shit. Do you hear me?"

"Whatever. Later," Rick said, and disconnected the call.

Rick's disrespectful attitude toward him pissed Gilbert off. His first instinct was to march across the street, snatch the boy from the house, and whip his ass until he realized that he had to respect him. That seemed to be the root of the tension between them. He'd been in Rick's life for four years and had been his stepfather for two; by now he'd hoped that their relationship wouldn't be so strained. He knew that once again he'd have to talk to Tabetha about being united when it came to disciplining Rick. Gilbert didn't want to continue thinking about that issue at the moment. He went back upstairs, took a shower, and headed out to the mall.

When Gilbert arrived at the mall, he located the boutique and found a saleswoman to assist him.

"Hello," he greeted the woman. "I had placed a mahogany female mink coat on layaway but returned it to the store," Gilbert explained. "Anyway, I'd like to fill out a credit application so that I can purchase the coat today."

"Sir, if we're thinking about the same coat, I believe one of the other sales associates sold it earlier."

"Don't tell me that." The thought that the coat had been sold distressed Gilbert.

"I'll double check, but I'm pretty sure the coat was sold. Hang on." The saleswoman walked around the counter, down an aisle, and through a door, which had a posted sign that read

EMPLOYEES ONLY. When she returned, she approached Gilbert with the bad news.

"Sir, that coat is gone. I'm really sorry. But the other associate sold it."

"Shit!" Gilbert hissed. "Don't you have another that I could buy?"

"No, that was the last one. We do have some others that are similar that I could show you," offered the woman, but Gilbert didn't want to do that. He didn't feel comfortable just picking out a coat and running the risk of having it be something that Tabetha didn't particularly like.

"That's okay." Gilbert slumped his shoulders. "Thanks for your help." He drove back home to consider what other options were available to him.

When he entered the house, neither Rick nor Tabetha had returned yet. He opened the refrigerator, which was packed with all of the unprepared ingredients for the large Christmas dinner they were supposed to sit down and enjoy. He grabbed a beer from a side door, headed to the basement, and plopped down on the sofa. Gilbert twisted the bottle open and guzzled down half of it before stopping.

"Music," Gilbert said to himself. "It's a good day to sit around and listen to music." He retrieved the stereo remote from atop the stereo case and pressed the on button. Rick had set the channel on one of the hip-hop stations, and some rapper began shouting out raunchy lyrics.

"Lord have mercy," Gilbert condemned the loud ruckus. He switched the channel and found something that fit his current mood. He located his easy-listening station and relaxed as Janet Jackson cooed about the way love goes.

A few hours later, Gilbert heard the garage door open, signaling that Tabetha had returned home. He waited in the family room for her so that they could talk. He wanted to explain to her how he'd gone to the mall to purchase her gift only to discover that someone had purchased it already. Gilbert had rehearsed his words in his mind over and over. When he saw Tabetha enter the family room through the garage, his words suddenly became trapped in his throat.

"What are you staring at?" Tabetha snapped at him.

"You got the mink coat." Gilbert's words finally freed themselves.

"You're damn right I did," Tabetha said as she walked past him and entered the kitchen. She placed her keys on the countertop, and then hustled up the stairs to the bedroom.

"Where did you get the money to buy the coat?" Gilbert asked as she rested her coat on the bed.

"Don't worry about how I got it." Tabetha's tone was still filled with contempt. "It's just like my mother always said: Don't depend on a man for the things you want in life."

"That comment wasn't called for, Tabetha," Gilbert fired back at her. He knew that an argument was inevitable; he just wanted to get it over with so that she could vent her frustrations and he could apologize to her.

"Just so you know, I tried to go and buy the coat today but was told that it had already been sold," Gilbert shared.

"Well, it doesn't matter now. I have it. It's all mine, paid for in full," Tabetha said as she went into the master bathroom to begin changing her clothes.

The words "paid for in full" were caught by Gilbert's ears and stirred his thinking. "What do you mean paid for in full?"

"Just what I said. The coat has been paid for." Tabetha exited the bathroom and went to the closet to locate a hanger strong enough to hold the weight of the coat. "I have to take it back so that I can have it monogrammed."

"You used Marlon's money, didn't you?" Gilbert wanted to confirm his suspicion.

"You got that right." Tabetha wanted her words to sting him. She wanted him to feel how hurt and disappointed she was when she woke up yesterday and didn't have what she expected to have. She wanted him to feel the sting of insecurity.

"Tabetha, I thought we agreed that you'd give the money back." Gilbert tried not to raise his voice, but he couldn't help it, because anger, jealousy, and feelings of inadequacy had just taken control of his emotions.

"Well, there was a change of plans." Tabetha put her coat on the hanger and marched over to her closet.

"Tabetha, you're going to return that coat!" Gilbert barked at her.

"Like hell I am." Tabetha's facial expressions were full of unresolved conflict.

"Don't you understand? I wanted to buy you that gift. I didn't want you to get the money from your ex-husband. What are you going to do? Go thank him now? Huh? You're going to rush over to him in your hot little pajamas and thank him by tossing your legs up in the air. That's your plan, isn't it? Hell, for all I know, you could be just coming back from his house now." Gilbert's jealousy was in full command.

"Be careful of what you say to me, Gilbert. You're skating on thin ice." Tabetha pointed her index finger at him. "I gave you a chance to come correct on Christmas. I even offered to help you pay for the coat, but no, you wanted to get it on your own. So I was like cool, let you be the man and handle it. You knew how badly I wanted that coat, just like I knew how badly you wanted a home theater system. Just to show you how much I cared, I went and got in debt for that home theater system because I wanted you to have it." Tabetha's voice betrayed her by cracking. "I really wanted to give you a gift that would show you how much I cared about you. That system cost me twenty-five hundred dollars, Gilbert! But I didn't care, and I didn't go around tossing the fucking price up in your face. Because I know how you are."

"I don't want you taking money from Marlon." Gilbert stood his ground. He couldn't hear what Tabetha was trying to say to him. He was still transfixed on the money she'd gotten from Marlon.

"Marlon and I have been friends since grammar school. Even though our relationship didn't work out, Marlon has always cared for me. We have a son together, Gilbert, which means that we have a bond that will never be broken."

"That man is trying to take you away from me, Tabetha, and you know it. Is that why you don't want to have a baby with me? Is that why you don't want to give me a son or daughter of my own? Huh?" Gilbert couldn't contain his jealous words.

"You bitch and moan over the amount of money you have to spend at the grocery store for the three of us. You bitch and moan about the mortgage payment. Now you want to add the demands of a baby into the mix?"

"That's different, Tabetha. A husband expects his wife to provide him with the blessing of a child, not gallivant around the city with her wealthy ex-husband behind his back!" Gilbert continued to bark at Tabetha. They were arguing so loudly that neither of them heard Rick come rushing into the house and up the stairs.

"Don't talk to my mother like that!" Rick stood at the bedroom door, ready to defend his mother.

"Rick, baby, this doesn't concern you." Tabetha walked over to where he was.

"Yes, it does!" Rick argued back. "I heard you guys going at it all the way across the street. He acts like he wants to hit you, Mom. And that's not going to happen."

Gilbert turned and exploded toward Rick so swiftly that Rick didn't have time to react. Gilbert twisted Rick's clothing at the neck and trapped his gaze within his own. Gilbert had no intention of hitting Rick; he just wanted to set him straight. Rick had this coming to him.

"Boy!" Gilbert snarled. "Don't you ever think you're man enough to whip up on me in my own house. In fact, if you ever dream of whipping up on me, you'd better wake yourself up."

"Gilbert, let him go!" Tabetha quickly positioned herself between them. "Let him go now!"

"No," Gilbert said, unwilling to disengage. "We're just getting some things understood between us. This has been brewing for some time now."

"You've made your point, Gilbert. Now let my baby go."

"Done." Gilbert released his grip now that he felt his point had been made.

"Rick, come on, baby." Tabetha lightly placed her hand on Rick's chest. She could feel the pounding of his heart in the palm of her hand. She knew that Gilbert had scared him half out of his mind, but Rick didn't want Gilbert to know that. He wanted to defend her honor at all costs. "Come on, turn around, Rick. Let's go," Tabetha said, guiding him out of harm's way. "I am not going to have the two of you in here fighting." Rick listened to his mother and allowed her to guide him out of the way of danger.

Gilbert stood in the center of the bedroom floor and calmed himself down. He began to think. One philosophy, which was a necessary evil, was to let Rick know that Gilbert was king of the hill. However, Gilbert really didn't want to go there with him, but Rick had gotten way too cocky and had to be brought down a notch.

Gilbert couldn't stand the thought of Marlon and his wealth taking Tabetha away from him. He didn't want to compete for her loyalty. He needed reassurance from her. Gilbert needed to know that he was number one in her life. He wanted her to convey that to him so that their relationship wouldn't get destroyed by distrust. He wanted Tabetha to want a family with him, and the fact that she wasn't willing to have a child with him was gnawing away at him on the inside.

"She talks about Marlon like she's still in love with him," Gilbert whispered to himself. "After all this time. After all the mean and low-down things he's done. She has the nerve to still care for and defend him. "What the hell!" Gilbert said, bewildered by how she could possibly still care for Marlon.

7

Veronica

Veronica dragged her suitcase up the steep snow-covered front porch steps of Lenny Gray's home. When she got her suitcase up the landing, she paused for a moment to catch her breath.

"Whew, my legs and arms are killing me," Veronica said. She walked over to the door, which was all glass with wood trim. She peered inside for signs of activity, but the only thing visible was a small vestibule with wooden doors on the right- and left-hand sides.

It still looks the same as it always has, Veronica thought. She rang the doorbell and waited for what seemed like a longer-than-necessary period of time.

"What the hell," Veronica grumbled. "I called her and told her that I was coming." A few moments later, she saw the door on the left-hand side creep open. She studied her godmother, who she had not seen in some time. The full-bodied woman she once was now appeared frail, waiting for the arrival of the in-evitable.

"Give me a minute, I'm getting there," Lenny Gray said. She

moved about as if the very act of walking was painful. She unlocked the door and allowed Veronica to enter.

"Come on in here and get yourself out of the cold," she welcomed Veronica.

"How are you doing, Lenny Gray?" Veronica hugged her.

"Be careful, now. I am not what I used to be. I've had three
hip surgeries. All of the hugging and squeezing isn't necessary.
Besides, I know you don't mean it anyway."

"Thank you for letting me stay with you for a while. My
roommate and I just couldn't get along." Veronica recapitulated
the lie she'd told in order to get Lenny Gray to agree to let her in.
Lenny Gray took a seat in her favorite chair, which was positioned in front of the television. Veronica had interrupted Lenny
Gray's routine of watching *Dr. Phil*.

"Sit down a minute." Lenny Gray invited her to take a seat
on the blanket-covered sofa to the right of her. "You not in no
rush, are you?"

"No, I'm not in a rush," Veronica stated, and took a seat.

"Veronica, I may be old, but I'm not dumb." Lenny Gray
looked at Veronica with judging eyes. Veronica refused to meet
her gaze, so she lowered her head and looked at the floor because she knew Lenny Gray was about to speak her mind.
Lenny Gray's raspy voice of truth and wisdom was about to tell
it like it was, and when the truth came from Lenny Gray's
mouth, it had a way of cutting straight through to Veronica's
soul.

"My mind is still sharp. I know who you are. I also know all
about the underhanded things you've done." Lenny Gray paused
to take in air. "I know what you're capable of doing. I know
how you set up your own mother. God rest her soul. It broke
her heart when her lover put her out because of his stolen income tax money."

"I don't know what you're talking about," Veronica lied yet
again.

"Veronica, there comes a point in a person's life when they got to stop bullshitting. There comes a point in a person's life when they have to find out about living for their self. The world sure doesn't owe you a thing just because you're here."

Veronica couldn't stand listening to a lecture from Lenny Gray. However, she took the scolding so she wouldn't be put outdoors. *One thing is for sure,* Veronica thought, *her mind is still sharp as a razor.*

"I am not in the business of raising grown people. But, child, you've been running, lying, cheating, and stealing for a long time."

"Lenny Gray, I haven't been doing all of that." Veronica stuck to her lie.

"Baby child, don't sit here and lie to me or to yourself. I can see right through you, Veronica. You can't bullshit somebody who was bullshitting long before you were swimming around in your daddy's nut sack."

"Excuse me!" Veronica held her head up and met Lenny Gray's gaze.

"Uh-huh. Yeah, I said it." Lenny Gray didn't take back her words. "I told you, I may be old, but I'm not a fool."

"I never said that you were," Veronica shot back.

"Still got that snakebite in you, don't you?" Lenny Gray studied Veronica. "After all you've been through, being tossed out on the street, you still believe that you and your clever mouth can get you anywhere you want to go in life. You must be a proud graduate of the school of hard knocks." Lenny Gray paused, and Veronica watched her as she searched for the correct words. "Your grandmother took me in once when I had no place to go. I'm taking you in out of a sense of obligation to your grandmother. I know what it feels like when you have no place to go."

"I had someplace I could have went," Veronica lied yet again. "I mean, I don't have to stay here." She tried to be truthful, but her words still came out sounding like a lie.

"There you go again, lying to yourself. Veronica, you can run all you want. But you can't run away from the truth, and you can't run away from yourself."

Veronica exhaled because she realized that she couldn't out-fox Lenny Gray, even at her advanced age.

"Family, Veronica. That's what's important. Did you know that Gilbert drops in to see about me?"

"No, I didn't know that," answered Veronica.

"Yeah, he drives the Austin Boulevard bus route. So, since he's over this way, he drops in to check on me. We talk. He told me all about how you got caught up and eventually locked up. He worries about you, Veronica. Ever since you were children, Gilbert has been trying to put your hardheaded behind on the right path. He wants you to have a good life. Gilbert believes in you. He believes that there is good in you, and the only person who can change his mind-set about you is you. Gilbert is the type of man who puts family above everything else. Bless his soul. He's a nurturing man. It's a shame that his high-strung and confused wife doesn't see how blessed she is to have a man who loves so unconditionally."

"Yeah, I never did like that b—" Veronica caught the profanity in her throat before it escaped her lips. Lenny Gray leaned back in her seat.

"Run into the kitchen and put me on a pot of water for some tea. Go on, do that for me real quick," Lenny Gray requested.

Veronica went into the kitchen and did as Lenny Gray asked. When she returned, she found that Lenny Gray had fallen fast asleep. Veronica approached her and kissed her on the forehead.

"Don't you be in here stealing from me. You hear me, Veronica?" Lenny Gray surprised her. "I'm no old fool."

Veronica wanted to be insulted at being accused of thievery but decided she'd let Lenny Gray's comment go unchallenged. "You're right. You're nobody's fool," Veronica agreed with her.

"There is a spare bedroom down in the basement. You can put your things there."

"Okay," Veronica said, then grabbed her suitcase with her belongings and took them to her room.

Veronica entered the bedroom, turned on the light, and found that the accommodations were sufficient. There was a bed with an old-looking bedspread on it.

"Lenny Gray probably knitted that ancient thing," she said aloud as she noticed an old black Singer sewing machine situated near the closet. The room was a bit drafty, and Veronica made a mental note to ask Lenny Gray for an additional blanket. She opened the closet door and found a small space heater with metal coils sitting on top of the closet shelf. She took it down and plugged it in. She sat down on the edge of the lumpy bed and studied the space heater until the coils heated and turned bright red. Veronica walked around the basement and found the laundry room.

"Perfect," she said to herself. "Now I can get some of my things washed up." She walked to another side of the basement and found a bathroom with a shower. Lenny Gray had even thought enough to place fresh towels, soap, and cocoa butter skin moisturizer down there for her.

"Home sweet home," Veronica whispered to herself. "At least for now."

Veronica unpacked her suitcase and took a nice long shower. The water pressure wasn't that strong, but it was relaxing. When she came out, she spread a drying towel out on the bed and sat down nude on it. She took the cocoa butter and began spreading it on her body. The scent of the cocoa butter reminded her of her mother, Joyce, because she always used it on her skin. The scent of the cocoa butter and the thought of Joyce stirred Veronica's emotions unexpectedly. She stared at the space heater once again, and the coils reminded her of the skin welts she'd seen on her mother's skin. Another torturous memory attacked Veronica and made her think about how treacherous she had been.

*   *   *

When Veronica was thirteen, she had convinced her best friend Bonnie to ditch school and spend the day at the mall shopping.

"Spend the day at the mall shopping?" Bonnie said with surprise. "I don't know about that one, Veronica. I mean, what are we going to do?"

"Spend all of this money on clothes." Veronica removed a billfold from her purse and displayed it to Bonnie.

"Girl, where did you get all of that money?" Bonnie snatched it from her hand and began counting it in a rush.

"There has to be at least five hundred dollars here."

"Yeah, I know." Veronica chuckled. "Are you going to help me spend it or what?" she asked. "We could have a girls' day out and shop until we drop. Girl, we could come back to this school tomorrow dressed to a T. Not to mention we could pick out some outfits for the upcoming school dance and get our hair and nails done. Come on, Bonnie, ditch school with me so that we can have a good time."

"Where did you get the money, Veronica?"

"Hell, does it matter? I have it, and it needs to be spent. Are you game or what?" Veronica placed her hands on her hips.

"Okay," Bonnie agreed with excited anticipation. "When do you want to go?"

"Tomorrow. I have it all planned out. We'll get up and act like we're going to school, just like normal. I'll lie to my brother, Gilbert, and tell him that I'll be going to the library after school to study with you."

"Yeah, and I'll lie to my mom and tell her that I'll be at the library with you; that way she won't worry about me."

"Exactly. Tell your mother that Gilbert will bring you home. I'll have him pick us up from the library around eight PM. That should give us enough time to get back from the mall."

"But we'll have a bunch of shopping bags," Bonnie pointed out. "We'll get busted if we have shopping bags from the mall."

"No, we won't," Veronica said. "The library gives out carrying bags when you check out books. We'll check out a few books and get the bags. We'll place our clothes at the bottom of the library bags and place the books on top of them. Problem solved. We'll get the clothes in the house without any problems."

"Okay, I like that. It could work. But how are we going to explain all of the new clothes?"

"Girl, that's easy. I'll just say I borrowed some clothes from you, and you do the same. End of story."

"Wow, Veronica. You're slick as hell. How do you think of all this?"

"Shit, girl, my brain is always working. Stuff just comes to me out of the blue, and I roll with it." Both Veronica and Bonnie laughed.

Veronica and Bonnie's day at the mall was pulled off without any glitches. They squandered five hundred dollars on clothes, shoes, food, and cosmetics, and manicures at the beauty salon. At the end of their adventure, they had just enough money to catch public transportation back to the library. Like clockwork, Gilbert showed up on time to pick them up.

"Dang, Gilbert. Where in the world did you get this jalopy?" Bonnie asked, laughing at the car that was clearly one false start away from the auto graveyard.

"Hey, this car is a classic; it's a 1968 Mustang. I worked hard and saved my money and purchased it from this old dude who was letting it sit in his yard collecting rust."

"Well, that's where you should have left it." Bonnie laughed.

"Hey, you can always walk home, you know," Gilbert said, not appreciating her criticism of his first car.

"I'm just saying, you need to get out of the sixties and come up to the eighties," Bonnie continued to tease him.

"He's working on it, Bonnie," Veronica defended her brother. "He's taking automotive courses at school, and they give him credit for bringing the car in to be worked on by other students."

"Yeah. When my automotive class is done with this car, Bonnie, it's going to look sharp, and you'll be dying to get a ride with me," Gilbert added.

Veronica sat in the front seat and watched as Gilbert continually pumped the gas pedal while turning the ignition switch. The car kept sputtering, refusing to start up.

"Come on now." Gilbert hit it again, but the car was still being stubborn.

"Oh God, please don't tell me we have to walk home," Bonnie blurted out.

"Just give me a minute," Gilbert said. "You have to crank it up just right." Gilbert hit it again, and the old Mustang finally fired up.

"Oh God, roll down a window. The entire car smells like gasoline now," Bonnie complained as Gilbert jerked the car into gear and pulled off.

Gilbert dropped Bonnie off and waited for her to enter her apartment building and give a signal from the window that she'd made it inside safely. Veronica and Gilbert then headed toward home. As they walked up the stairs, they heard Fred shouting at the top of his voice over the loud clatter of objects crashing.

"What the hell is going on in there?" Gilbert said, fumbling with his door keys.

"I don't know," Veronica quickly said. "Maybe we should leave them alone."

"No. It doesn't sound good. Mom is screaming like she's in danger. I hope Fred isn't hitting her or something."

Veronica saw Gilbert's hand nervously fumble with the lock. Veronica let Gilbert rush into the house first. She felt her nerves on edge; they were tingling with fright. She swallowed hard. She felt her pulse quicken as she entered the house, uncertain of what she was walking into. When she walked into the family room, everything was in disarray. She saw Fred continually trying to hit her mother with his belt while Gilbert held his arm to prevent another blow from landing.

"Don't you know how much I care about you?" Fred howled out. "I love you. How could you do this to me, huh? How could you steal money from me?"

"Stop it!" Gilbert wrestled Fred to the floor and began to drag him away from his mother. "Don't you hit her!" Gilbert got Fred away from her and confronted him.

"What the fuck is wrong with you, hitting on my mother like that? Huh?"

Veronica saw the fury in Gilbert's eyes. To her, all of the drama was exciting to watch unfold.

"She stole my fuckin' income tax money from me!" Fred barked.

"Hey, man, my mother doesn't have to steal anything!"

"Yes, she did! I'm going to beat her ass!" Fred was so angry that he made another lunge for her, but Gilbert stopped him with a bear hug and wrestled him to the floor yet again. Gilbert made the mistake of letting Fred get up a second time. Fred wasn't about to allow Gilbert to manhandle him, so he took his vengeance out on him.

"Boy, I will kill you." Fred clutched his hands around Gilbert's throat and began to squeeze with all of his might. Gilbert quickly dropped to his knees but continued to try and free himself from Fred's murderous grip.

"Let him up, Fred!" Joyce, their mother, began pulling herself up off the floor.

Veronica looked at her mother's bare arms, which had red welts all over them from being lashed with the belt.

"You will not whip on me in my own house, boy!" Fred continued his brutal assault on Gilbert, who was clearly beginning to black out from lack of air.

"Baby, he's just a boy!" Joyce tried to pull Fred's hands away from Gilbert's throat. Veronica rushed over to the kitchen. She searched the cupboard for her mother's black iron skillet. When she found it, she grabbed it, rushed up behind Fred, closed her eyes, and swung it at his head. The sound of the iron skillet connecting with Fred's skull made a haunting and eerie sound. Veronica moved out of the way as Fred's body collapsed.

"Gilbert, baby, breathe," Joyce pleaded with Gilbert. "Breathe, baby. Come on, breathe." Gilbert finally coughed and gasped for air.

"Oh, my head," Fred groaned.

"Veronica." Joyce caught her gaze. "Go get a cold towel and wrap it in some ice for Fred."

"What?" Veronica didn't understand why she had to help him.

"Do it now, Veronica!" her mother insisted.

After all was said and done, Fred, their mother's boyfriend, ended their relationship and asked Joyce to leave. Veronica eventually confessed about taking the money, and as a result, a wide valley formed between Veronica and her mother that could never be repaired or healed. The memory of the incident was like pieces of shattered and jagged glass in her mind.

8

Tabetha

The tension around Tabetha's house had subsided over the past few days, and life was returning to its usual routine. Gilbert apologized for messing things up on Christmas morning and for losing his temper and taking out his frustrations on Rick.

"You know I'd never harm him or you, right?" Gilbert reassured Tabetha.

"Are you sure, Gilbert? You had a murderous look in your eyes the other day."

"Tabetha, I was angry. More angry with myself than with anyone else. I get jealous of you and Marlon."

"Why?" Tabetha asked.

"I guess the selfish part of me would prefer it if he was a deadbeat father; then we could both bad-mouth him together. We could both dislike him and remove him from our lives. But that's not the way it is. You guys have a parental relationship, and I have to keep reminding myself that your relationship with him is necessary and that there is no romantic interest in him on your part—right?" Gilbert asked, looking for reassurance.

"Yes, Gilbert. I've told you that a thousand times. You don't have to worry about that."

"Okay, that's all I need to hear," Gilbert said. "I trust you, and that's all that matters." Gilbert embraced Tabetha and whispered, "I love you."

It was 2:00 PM on New Year's Eve, and Tabetha had just completed her annual ritual of going through her closet and removing clothes and shoes that she would be donating to the local charity organization. She'd packed up the garments and placed them in a box. She dragged the box over to her bedroom, then walked down the hall and entered Rick's room without knocking.

"Hey!" Rick complained about the intrusion. Tabetha could have cared less about Rick having a problem with her not knocking.

"What are you doing in here?" she asked, peeking into his room suspiciously.

"Lifting weights," Rick answered.

"With your shirt off?" Tabetha asked.

"Yeah, I'm getting my pump on," Rick answered.

"Well, come on down to my room and carry this box of clothes out to the garage and put it in my car."

"Right now?" Rick complained.

"Yes, right now. Lifting a heavy box should help you maintain your pump," Tabetha teased him. She turned around, walked down the steps, and made her way around to the family room. Gilbert was sitting on the sofa reading the hook-up instructions for the new plasma television.

"Aren't you done hooking that thing up yet?" asked Tabetha.

"No, not just yet," Gilbert answered. "I'll let you know when I have it all hooked up."

"I'm about to go upstairs and balance the checkbook for our joint account. Have you written any checks I need to know about?"

"No," Gilbert answered as he continued to remove additional items from the box that the television came in.

Tabetha picked up a stack of bills that were sitting in a basket on the countertop. She opened the refrigerator and removed one of her Clearly Canadian bottled waters. She went back upstairs and into the third bedroom, which was the home office, and booted up the computer. Tabetha went about the business of balancing the joint account and her personal account, which at the present time was in a sad state because of the money she'd spent on the home theater system and on her fur coat. Once she was finished, she came downstairs again to see if Gilbert was done hooking up the television. She noticed that Rick was helping him.

"Are you guys done yet?" asked Tabetha. "I want to see how well the television plays."

"Not yet, Mom. We're trying to hook up the DVD player and the VCR to the theater speakers," Rick answered.

"Well, I'm going to go surf the Internet then," Tabetha said, and then went back into the home office.

Tabetha checked her e-mail and noticed that she had several from her girlfriend Lynise, who lived online. She opened up various e-mails, which had bad photos of celebrities, and responded to them. She decided to log onto her work e-mail to see what type of drama she'd be dealing with once she returned to the office. Just as she was about to open up an e-mail from her boss, she received an instant message.

Marlon38: I was just thinking of you. How are you doing?
LadyTabetha: Oh really, that's nice to know.
Marlon38: How was your holiday?
LadyTabetha: Good, and yours?
Marlon38: I can't complain. I'm in paradise right now.
LadyTabetha: Paradise?
Marlon38: Yes, I'm spending New Years in the Florida Keys. I recently purchased a vacation home here.
LadyTabetha: Well, I'm sure it's a nice one.

Marlon38: Would you like to see it?
LadyTabetha: Sure, e-mail me a photo.
Marlon38: Why send a photo when I can turn on my Webcam.
LadyTabetha: Okay, let's see.

Tabetha accepted the notification that Marlon wanted to do a video conference with her. Her computer opened up an additional window that displayed the video feed coming from Marlon's computer. He appeared to be located in one of the bedrooms of his tropical home. He panned the camera around and stopped it so she could see the view of the patio, the palm trees, and the ocean.

"Oh, that looks nice," Tabetha mumbled to herself. Marlon moved the camera again and set it back on top of his computer so that Tabetha could see his face as they continued to communicate with each other.

Marlon38: If you and Rick ever want to come down, let me know, and I'll arrange it for you guys.
LadyTabetha: Well, maybe not me, but I'm sure Rick would love it.
Marlon38: I'm sure he would. Perhaps I'll bring him down after he graduates from high school. It would be a nice graduation present, don't you think?
LadyTabetha: Yes, it would. So, what woman are you down there with?
Marlon38: I'm not with anyone. I'm alone down here.
LadyTabetha: Yeah, right. I don't believe you.
Marlon38: Well, it's the truth.
LadyTabetha: Why are you there alone?
Marlon38: Because I needed time to reflect.
LadyTabetha: Reflect on what?
Marlon38: My life. And my career. I have a new goal I want to achieve. It may be of interest to you.

LadyTabetha: I doubt it.
Marlon38: Perhaps. But are you so sure you'd turn down an opportunity to be wealthy?
LadyTabetha: Marlon, what are you talking about?
Marlon38: Just think about what I said and consider what it would feel like to never have money problems. When I return, we can chat about it.
LadyTabetha: Yeah. Whatever.
Marlon38: I just sent you a photo. Take a look at it.

Tabetha went to her in-box and downloaded the photo. When the photo opened, she saw that it was a picture of her when she was nineteen. The photo was taken during the summer as the sun was setting at Sixty-Third Street Beach off of Lake Shore Drive. She was wearing white shorts and a yellow summer top. She was sitting on the back of Marlon's motorcycle. She had her fingers locked around Marlon's waist, and her face was pressed into his back. Marlon was clutching the handlebars, keeping the motorcycle balanced as they both looked in the direction of the camera. Tabetha studied her mahogany legs and arms and recalled how she felt during that time period in her life. She studied the photo a little longer and could almost feel the buzzing vibration of the motorcycle between her legs.

LadyTabetha: What are you trying to do, Marlon? This photo is so old. You need to stop living in the past.
Marlon38: I know that, Tabetha. I just reflect sometimes and think that if I could do things over again, let's just say things would be much different.

Tabetha shrunk the photo window and studied Marlon's face on the Webcam. She was trying to determine if he was losing his mind or was in some type of depressed state. However, she couldn't tell if he was depressed or not. She had to admit that she wouldn't know the signs of depression if they presented themselves to her.

Marlon38: Do you need anything? Do you need any money or—

LadyTabetha: Marlon, I don't need anything, okay? I can take care of myself.

Marlon38: I wasn't suggesting you couldn't. You've proven that beyond doubt. I just want you to know that if you ever need anything, all you have to do is ask.

LadyTabetha: Thanks.

Marlon38: You and Rick really should come down here. The house has its own theater room with a screen as big as the ones you find in movie theaters.

LadyTabetha: You sound as if you're lonely in your big home. I'm sorry, I shouldn't have said that. It sounds as if you spared no expense.

Marlon38: It's okay. It is a little lonely down here. Anyway, I had a design company build the house from the ground up. I know you'd fall in love with it if you saw it.

LadyTabetha: Like I said, Rick would probably love your cozy bachelor pad, but I'm not setting one foot in your home. I'm married, remember.

Marlon38: Oh yeah. I forgot about that.

LadyTabetha: How could you forget that I'm married?

Marlon38: Easy. Especially when I hear that things aren't going too well in your home.

LadyTabetha: Things are great here, Marlon. I don't know where you're getting your information.

Marlon38: If you say so. Perhaps when we talk you'll seriously consider my offer.

LadyTabetha: Marlon, you're not making any sense.

Marlon38: I know. I'll explain it all to you when I return. Happy New Year.

LadyTabetha: Happy New Year to you too.

Tabetha deleted the text of their conversation before she called Rick up into the room so that he could chat with his father via the computer. Tabetha went back to her bedroom and sat down in front of her makeup table. She took a headscarf from the drawer and placed it around her head. She studied her diamond face in the mirror and began to think about the photo Marlon had shown her.

"I was so young then," she whispered to her reflection. Tabetha felt the door of an old chamber in her heart open that hadn't been unlocked in years. It was a door to old memories. At first she was going to close it back up, but she decided to take a good look around. Tabetha went up to the attic where all of her priceless memories and possessions were stored. Once up there, she pulled the string of the light switch so that she could see. Over toward the corner of the attic were several trunks and boxes. She walked over to an old trunk, which contained memorabilia from her past. Tabetha sat down on an old chair and opened up the first trunk.

"My roller skates," Tabetha said aloud as she pulled them out of the box. "My white roller skates." She laughed. She spun one of the squeaky wheels and visualized herself at her tenth birthday party at a local roller-skating rink. She'd invited all of the kids in the neighborhood, including the new boy Marlon, whose family had just moved next door to her. Tabetha closed her eyes and could hear the song "Boogie Nights" by Heatweave playing in her mind.

"What's the matter with you?" She had rolled up with two of her girlfriends and asked Marlon, who refused to come out onto the floor and roller-skate. "Don't you know how to roller-skate? Everyone is out here having fun, and you're standing around with your lip poked out."

"I can do anything," Marlon answered confidently. "I just don't want to skate right now."

"Well, it sounds to me like you're a chicken." Tabetha challenged his ego.

"I'm not a chicken." Marlon denied her claim.

"Then what are you?" Tabetha questioned him as she curled her lips into a sour expression.

"I just don't want to make y'all look bad. I know how to roller-skate," Marlon boasted.

"Yeah, right. Let me see you do it."

"This isn't my song," Marlon stalled. "When my song comes on, I'll do it."

"Boy, please. It doesn't take all of that to show someone you know how to roller-skate," Tabetha said, and then rolled away with her girlfriends. As she and her girlfriends rolled around the rink, she saw Marlon come out onto the floor and try to roller-skate. It was clear to her by the way he was fanning his arms like a chicken that he didn't know how to balance himself very well. As Tabetha approached him, she decided to spin herself around and show him how well she could roller-skate backward.

"What's the matter, hot shot?" she blurted out as she zoomed past him. Tabetha realized that she must have embarrassed him because he quickly got off the floor. She decided to be nicer to him and at least show him how to move without falling.

"Come on," she said as she rolled up to him.

"What?"

"Come on, I'll show you how to roller-skate." Marlon didn't move. "I promise I will not let you fall," Tabetha assured him. "Take my hand; trust me. I've taught three friends how to do it already."

Marlon stood up and followed her. She instructed him on how to balance himself and then held his hand as they slowly moved around the edge of the rink, out of the way of the other skaters who were zooming by.

"I don't roller-skate much," Marlon admitted as he kept looking at his feet.

"Duh, I know that," Tabetha responded obnoxiously. "I should start charging people for showing them how to do this."

"You should, I mean, I would. When I grow up, I'm going to be a businessman and own all types of companies. I might even own a bunch of roller-skating rinks. I'm going to have a bunch of money and people who work for me. One day I'm going to have millions of dollars and never have to work. The only thing I'll do is count how much money I'm making."

"Okay, obviously you don't get out much. You must be a major bookworm, because you're lost in your own world."

"I am not lost in my own world," Marlon raised his voice.

"Jeez, relax, and stop clutching my hand so tightly. I'm just saying you sound like Scrooge when you talk about counting your millions of dollars."

"What do you know about Scrooge?" Marlon had heard a bit of sarcasm in her voice.

"I read the book, thank you very much," Tabetha replied.

"Yeah, right. You probably saw the movie." Marlon didn't believe her. "No one our age reads books like that."

"It was written by Charles Dickens. He was born in 1812 and died in 1870. At the age of twelve he was sent to work in a factory to help support his family."

Marlon gazed at Tabetha with surprise.

"Shocked?" Tabetha glared at him.

"I'm not sure yet. Let's see how well-read you really are. Who wrote *Little Women?*" Marlon challenged her knowledge.

"That's easy. Louisa May Alcott," answered Tabetha.

"Come on. Impress me more. Tell me about her."

"Please, you can't stump me. She was born in Germantown, Pennsylvania, in November of 1832. She and her three sisters were schooled by their father, who was a philosopher and a teacher."

"You're good," Marlon admitted. "Most kids I know don't even like to read."

"I'm not most kids," Tabetha stated.

"Yeah, I see that now." Marlon said.

"My mother is an English professor at the university,"

Tabetha shared. "We love to read. My father used to play professional football. He's retired now but is assistant coach for our city's team. What do your parents do?"

"My dad is a state congressman. He travels a lot and deals with a lot of businesspeople. My mother is a judge for the fifth district circuit court of appeals."

"Do you have any brothers or sisters?" Tabetha asked.

"Yes, I have an older sister. You?" Marlon asked.

"No. I'm the only child. I think that you've got it now," Tabetha said. "We've been skating in circles for some time now."

"Yeah, I think you're right." Marlon smiled, pleased that he was able to get around better.

"I need to go to the ladies room," Tabetha said as she rolled away from him. "I'll be back."

Tabetha remembered thinking even back then that Marlon was different from other boys. She reached into the trunk again, and this time she removed several diaries that she'd kept from junior high through high school.

"Oh my God. I haven't seen these in ages," Tabetha said to herself as she brushed the dust away. "I forgot that I had these." She opened to the first page of her very first diary and read what she wrote.

Dear Diary,

I feel really silly writing to you like you're a real person, but I suppose that's how a person is supposed to make an entry. I guess I should start off by saying that I'm thirteen years old and in the eighth grade. I'm one of the most popular girls in school, thank God, because I would end my life if I looked like Shanita Gravey. That girl's face looks like pimple paradise. Anyway, I'm not writing to talk about Shanita because I could care less about her. I'm writing to talk about Marlon Wayne. He is like the most drop-dead gorgeous boy in the entire region. No, the entire planet.

Well, maybe not the entire planet; Todd Bridges holds that title. But Marlon and Todd Bridges could be brothers. Marlon used to live next door to me, but he moved to the other side of town into a much bigger home. Although we go to the same school, I just don't see or talk to him as much as I'd like to. Anyway, Marlon showed up last night at the school dance looking like a million bucks. I couldn't wait to talk to him and catch up on things as well as sneak in a slow dance with him. I stood in the center of the gym with all of my girlfriends, just waiting for him to notice me and come over. But before he even saw me, Raggedy Rita Turner got all up in his face. Now, everybody knows that Raggedy Rita is overdeveloped and lets boys feel her up all the time. I can't stand Rita. Anyway, I saw that I'd have to get Marlon's attention. I knew that once he saw me, he'd be happy to see me, and we'd catch up on things. I moved around the gym and got closer so that he would notice me. But Raggedy Rita kept distracting him by pushing her over-developed boobs in front of him. Just when I was about to give up, Marlon saw me and called my name. He excused himself from Rita and came over to me. I was so happy. We stood and talked about which teachers were too hard, and stuff like that. Then a slow song came on, and he asked me to dance. I swear my heart must have stopped beating. I didn't know much about slow dancing, but I was more than willing to give it a try with him.

"Come on," he said to me. "If you can teach me how to roller-skate, I can teach you how to slow dance." It was magic dancing with him. I don't even remember the song we were dancing to. All I do remember is the way he gazed into my eyes and how much I wanted to kiss his smooth chocolate lips.

Dang, I have to go, my mother is calling me. But I'm going to dream about him tonight. He is so cute!

Tabetha closed the dairy and laughed at her writing. She recalled how badly she wanted Marlon to kiss her that night, but he didn't. Tabetha decided to put the diaries back and read another passage at a later time. She dug a little deeper into her memory chest and found an old wedding photo of her and Marlon. "We used to be so happy together," Tabetha mumbled as she studied the picture. "We were so young," she whispered as the horrible memory of how they split up came forth.

They were both in their early twenties and living in a small one-bedroom apartment with their son, Rick. Marlon had a job that didn't pay much, as did Tabetha, but she didn't care. She was so in love with Marlon and wanted to make their young marriage work. However, Marlon started changing on her. He became mean, started arguments all the time, and was very suspicious and critical of her.

"Why did you get pregnant on me anyway?" he howled at her during the argument that ended their marriage. He'd just returned home from the bank, where their account had zero funds in it, even after he'd deposited his paycheck. He wasn't making the type of money that he wanted to, and now he wanted to blame it on her.

"I didn't do it on purpose, Marlon. It just happened." Tabetha felt her heart aching at his accusation of entrapment.

"Our marriage isn't going to work. I can't live like this. Struggling from one paycheck to the next. A high school education isn't enough for me to go where I want and need to go."

"Baby, you can go to college. We can make this work," Tabetha assured him.

"No, we can't, Tabetha. How can you say that? I bring home five hundred dollars every two weeks. Rent here is six hundred dollars. It takes two of my checks to cover our living expenses. And your part-time job at night barely brings in two hundred additional dollars. Rick's food, medical, and clothing expenses outweigh our income."

"What do you want, Marlon? Huh? Do you want me to make Rick disappear or something? Well I can't. We just have to deal with this baby. We can make it." Tabetha tried to comfort him.

"No, we can't, Tabetha. Not like this. I can't live ghetto fabulously like this any longer. I don't want to continue on with you."

"Don't you say that to me, Marlon." Tabetha trembled uncontrollably. "Don't say that to me. Don't you know that I love you? Don't you know that I've loved you ever since we were children? Ever since that day we were at the roller-skating rink? Don't break up our family, baby. Am I doing something wrong? Is there another girl? Tell me, Marlon. I'll make changes."

"I have to do this. I've already talked it over with my parents. They're going to help out financially while I go to college."

"I don't want money from your parents! I want my husband. I want my family. Don't you know that? I will do what I have to do to keep you, Marlon. I just can't turn my love for you off."

"This has to be done, Tabetha. I made a mistake. No, we made a mistake. It happens. I'm not going to allow this mistake to ruin my life, though."

"Ruin your life?" Tabetha began sobbing. "I didn't want to ruin your life. Is that what you think of me? I'm just some dumb girl who ruined your life? Oh God, Marlon." Tabetha cried hard and loud.

"Tabetha, listen. This is what is best. I'm sorry, but I don't want you." Marlon's words crushed Tabetha's heart in a way that it had never been hurt before. "Look, both of our parents decided to let us give it a shot and try to make it on our own. But we can't. A blind man can see that we're in over our heads. I don't know about your parents but mine were extremely disappointed that this pregnancy and marriage occurred sooner than anticipated."

"Please don't go. Please don't leave us. Please, Marlon. I love you so much. Tell me what I can do."

"There is nothing you can do. This is just the way it is."

"Why are acting so cold toward me?"

Marlon shrugged his shoulders. "I'm not going to sign the new lease when it comes next month. You should call your parents and move back in with them. I'm going back to my parents, and I'm going to finish college and make something of myself."

"Marlon, we can do this, baby," Tabetha said.

"No, we can't. I don't want to. Get it through your head, Tabetha. It's over."

"So you're just going to leave me and your son out in the cold?"

"I told you. My family has money, and they'll help out. I'll do what I can and come around when I can."

Tabetha tossed the old wedding photo back into the trunk.

"Low-down bastard!" Tabetha mumbled as she continued to dig through the box. She came across an old issue of *Black Entrepreneur Magazine*, which had a feature article on Marlon. He was standing on the cover smiling and looking wonderful in his blue pinstriped business suit. Tabetha opened up the magazine she'd saved and read a little bit of the article.

Marlon Wayne has a lot to smile about these days, because his small company that he started ten years ago is finally turning a profit. Nolram Holdings Company and its two subsidiaries earned eight million dollars in revenue last year. "Nolram Holdings Company specializes in the acquisition and development of high-end real estate properties," said Mr. Wayne, who has two independently operating subsidiaries as well. Career Works, Inc., is a career services portal and network for recruiting firms, hiring companies, and job-seekers; and IMC Entertainment is a company that develops Internet-based computer gaming software. "Sometimes I sit in my office and smile at my success," said Mr. Wayne, who was confident that his small company would eventually turn a profit. "I always knew

*that I'd do well in business. It's in my blood, and success
runs in my family. I'm just doing what I've always wanted
to do, and that is live the American dream." Mr. Wayne's
father, who is a former congressman, works for his son
now and has aided in securing business deals through his
political connections with business leaders and investors
who were hungry to tap into the markets that Marlon indicated would be booming.*

God he sounds so cocky, Tabetha thought as she closed the
magazine. She shut the trunk and went back downstairs.

"Tabetha, I have it hooked up; come take a look at it,"
Gilbert called to her.

Tabetha went into the family room to view the television.
"That's a beautiful picture," Tabetha said.

"Yeah, it's nice," Gilbert said, stepping back to admire the
sharpness of the picture.

"Come snuggle up with me on the sofa," Gilbert suggested
as he took a seat on it. "I know how much you love classic
movies, so I rented *Little Women* for you."

"Really? I love that movie," Tabetha said.

"I know you do," Gilbert said, and kissed her on the forehead.

9

Gilbert

Gilbert didn't remember exactly when he and Tabetha had drifted off to sleep on the sofa. When he woke up, the movie they'd been watching had ended. He took the television remote that was in his hand and pointed it at the television. He clicked the clock button to check the time. It was three-thirty in the morning. He exhaled and set the remote on the back of the sofa. He glanced down at Tabetha, who was resting comfortably against his chest. Her head was turned to the right and faced the inside of the sofa. He could see her inhaling deeply before exhaling and knew that she was in a deep sleep. Gilbert loved moments like this with Tabetha. These were the moments that weren't so strained or tense with some type of conflict. Gilbert stroked her hair lovingly, not wanting to disturb the peaceful moment.

"What was this episode that we just went through all about, Tabetha?" Gilbert asked in a soft voice, not really seeking a response to his question. He was tossing his question in the air just to study it.

"Money isn't everything," Gilbert said as he continued to

stroke her hair. "Family is what's important. Good health is important. Having someone who loves you without question is important. Don't you know that?" Gilbert asked.

"You know, I was so happy when your car had a flat tire. If you had not gotten a flat tire at Rick's Little League game, we probably wouldn't have a relationship. I still remember the day as if it were yesterday." Gilbert squeezed Tabetha with affection.

Gilbert had been volunteering his free time as the Little League coach for the local park district. After a game one Saturday afternoon, he went inside the field house to finish up some paperwork. He'd just gotten started when he heard a knock at the door.

"Excuse me, Mr. Murphy." Tabetha peeped inside the office.

"Yes," Gilbert answered without looking.

"I am really sorry to disturb you, but I'm in kind of a jam."

Gilbert looked up from his stack of papers and saw Tabetha standing in his doorway. He couldn't help but study her long shapely caramel legs, her sexy hips, beautiful breasts, and attractive face. He knew exactly who she was.

"What can I do for you?" Gilbert asked as he stood up and came around from behind his desk. "Did one of my boys do something or say something that wasn't polite?" Gilbert asked, ready to get the name of the offender.

"No, it's nothing like that," Tabetha assured him. "My name is Tabetha West. I'm Rick's mom."

"Yes! Miss West." Gilbert smiled at her.

"Oh, okay. I wasn't sure if you remembered me from orientation back in the spring."

"Trust me, I remember you. I could never forget someone like you," Gilbert informed her, hoping that his comment wasn't offensive to her. He studied Tabetha as she smiled and then laughed a little. Gilbert took her relaxed demeanor as an invitation to continue his lighthearted flirting.

"No, Miss West, even if I was struck by a bolt of lightning, my memory of you would remain. I may not recall my own name, but I'd remember yours."

Tabetha laughed. "It's nice to know that I left an impression on you," Tabetha answered him. "Look, I came in here because I'm in a bit of a jam. My car has a flat tire, and I don't have a clue as to how to change it. I tried to get one of the other dads to help me, but before I could get anyone's attention, they were all driving off. I called my motor club service, but it's going to take them about two hours before they get here, and I just don't have that type of time to waste. At least not today. So, if it's not too much trouble, I could really use your help," Tabetha pleaded.

"No problem, Miss West. I'd be more than happy to change that tire for you. Let me just grab my keys and lock up the office," Gilbert said as he went around the desk, opened the top drawer, and retrieved his keys. "Where is Rick? Doesn't he know how to change a flat tire yet?"

"Rick knows about as much as I do," Tabetha admitted. "Besides, I'd be afraid to let him do something like that. It'd be just my luck that some freak accident would happen, like the car tipping over on him."

Gilbert chuckled at Tabetha's unwarranted fear. "Where is Rick at now? With your permission, he can watch me do it so that he learns how," Gilbert offered.

"He rushed over to the batting cage to practice," Tabetha informed him. "The minute he knew we wouldn't be leaving right away he rushed off."

"Well, I'll be the first to admit that he does need the practice," Gilbert said as he locked the door and followed Tabetha out to his car. "Rick has phenomenal leg speed, which makes him a great outfielder, but his hand-eye coordination hasn't developed just yet."

"Yeah, I noticed that as well. He's all set to give up on the sport and try something else, but I keep telling him that he has to learn how to see things through. Rick wants to be able to do everything instantly, and when he discovers that he's not so good at something, he loses interest."

"Well, I think it's good that you're making him stick with it. At a minimum it will teach him to be disciplined," Gilbert said as they walked past the baseball diamond and across the green field toward her car.

"You must have boys of your own?" Tabetha concluded.

"Actually, no, I don't."

"Oh, so you have girls," Tabetha corrected herself.

"No, actually, I don't have any children. But I'm in the market for a wife," Gilbert shared. "I'm looking for the right woman to build a strong black family with."

"So you look forward to becoming a family man?" Tabetha restated.

Gilbert noticed the tone of Tabetha's voice; she seemed perplexed by his position.

"Oh yeah," Gilbert admitted without hesitation. "You sound as if you're surprised by that," he said as they reached Tabetha's car.

"Well, you're certainly not like the men I've come across. Settling down is the furthest thought from their minds. I honestly didn't think men such as yourself were still around."

Gilbert laughed. "Trust me, we're still around. Forgive me for being bold, but I thought you were married."

"Who, me?" Tabetha smiled at Gilbert's assumption. "No, I'm not married."

"Sorry, I didn't mean to strike a tender spot," Gilbert apologized.

"Don't be," Tabetha said as she opened the trunk of her car so that Gilbert could pull out the spare tire. "It didn't work out with Rick's father and me. He wasn't ready to be a father. He wanted to pursue other things, blah, blah, blah. You know the story; I'm sure of it."

"So he left you high and dry?" Gilbert said what she wouldn't.

"Yeah, kind of, but not exactly. It's complicated," Tabetha said.

"Does Rick see him at all?" Gilbert continued to pry into Tabetha's personal affairs.

"Yeah, Rick sees him, just not as much as he should. His dad is off building his empire." Tabetha mocked Marlon's words.

"Empire?" Gilbert asked, confused as he removed the spare tire and jack.

"Like I said, it's sort of complicated."

"Well, as long as his father is still around, that's the important thing," Gilbert said. "Young boys need a father."

"And their mother," Tabetha quickly added.

"That is correct," Gilbert agreed. He changed Tabetha's tire and placed the bad one along with the equipment back in the trunk of her car.

"Let me pay you for your time," Tabetha offered.

"Oh no." Gilbert tossed the palms of his hands up. "There is no need to pay me."

"Come on, don't do this," Tabetha pleaded. "I would have tipped the Triple A guy. Let me tip you."

"No," Gilbert answered defiantly. "Use the money for something else. I'm sure that a single mom could always use a little extra cash."

"Isn't that the truth," Tabetha agreed with him. "Look, I feel bad for not giving you something. Maybe we could have lunch after one of the games or something."

"I would like that, Miss West." Gilbert smiled at her. "I'd like that a lot."

"Good. Then next Saturday after the game, we're having lunch, okay? Is there any place in particular that you'd like to go?"

"Not really." Gilbert watched the expression on Tabetha's face switch to embarrassment.

"I'm sorry, how rude of me. If you have a lady or something, it's okay, I understand." Tabetha said.

"No," Gilbert quickly corrected her. "It's nothing like that to worry about. I was just being coy. Do you like soul food?"

"It really depends on how it's cooked," Tabetha said.

"There is a new soul food place that opened on Stony Island Boulevard just past Eighty-Seventh Street. It's a great place. I'm sure you'd like it," Gilbert assured her.

"All right," Tabetha said, "I'll trust your judgment." Tabetha shifted her attention from Gilbert to the batting cage. "Well, let me go and get my child. We have a ton of running around to do this afternoon."

"All right, Miss West. You take care, and I'll see you next Saturday."

Tabetha stirred in her sleep before she woke up and rose from Gilbert's body.

"Oh, my neck has a bad catch in it now," Tabetha complained.

"I'll rub it out for you," Gilbert offered, and began massaging her shoulders.

"Ooooh, that's too hard. Do it softer," Tabetha instructed.

"We slept right through the New Year," Gilbert said.

"Oh, man. I wanted to watch the countdown," Tabetha said.

"Well, happy New Year," Gilbert said as he hugged Tabetha and forced her to lie back down on the sofa with him.

"Happy New Year," Tabetha replied back. "Do you have any resolutions?" she asked.

"Only one," Gilbert said.

"What is it?" Tabetha asked.

"For us to have a baby together," Gilbert answered, hoping to begin a meaningful dialogue about planning a pregnancy.

"Gilbert." Tabetha sat up. "I'm not going down this road with you again. You know my position on having another child. I don't want to have another one." Tabetha got up from the sofa and began to walk away.

"Can't we at least talk about it some more?"

"No, Gilbert," Tabetha answered conclusively as she went upstairs to the bedroom. Gilbert turned off the television and sat on the sofa trying to figure out why Tabetha was so unyielding about providing him with a child of his own.

"This isn't right," Gilbert whispered. "If she doesn't change her mind soon, something is going to happen that we'll both end up regretting."

10

Veronica

Three weeks into the new year, Veronica figured that enough time had passed for Bonnie to calm down. Bonnie still had items at her house that Veronica wanted back. Veronica decided that she'd pay Bonnie a visit during the daytime when she was normally asleep and her kids were at school. Veronica knew that she'd disturb Bonnie's rest by visiting her at ten o'clock in the morning but thought it would work to her advantage because Bonnie would not be so quick to get into another physical confrontation with her. Veronica took the bus over to Bonnie's place and hustled up the porch staircase and to her back door.

"Well, here goes," Veronica mumbled to herself as she prepared for the worst. She began banging on the back door fast, hard, and loud as if she were the police trying to gain access into her home. She continued banging loud and hard on the door with both her hand and foot. She finally heard Bonnie ask who was at the door.

"Who is it?" her voice sounded heavy, as if she'd just awoke.

"It's me, girl, open the door. It's cold out here," Veronica said, trying to gain some sympathy from Bonnie.

"Do you have my damn money?" Bonnie asked.

"Girl, come on. Open the door. Let's not talk about that right now," Veronica answered, hoping to persuade her once again. There was a long pause of silence before Veronica heard the door tumblers being unlocked.

"I take it you're here for the rest of your things," Bonnie concluded. Veronica noticed how she folded her arms across her chest and glared at her with contempt.

"Yeah, can I come in and get them?" Veronica asked.

"Yeah, I packed your stuff for you. I should have just tossed it in the alley or, better yet, burned it up."

"Well, thank you for not doing that," Veronica voiced her gratitude as she entered. Bonnie shut the back door.

"I'm never going to forgive you for what you did, Veronica. I want you to know that."

"Bonnie, I told you. I didn't do that," Veronica boldly lied to her.

"Veronica, stop lying. This is me you're talking to. Remember, I've been around you for a long time. I remember when you stole your mother's boyfriend's income tax money and caused him to go crazy and beat her up and then almost kill your brother Gilbert. So don't tell me what you didn't do, because I know you too well."

"Bonnie, I'm telling you, girl. I didn't take your money." Veronica stuck to her story.

"There's just no helping you," Bonnie said, accepting Veronica for what she was, a lying thief through and through. "Wait right here. I'll go and get your things."

Veronica waited in the kitchen for Bonnie to return. When Bonnie came back, Veronica saw that she'd placed the rest of her belongings in two large duffel bags.

"Here you go," Bonnie said. "If you ever find it in your heart to return my money, I'd appreciate it."

Veronica didn't know how to respond to her, so she just nodded her head in agreement.

"Does this mean our friendship is over? I mean, it's not totally over, is it?"

"Veronica, you have to grow up. You can't keep running from one person's house to the next and expect them to help you out while you steal from them. You're not welcome in my home anymore, that's for sure. If I see you on the street, I'll speak, but that's about it."

"Come on now, Bonnie, we——"

"Save it, Veronica," Bonnie cut her off before she could get started.

Veronica took her belongings and headed out the way she came in. As she approached the staircase, her heart skipped beats when she saw Big Money Chuck coming through the gangway. Veronica quickly ducked down and scurried back over to Bonnie's back door. She knocked a few times quick and hard, and then whispered loudly, "Bonnie, open up." She tapped on the back door again. "Bonnie, open the door."

"Veronica, what the hell are you doing? Why are you squatted down like that?"

"Bonnie, let me in, please."

"Hell, no. What in the world has gotten into you?" Bonnie asked. "Did you smoke some bad shit again?"

"No! Big Money Chuck is coming through the gangway. If he sees me, I don't know what he'll do. I'm dead," Veronica uttered softly. "Please, Bonnie. Let me in."

"He's coming here looking for you. I told you that. I don't want shit to do with him anymore. I left that lifestyle alone, Veronica. I'm not about to get caught back up in that crazy lifestyle." Bonnie was about to shut the door.

"Bonnie, please. I don't want to see him right now." Veronica gazed up at Bonnie. "If you were ever my friend, do me this one last favor. Let me cut through the house and go out the front door. I promise you, I will never bother you again."

"No," Bonnie said, but then paused. "I don't know why I'm

helping your black ass. Hurry up, get in here and go out the front door."

"Thank you so much, Bonnie," Veronica said as she stepped inside. She watched as Bonnie quickly locked the door.

"He can stand there and knock all day if he wants to. I'm not answering that door," Bonnie said, and moved toward the front of her apartment with Veronica.

"Come on." Bonnie signaled for Veronica to follow her.

"I'm staying with my godmother, Lenny Gray. That's where I'll be if you—"

"Good-bye, Veronica. I hope you get your act together one day. I'd hate to have to read about you in the newspaper. Or see you standing at a traffic light with a message written on a cardboard box."

Without saying another word, Veronica flung a duffel bag over each shoulder and rushed down the steps of the narrow hallway. When she got to the bottom, she flung open the vestibule door and rushed away from Bonnie's apartment as quickly as she could.

Veronica hustled through Lenny Gray's backyard and entered the house through the kitchen, which was situated at the rear of her home. She shut the door and made sure that it was locked securely before plopping down on one of the antique red and silver kitchen chairs, which appeared to have come from a fifties diner. Her heart was pounding rapidly, and her skin was slick with sweat from making such a hasty exit. Veronica was about to call out Lenny's name to let her know that she had returned but noticed a handwritten note posted to an ancient-looking white refrigerator door. She got up, pulled the note down and read it.

Why did you leave the house this morning? You knew that I wanted you to come to church with me today.

Veronica crumpled up the note and tossed it in the trash can.

"Church is about the last place I'm going," she said aloud as she pulled the silver handle of the refrigerator door. She glanced inside and searched for something to snack on.

"This refrigerator is always empty," Veronica complained, and slammed the door shut hard. She had become extremely irritable by the fact that Big Money Chuck was searching for her. *Doesn't he realize that I don't want anything to do with him?* Veronica thought. *Doesn't he realize that I'm not working with him anymore and that I don't have plans to ever work with him again? My God, Veronica, you know good and well that when Chuck catches up with you, there may be hell to pay.*

Back when Veronica was twenty years old, she was living on her own and attempting to complete her college education by attending classes in the evening. She worked as a saleswoman and cashier for a clothing retailer located in her favorite shopping mall. Veronica had been employed at the retailer for eight months and had gained the confidence and trust of the store manager and was eventually given a slight increase in pay and additional responsibilities. Veronica enjoyed working at the store and the discounts that she was afforded, but as she learned more about the business, she discovered loopholes in the way the store manager accounted for money and inventory. It wasn't long before she began to take advantage of her opportunity to steal. When the time was right she coached Bonnie on exactly how to steal items from the store.

"Bonnie, all you have to do is go to the sale rack at the rear of the store. There is a big red sign that says 'sale' hanging above the rack. I've placed some very nice items back there. They're the only items on the rack."

"You've gone over this with me already, Veronica. I can handle this," Bonnie assured her.

"I'm just making sure of it, okay?" Veronica was irritated by the interruption.

"Bring all of the items up to my register. There will not be a line when you come, because we're doing this transaction first thing this morning. I'll ring you up with the coupon that I gave you. With the discounts that I'm going to give, you'll get to walk out of the store with a load of expensive clothes for less than twenty-five dollars."

"Did you get the skirt suit that I wanted?" Bonnie asked.

"Yes, it's mixed in with the clothes. Just make sure you're the first person in the store so that no one else goes to the rack and picks up our shit." Veronica reinforced her position.

When Veronica opened the gate of the store, Bonnie wasn't standing there like she had instructed her. She went over to the sales rack to remove the clothes that she'd placed on the rack so no other customer would get them. Just as she was about to remove the clothes, the bell chimed, signaling that someone had entered the store. Veronica turned around and saw Bonnie and a slim man with gingerbread skin enter the store. Veronica caught Bonnie's gaze and trapped it for a moment so that she could read her eyes before assisting the man who'd come into the store.

"Can I help you locate something?" Veronica asked the man.

"I'm just browsing right now," the man informed her. "When I need a little help, I'll call on you," he said.

Veronica went back to the cash register to ring up the items that Bonnie had placed on the countertop. Veronica kept a suspicious eye on the man because of a strange vibe she got from him. As she began ringing up the items, the man approached the register.

"Excuse me, miss," he addressed Bonnie. "What rack did you get these items from? I'm looking for that exact suit," the man explained. "It's for my baby sister. She's graduating from nursing school, and I told her that I'd buy her a nice graduation outfit."

Veronica didn't believe the man for one moment.

"Sir, these are closeout items. What she has here is the last of it."

The man popped his fingers. "I guess I wasn't quick enough," he said, and continued to browse around the store.

"Hurry up and get this shit out of here," Veronica whispered to Bonnie as she quickly rang the items up and placed them in a bag. "He could be from the corporate headquarters," Veronica said. "Go." She rushed Bonnie out of the store. Her heart was pounding hard from the excitement of getting away with what she'd done. She couldn't wait to get home and try on the items that she'd taken illegally.

"You like the rush and excitement of it all, don't you?"

Veronica hadn't noticed that the man had approached her. She studied him more closely this time. He was tall and menacing, with a well-maintained haircut, rich black eyebrows, and distrustful eyes.

"Excuse me?" Veronica's tone was stern with him.

The man laughed. "There is no need to get all uptight. I'm not mall security." He smiled, and Veronica didn't like the way his grin formed on his face.

"My name is Chuck," he introduced himself. "My friends all call me Big Money Chuck."

Veronica looked at him suspiciously. She recognized his name; she knew that Chuck was a street thug with a reputation for getting merchandise. It was also rumored that he was very ruthless.

"Did you find something for your sister, Chuck?" Veronica captured his gaze and held it in her own. She could read his eyes very well. It was something that came naturally to her. She had always been able to read a person's eyes. She knew that he was trying to determine if he should share what the real nature of his visit to this particular store was.

"You didn't answer my question. Do you like the excitement of what you do?" He asked again.

"I like my job," Veronica answered. "It pays my bills."

"No, it doesn't," Chuck boldly stated. "You're probably barely surviving on this dead-end job. But like me, you find ways to make your stay worthwhile." Chuck smiled and winked at her with a sly sense of knowing.

"What do you want?" Veronica asked him directly.

"Well, would you look at this." Chuck removed an item from the rack before him. "You know, this looks just like that suit girlfriend walked out of here with a few minutes ago. This suit is"—he glanced at the price tag—"two hundred dollars, and she had about four of them. I don't claim to have super hearing senses, but I swear I heard you say that her total was twenty-five dollars."

"You know what, I'm calling security." Veronica was about to march over to the counter and hit the silent panic button.

"Don't do that," Chuck advised her. "It's not necessary. You and I have a gift for getting items at bargain rates. Right now, you're small-time, but me, I do it professionally. I have clients who reward me for my services," Chuck boldly stated.

"What type of services?" Veronica's curiosity cord had been pulled.

"What time do you get off from work?" Chuck asked, re-directing the conversation.

"Four o'clock," Veronica answered.

"If you're truly interested, I'll be sitting down in the Chinese restaurant in the food court when you get off from work. I think that you'll find what I have to say exciting." Chuck winked at Veronica once again before he exited the store.

At four o'clock when Veronica left the store as she normally did, she decided that class that evening could wait while she in-vestigated what Big Money Chuck was into. She walked down to the food court, and sure enough, he was sitting at a table waiting for her.

"Have a seat," Chuck offered. Veronica sat down quietly. "So, it looks as if I was right," Chuck stated.

"Who knows, maybe you were wrong," Veronica shot back.

"Darling, I'm rarely wrong when it comes to selecting members of my team. I've been doing this for years and know how to spot new talent."

"What is it exactly that you do?" Veronica asked directly.

"The same thing you do. I steal stuff and sell it at reasonable prices. I'm a fence."

"Really?" Veronica asked, filled with intrigue. She leaned closer to him and whispered, "What exactly does a fence do? It sounds like it's dangerous." Veronica shifted her eyes to see if anyone heard what she said.

"I was right then," Chuck stated. "You like the excitement of doing this kind of work."

"Well, I'm no pro at it," Veronica admitted.

"Would you like to become one?" Chuck asked.

Veronica laughed nervously but then thought about it. "It depends on how much fun it is and how much money I can make at it."

"Is money an issue for you right now?" asked Chuck.

"Shit yeah. I'm working this bullshit job that barely pays my bills. I'm trying to go to college, but the shit is just way too damn expensive. At least once a month I call my brother to ask him for money. He's trying to make it himself, but he gives me what he can. My brother is giving like that. At first, I used to feel bad always asking him for money, but then it got to the point where it was all too easy to ask him, because I knew he'd give it to me."

Chuck nodded his head knowingly. "Have you ever been arrested for stealing?" he asked.

"Oh, hell no," Veronica quickly answered. "I'm not trying to go to jail."

"Neither am I," Chuck answered. "Right now I'm not going to tell you all of the details of my operation, but I will give you a brief overview of how it works. Professionals like me are thoughtful, and we're very difficult to stop. In fact, my operations are credited with shutting down five retail stores," Chuck said. "That's a fact that I'm proud of. I'm a smooth operator. I don't do that crude snatch-and-grab shit. I work below the radar and hit retailers through a variety of techniques ranging from misuse of employee discounts, like what you did today, or through distraction techniques."

"How does that work? The distraction thing, I mean?" Veronica asked with a perky voice filled with energy. She felt herself buzzing all over as Chuck explained his methods to her.

"I can't just tell you how to do it. That, my dear, is something you must be trained to do."

"Okay, then train me," Veronica said without thinking about what she was asking.

Chuck laughed. "You're an eager one, aren't you? Baby girl, we just met." Chuck swept his tongue across his lips. "But if we get together, I'm sure things will work out."

Veronica read Chuck's eyes and knew that he was talking about more than stealing. He was searching for sex as well.

"I'm available," Veronica answered the unspoken question. "I'm twenty years old with no kids. I love to have fun. Do you think you can handle me?" Veronica asked.

"Damn right I can," Chuck responded. "But you have to gain my trust. One dumb move can fuck up an entire operation. And I'll tell you this, all bullshit aside. If I train you, I own you." Chuck's words were direct and clear.

"What do you mean by 'own me'?" Veronica needed more clarification.

"Just what I said. There is no hidden meaning behind my words. When you get with me, it's a lifetime contract."

"Yeah, right." Veronica laughed, believing that Chuck's comment held no real merit. "Okay," Veronica answered. "I can live with a lifetime contract." She lied to him and believed that she was just telling him what he wanted to hear in order to gain his trust.

Chuck pulled out his wallet, removed two business cards, and handed one to Veronica.

"Pawnshop," Veronica read the card.

"Write down a number where I can reach you."

Veronica did as he asked and handed the card back to him. Chuck then gave her the second card for her to keep. "I will be in touch. I have an order that needs to be filled by your store."

"What? You're going to do it, just like that?" Veronica asked, still buzzing with untamed energy.

"If you do good with this assignment, others will follow."

"Now wait a minute." Veronica suddenly developed concerns. "My job is my livelihood. It pays the bills. You know what I mean. I can't just go around hooking you up. I may get caught and lose it. I don't know about that. Shit, I have rent to pay."

"When you work for me"—Chuck was once again very direct and clear with his words and intentions—"you don't worry about paying your rent, because I take care of that. If you get arrested, I'll take care of your attorney and your legal fees. I'm a smooth operator, Veronica. I'll teach you how to defeat the antitheft technology that the stores have as well as send you out on assignment with a team."

"A team?" Veronica asked.

"Yes, a team."

Veronica squirmed in her seat as a way to contain the strange sensation washing over her. *Finally,* she thought, *I've met someone just like me.*

"Are you bad enough to handle all of the excitement that comes with this territory?" Chuck asked.

Veronica's twisted heart loved the idea of being part of a large operation. "How much money will I make?" Veronica asked. "I'm not going to do this if I'm not going to get paid."

Chuck smiled a sinister grin. "You'll be paid fairly," he answered. "You won't be disappointed with the amount of money you can make." Chuck stared at Veronica for a moment before he broke eye contact.

"Okay. So you'll call me tomorrow, right?" Veronica asked.

"Yeah, at nine o'clock. Make sure you're at this number." Chuck held up the card she'd written her number on.

"Don't worry, I'll be there," Veronica said as she stood up and excused herself.

"Oh, one more thing." Chuck stopped Veronica before she walked away. He stood up, walked over to her, and whispered in her ear, "Nobody ever screws me over and gets away with it. Anyone who tries to will get a one-way pass to the underground motel. Do you understand what I'm saying?" Chuck asked.

"Yeah, I hear you." Veronica pulled away and looked him in the eyes. "Just make sure you don't try to bury the wrong snake," Veronica countered with a proclamation of her own.

"I like you." Chuck nodded his head as he agreed with his own words. "You have balls. So, we understand each other then?"

Veronica studied Chuck's eyes.

"Yeah, we understand each other," she answered him, and continued on her way. As she walked away from Chuck, she wondered if he was any good in bed.

Veronica placed her fingers in her hair and began scratching her scalp. "I thought for sure that by now Big Money Chuck would let shit go. I thought for sure that he'd cut his losses and move on. Why did I screw him over? Of all people, why did I screw over Chuck to save my own ass?" Veronica asked, but got no answer from herself.

"I have to get away from this side of town," Veronica said aloud. "Perhaps Bonnie had a point." She began to think. "Perhaps I need to be like her and get my life together." She unzipped the other duffel bag and pulled out a purple pouch with a gold drawstring. She opened it up and found what she'd really gone back to Bonnie's house for.

"Thank God," Veronica said as she removed several thick sticks of marijuana. "This will most certainly relax my nerves," she said as she went over to the stove and turned the knob. The flame leaped up, and she lit her joint. Veronica took a hard drag and waited, anticipating the mellow feeling that was soon to come. She went into the basement where her bed was and sat down. Big Money Chuck's pursuit of her was heavy on her mind. She knew that if he caught her, he'd probably make sure that she checked into the underground motel, and she wasn't ready to get there just yet. If and when Chuck did catch up with her, she'd have to really come up with a way to smooth things over with him. Veronica hoped that her game was good enough to save her ass a second time.

11

Tabetha

Tabetha was sitting in a conference room listening to the phone conversation of a sales call that one of her sales representatives was handling. She was making notes about the call so that she could offer more useful techniques to the sales representative when trying to sell a customer additional listings in the yellow pages. Tabetha enjoyed her job as the regional manager of sales for the Chicago market. She was responsible for yellow page ads for the Chicago neighborhood markets and the surrounding suburbs. She had a staff of fifteen telephone sales representatives, five mobile sales representatives, and two managers. Her job was demanding, but she loved what she did for a living. Her career was important to her, and she wasn't about to give it up to have a baby. As she continued to make notes regarding the call, she was interrupted by the buzz of her cell phone, which was attached to her belt. She pulled the phone out of its carrying pouch and saw that it was Lynise.

"This is Tabetha," she answered.

"Hey, T. I was just calling to make sure we're still on for happy-hour drinks," Lynise said.

"Yes," Tabetha answered. "I need to talk to you about some things that are on my mind."

"Oh boy. What happened now?" Lynise wanted the scoop.

"I'll tell you when I see you," Tabetha said. "Just make sure you arrive at Bandera's on time."

"I'll probably beat you there," Lynise assured her.

"Whatever," Tabetha joked. "I'll see you there this evening," said Tabetha before she disconnected the call.

When Tabetha arrived at Bandera's restaurant on North Michigan Avenue, Lynise was already seated at the bar, nursing a drink and awaiting her arrival.

"Sorry about being late," Tabetha said as she quickly sat down on the bar stool next to her. "My sales meeting went longer than I anticipated."

"It's not a problem." Lynise eased Tabetha's regretful feelings. "I took the day off for a doctor's appointment."

"Oh really?" Tabetha commented. "It's nothing serious, right?"

"No, it's just time for that yearly exam. The doctor has to go and peep around in my ass. You know the drill." Lynise laughed.

"Yeah, I know the drill. You still have the male gynecologist? What's his name." Tabetha popped her fingers as she tried to recall his name.

"Payne," Lynise answered. "Dr. Phillip Payne."

"It must have been difficult for him to get his practice going," Tabetha concluded.

"Why do you say that?" Lynise asked. "He's a handsome brother who resembles Will Smith. I highly doubt he had any issues getting started. Sometimes I wish he didn't have to have a nurse in the room all the time, because I'd certainly try to take advantage of his fine ass." Both Lynise and Tabetha laughed.

"No, I'm not talking about the way he looks, silly. I'm talking about his name. I mean, who would go to a doctor named Payne?" Tabetha paused. "Well, besides you. You like pain," Tabetha joked with Lynise.

"Hey, don't knock the pain-pleasure thing until you've tried it," Lynise quickly countered with a witty comment of her own. "So what's going on? What has your panties all tied up in a knot?" Lynise asked.

"Gilbert," Tabetha answered.

"I told you that I didn't think it was such a good idea to bring that fur coat back to the house, but I wasn't about to get all up in your business like that."

"Girl, that's old news. Gilbert is over that now." Tabetha made a waving-away gesture with her hand. "Shit, spending my money on a fur coat was fully justified in my opinion."

"Hey, if it works for you, then it works for me. Just be careful how you treat Gilbert," Lynise offered as a bit of advice. "He's a good guy, Tabetha. He's a little insecure about some things, but overall he's a good guy."

"Well, good guy or not, he's on my last nerve right now." Tabetha's words were edgy, and she wanted Lynise to pick up on it immediately.

"What did he do?" Lynise asked, concerned.

Tabetha huffed and then searched for the right words to describe her feelings. "He wants me to have a baby with him, and I'm just not going to do it." Tabetha's voice was filled with irritated emotion. "I'm thirty-eight years old with a seventeen-year-old son who, in a minute, will be out of the house and on his way to college. Once Rick turns eighteen and goes away to college, my time will have been served."

"Didn't you and Gilbert discuss this before? I mean, I know you did, but you never really went into details about what was said."

"Well, when we first got married, I told him that I'd think about it, but I really had no intentions of getting pregnant again."

"Oooh. You should have just flat out told him that there wasn't a snowball's chance in hell of you wanting to get pregnant again if you feel that strongly about it."

Tabetha paused in thought again as she considered what she

really wanted to say. "Let me rephrase that. When we first talked about it before we got married, I did say that if the circumstances were right, I'd consider having another baby with him. I didn't say I would; I said I'd consider it."

"And what are the right circumstances?" Lynise asked.

"First of all, he'd have to be making enough money to take care of me, the baby, and all of our other bills while I sit at home and play the happy fucking housewife. Second, in order to do this, I'd have to want to take a break from my career, which I don't want to do, by the way. I've worked my ass off to get to executive management, and I'll be damned if I'm going to waltz into my boss's office and tell him, 'Oh, I want to have a baby now. I'm sorry that I didn't tell you this before I took on the responsibility of this job.' I don't think so." Tabetha was passionate about her position.

"Well, perhaps you guys could adopt a child or, even better, become foster parents or something."

"Lynise, don't you get it? I'm done. I don't want any more children. I don't want to change shitty Pampers or worry about day care or go through grades one through twelve again. When Rick is gone, I want to run around the house naked and take romantic vacations or purchase a getaway home in the Florida Keys with a theater built inside of it." Tabetha caught herself and paused, wondering why the hell her last comment came flying out of her mouth without notifying her brain first.

"What's wrong with you? Why do you have a perplexed look on your face?" Lynise asked.

"Nothing," Tabetha said, searching for the answer to her own internal questions.

"Bullshit!" Lynise said. "It's written all over your face, Tabetha. Now tell me what else is going on in that head of yours."

"Lynise, I don't even want to know." Tabetha signaled for the bartender.

"What can I get you?" asked the young bartender.

"I'll have a strawberry daiquiri," Tabetha said.

"Come on, spit it out. What's on your mind?" Lynise asked.

"I'm trying to figure myself out, Lynise. I'm trying to figure out why I"—Tabetha trapped her words in her throat, then swallowed them down because she didn't want her ears to hear what her mouth had to say—"sometimes . . . I just . . . it's like, I love Gilbert, I really do. But I don't want to have his baby. Wait, that didn't sound right. I don't want to get pregnant and start another family at this point in my life. But he does, and I know that he has every right to want to start a family. What does that mean, Lynise? Does it mean that I'm a bad person or that I'm not committed to the vows I took? I'm confused about this. I mean, am I wrong for feeling the way that I do?"

"Look, I'm not the type of person who likes to get into other people's business, Tabetha, but you and Gilbert need to work this out before it gets out of hand."

"Lynise, every time we talk about it, we end up having a massive argument. When it comes to this topic, we end up barking at each other. Having another baby represents slowing down and missing out to me. It represents getting fat and dealing with car seats and strollers and going down a road that I've already traveled."

"What road do you want to go down now?" Lynise asked.

Tabetha smirked. "I want a man who has the power to whisk me away to some tropical paradise and romance me. I want a man who has wealth and power and can buy me whatever my heart desires."

"Tabetha!" Lynise called out her name loudly and snapped her out of her fantasy.

"What?" Tabetha answered.

"Did you just hear yourself?"

"What? I just said that I want Gilbert to romance me and buy me whatever my heart desires."

"That's not what you just said. You said that you want a man to do those things. You spoke as if Gilbert didn't exist."

"No, I didn't," Tabetha denied Lynise's claim.

"Yes, you did, Tabetha. My ears were not lying to me. Let me ask you something. This may sound far-fetched but stick with me. Are you in love with Marlon?"

"Hell no," Tabetha said with certainty.

"Do you want to be with Marlon?"

"No," Tabetha said.

"Do you wish that Gilbert was more like Marlon?"

"Gilbert could never be Marlon," Tabetha said.

"I didn't ask you if Gilbert could be him. I asked if you wanted Gilbert to be more like Marlon. In other words, do you still have feelings for Marlon?"

"I'll always have feelings for Marlon. We have a child together," Tabetha said truthfully. "I care about his well-being, but I'm not in love with him. I'll admit that I do enjoy seeing how successful he has become."

"Are you jealous of his success?" Lynise asked.

"No. Why would you ask a question like that?"

"I'm just asking questions that are obvious to me."

"So what are you trying to say or trying to imply?" Tabetha was set to get offended.

"Here's your drink, ma'am." The bartender set Tabetha's drink in front of her. She lifted the straw and took a sip.

"Mmm, that's good," she said as she savored the taste of the alcohol.

"I'm not trying to say or imply anything. I'm just concerned that you may be in denial about a few things."

"You know what?" Tabetha set the drink down. "I love my husband. He's a good family man, and I know this. That's one of the reasons I married him."

"Then if you know that, why don't you want to start a family with him?"

"Because it's not what I want to do." Tabetha raised her voice, which was verbal confirmation that she'd gotten upset. "I'm sorry, Lynise. I didn't mean to raise my voice at you."

"Hey, ain't no sweat off my nose; speak your mind."

"I guess what it boils down to is this. The thing that I loved the most about Gilbert has ironically become the thing that annoys me the most, and I'm not sure of how to fix it without doing something I don't want to do. Does that make any sense?" Tabetha studied Lynise as she considered her answer before she shared her thoughts.

"In my mind, you both have valid points, but I don't know how to fix a problem like this. I'm sorry that I haven't been helpful."

"No, Lynise. You've been helpful. Just listening to how I feel has been helpful."

12

Gilbert

The bitterly cold February wind nipped at Gilbert's uncovered ears as he walked up the front steps of Lenny Gray's home. He rang the doorbell, then covered his right ear with the palm of his hand.

"Whoa, it's cold," he hissed as he shivered and waited for either Lenny Gray or Veronica to come to the door. He pressed the doorbell again, and a short moment later, Veronica opened the door for him.

"There's my big brother," Veronica greeted him jovially as she locked her arms around his neck and hugged him while she rocked him from side to side.

"Quick, let your big brother come in out of the cold," Gilbert said as he stepped inside where it was warm.

"Yeah, sure, come on in." Veronica stepped aside and allowed him in. "Go on up in there. Lenny is back there in the kitchen frying up some chicken wings."

"Yeah, I can smell them," Gilbert said as he walked back toward the kitchen. When Gilbert entered, Lenny was standing at the stove turning the chicken wings over onto the uncooked side. She was wearing a comfortable-looking green fleece housecoat with matching slippers.

"Come here, baby, and give me sugar," Lenny said as she set her cooking utensil to the side and stepped carefully over to Gilbert to hug and kiss him. "It's so good to see you," Lenny said.

Gilbert held on to Lenny's embrace a little longer than necessary. He could feel the frailness of her body and made a mental note to himself to savor every moment, because her time here was approaching its end.

"Have a seat over there at the table. Let me put on a few more wings for you."

"No, that's okay, you don't have to do that," Gilbert said, feeling guilty about her standing at the stove at her age wanting to cook for him.

"It's no problem at all," Lenny said as she opened the refrigerator door.

"Veronica, help her out," Gilbert said. Veronica glared at Gilbert as if he was speaking a foreign language.

"It's okay, I don't need any help. I was frying chicken long before you were even a thought in your mother's head."

"She don't need my help," Veronica stated.

Gilbert shot daggers at Veronica with his eyes. In his mind, it was clear to him that Veronica was perhaps taking advantage of Lenny Gray, and he didn't like it.

"Lenny, you must be tired from standing on your feet. Let me do that for you." Gilbert stood up and went over to the stove. "Here, have a seat right here. As soon as a few of these wings are ready, I'll serve them to you with a side of hot sauce."

Lenny coughed a little as she honored Gilbert's request to take a seat.

"I put some frozen French fries in the oven," Lenny said. "It's hard to get people to help you out around here, Gilbert,"

Lenny complained to him. "I've got grown able-bodied people around here who don't like to lift a finger; they're too busy puffing on those funny-smelling cigarettes."

Veronica tossed an ugly expression in Lenny Gray's direction. The last impression that she wanted Gilbert to have was of her leeching off Lenny Gray. Even if it was true, he didn't have to know about it.

"I know what you mean, Lenny," Gilbert validated her comments.

"People around here act like a job is going to come knocking on the door looking for them by name."

"You don't have to talk about me as if I'm not sitting right here." Veronica caught a quick attitude.

"I can talk however I want to talk in my own house," Lenny barked back.

"Veronica." Gilbert caught her attention and gave her a threatening glare.

"I don't have to sit here and listen to this shit. I'm going downstairs to my room," Veronica said, and went into the basement.

"She ain't going to do nothing except smoke those funny cigarettes and drink that alcohol. You know the smoke from those things kills people," Lenny complained. "I think she in here trying to kill me. You know I'm too old to be around here inhaling smoke. She's my goddaughter and all, but, Gilbert, I'm not going to take much more of this from her. You know I'm not a fool. I tell it like it is."

"I'll talk to her, Lenny," Gilbert said sympathetically. "Veronica is lost and doesn't know where she's headed," Gilbert began defending her. "You and I both know that ever since Veronica was a little girl she always marched to her own tune. She's always gotten into mischief and would do some of the dumbest things. Even when our mother would tell her not to get into mischief, Veronica had a way of twisting the meaning of what Mom was saying. I think in her mind it just meant do anything you want to, just don't get caught. Once, when she was about six years old, we were at a summer family get-together, and Veronica saw our mother smoking. When our mother tossed the half-smoked cigarette away into the grass, Veronica went to pick it up, but our mother caught her before she did and scolded her for wanting to try it. Veronica cried and rushed away. But as the gathering continued, I noticed that Veronica had disappeared. I went searching for her, because I knew she had a tendency to wander off without permission. When I located her, she was squatting down behind the garage with our mother's purse. She'd found her cigarettes and had lit several sticks at once and tried to smoke them all at the same time.

" 'Veronica!' I practically screamed her name.

"She looked into my eyes as if she truly had no idea of what she was doing or why." Gilbert paused as words formed in his mind. "Veronica should have gotten more attention, I think. She just needed a little extra love, that's all."

"Well, she's not going to find too much more love here with me," Lenny proclaimed.

"I understand," Gilbert answered. "I'll talk to her and find out where her head is at."

"Probably still stuck inside of a jail cell." Lenny's words were sharp and full of truth.

"Maybe not." Gilbert was being optimistic. "Maybe she just needs someone to show her the reality of her situation."

"Well, good luck," Lenny said sarcastically. "Before you go and talk to her, put me a few of those wings on a plate and grab the hot sauce from the refrigerator door."

Gilbert did as he was instructed, then kissed Lenny on the forehead before heading down to the basement where Veronica was. "I'll go talk to her, Lenny," Gilbert said.

"Good, because I don't know how much more of her I can take. Maybe she would do better if she had someone like you encouraging her. You just said it yourself. Veronica needs a little extra seeing after."

"Perhaps you're right, Lenny," Gilbert agreed, although he had his reservations. "I'm going down into the basement to see her now. You just sit tight and enjoy your food," Gilbert said as he walked down the basement stairs.

As Gilbert made his way into the basement, the foul stench of marijuana assaulted his nose along with the muffled sound of some hip-hop artist bellowing about smoking his chronic. He walked toward the rear of the basement where smoke was wafting through the air.

"Veronica," Gilbert called her name.

"What?" she answered back defiantly.

"What are you doing back here?" He waved his hand in front of his face to clear away the smoke.

"What the hell does it look like I'm doing? Shit, I'm smoking."

"Veronica, put that out. You know that shit isn't any good for you. Besides, the smoke bothers Lenny."

"I'm not a kid anymore, Gilbert. You can't tell me what and when to smoke." Veronica glared at him rebelliously.

"You're right, I can't treat you like a kid. But the least you could do is show a little respect for Lenny. You know the smoke bothers her."

"Fine," Veronica said as she extinguished her smoke. "So let me get this straight. You came all the way down here just to put me in my place, right? You're not happy to see me or anything. All you want to do is set me straight, right?"

"Ronica," Gilbert called her by her nickname, "I don't want to sound like a broken record, but you've gotten too old for this mess."

"What mess? I haven't done shit."

"This," Gilbert said generally. "You're leeching off an elderly woman."

"Would you feel better if I was leeching off you?"

"You wouldn't leech off me. I'd put your lazy behind to work," Gilbert said.

"And what type of work do you think an ex-convict is going to get?" Veronica used her past as a crutch for her lecherous behavior.

"Veronica, I know you can do anything you set your mind to."

"Yeah, whatever, Gilbert."

Gilbert paused for a moment, and the silence between them seemed to last an eternity. Gilbert sensed the delicate tension between them, which lingered in the air like an echo that refused to fade away. "Come take a ride with me," Gilbert finally broke the silence.

"Take a ride with you?" Veronica asked, puzzled. "Where to?"

"You're hungry, aren't you?" Gilbert stated as more of a fact than a question.

"Yeah," Veronica answered.

"Then why don't we go and get something to eat. We could head over to the Brickyard Mall."

Veronica's disposition changed at that moment as the thought of stealing something swept over her. "That's so nice of you, brother dear," Veronica said as she searched her cluttered mattress for her coat. When she found it, she put it on and headed out the door with Gilbert.

Gilbert and Veronica sat at a table within the mall's food court. Veronica had ordered the five-item combo from the Chinese restaurant, and Gilbert had ordered two slices of stuffed pizza.

"This is so good," Veronica proclaimed as she dabbed the corner of her mouth with a white napkin. I haven't had Chinese food in ages."

"I'm glad you like it," Gilbert said as he thought of how to bring up her precarious situation without her exploding.

"You know Lenny is old and lives off of a fixed income," Gilbert said softly. "It would help her out some if more income were to come into the house."

"I'm not even thinking about Lenny right now." Veronica's tone was sharp. "And don't give me that look. You always make me feel bad when you give me that judgmental glare."

"How can you sit here and say that, Veronica?" Gilbert was trying not to be disappointed with her.

"Don't get me wrong, Gilbert. I appreciate Lenny for giving me a place to stay, but she came out of a bag on me today. She was acting all two-faced. I tried to help her cook, but she told me to sit down. Shit, then the minute you walked in the door, her damn tune changed. Then it was all about how wrong I was and all of that mess. Don't let that old woman fool you. She just wants me to get a job so that she can take a cut of my money. That's all she's after. Trust me. I know. She's a money-hungry old woman." Veronica wanted to change Gilbert's perception of Lenny Gray.

"Veronica." Gilbert was being patient with her. "Listen to yourself. You can't live anyplace for free. You have to pay one way or the other."

Veronica didn't respond to Gilbert. She decided that she'd tune him out because she didn't care to listen to his lecture about being responsible. Veronica knew that she was in a bad position, and the last thing she wanted right now was for him to make her face the truth. All she really wanted to do at that moment was eat her food and then walk around the mall as a way of easing her mind and perhaps spotting an item or two that was worth taking.

"What's it going to take for you to get your life back on track? You're out of jail now. Your parole period has passed; you don't have that foul man in your life anymore, or at least I hope you don't."

"No, I don't," Veronica answered. "Chuck is my man. But right now things aren't perfect between us."

"Good. I'm happy to hear that. Veronica, you've been given a fresh start. Can't you see that?"

Veronica captured her brother's gaze for a moment and held it. She didn't say anything because she didn't know what to say.

"I think you're doing great thus far."

Veronica laughed to herself because she knew that Gilbert was full of shit.

"Do you know what I want, Gilbert?" Veronica asked.

"No, what?"

"I want to stay with you. I could focus on what I really want to do with my fresh start." She lied to Gilbert with a straight face. She studied him for a moment and read his expressions. *He actually believes me*, she thought.

"I would have to speak with Tabetha about it. But I think we could work this out if you're serious, Veronica."

"Of course I'm serious." She lied again, thrilled at how trusting her brother was.

"Speaking of Tabetha. I heard that she refuses to give you a child." Veronica knew that she'd hit a tender nerve by the way he reacted. Gilbert shifted his eyes and body as if the very subject irritated him. Veronica decided to get all up in his business since he was so quick to jump into hers.

"You mean to tell me she refuses to have a baby with her own husband?" Veronica was getting a twisted kick out of putting Gilbert and his situation under a magnifying glass. "I told you a long time ago that snobbish girl was high-strung and superficial."

"Don't talk about Tabetha that way," Gilbert defended his wife. "She's a good woman."

"Whatever. I don't know why you can't see it. But take it from a woman who knows about things. Something isn't right about that woman. I knew it from the day I met her. Trust me, I'm your baby sister, and I know how women are." Veronica enjoyed the fact that she'd turned the tide of the conversation.

"So why won't she have a baby with you? Is she sick or something?"

"No, it has nothing to do with health," Gilbert answered Veronica but shifted his attention to the people heading toward them. "Well speak of the devil. Here comes Tabetha and Rick now."

"Where?" Veronica twisted herself around and focused on Tabetha and Rick, who were approaching them.

"Damn, that's a nice-ass fur coat she has on," Veronica said. "Did you buy that for her?" Veronica inquired.

"No." Gilbert felt his demons of jealousy and insecurity about the purchase of the fur coat surfacing. He cupped his hand and massaged the tension out of his neck. Tabetha and Rick approached the table and greeted Veronica and Gilbert.

"Is this your son Rick?" Veronica studied how handsome and more mature Rick had gotten. She stood up to give him a strong hug.

"Yes, this is him," Tabetha stated as she watched Veronica embrace her son.

"You're so handsome." Veronica kissed him on the cheek. "I know I've only been away for a year, but, man, you've changed so much. Boy, if you were a few years older and I was a few years younger—"

"Don't go there," Tabetha quickly interrupted Veronica before her lustful thoughts got the best of her.

"It's all good. I feel where you're coming from," Rick answered Veronica with a sly smile as he nodded his head.

"Boy, you'd better not know a thing about what she's talking about." Tabetha shot Rick a disapproving glare.

"Mom, lighten up. She knows a Mack when she sees one."

Veronica laughed. "All right, Mr. Mack." Veronica winked at him, then shifted her focus to Tabetha.

"Tabetha, that fur coat you have on is smoking." Veronica reached out and touched the fur fabric. "I love this mahogany brown color. You have the real deal too. No paw pieces on this coat." Veronica stopped fondling the coat when she noticed the unpleasant expression on Tabetha's face. She continued her inspection of the coat with her eyes. "Full lining and hooks to clasp it closed." Veronica quickly began adding up the worth of the coat in her mind. "At retail price, a coat like this had to hit you for around five or six grand."

"Yeah, somewhere around there, but I didn't pay full price for it," Tabetha stated.

"So what are you guys doing way out here?" asked Gilbert.

"I'm trying to find him some type of special running shoes that he says he must have."

"They're not just any running shoes, Mom."

"Anyway, we'll let you two catch up on things. Veronica, it was good to see you again. Gilbert, I'll see you when you get home." Tabetha excused herself, and Rick walked along with her.

"That's a nice-ass, coat." Veronica continued to talk about the value of the coat.

"Yeah, it is," Gilbert grumbled. "It's a little too nice," he said.

On the way back to Lenny's house, Veronica promised Gilbert that she'd really make an effort to get her life together.

"Veronica, I have faith in you. In spite of all the mishaps you've had and the mistakes you've made, I believe you'll turn yourself around. If you ever need me, I'm always here for you," Gilbert told her.

"Do you really mean that, Gilbert?" Veronica asked.

"Of course I do. It's just you and me now, and I could never turn my back on my own sister. Even if you do at times some crazy shit. You'll always be my sister. I'll always look out for you."

Veronica didn't expect Gilbert's words to hit her emotionally the way that they did. She felt her heart betray her for perhaps the first time in a long while. She decided to believe that she was worthy of living an honest life.

When Gilbert dropped her off at Lenny's, she watched him as he pulled away. She decided that she'd walk down the street to a local quick mart to pick up some personal items she needed for herself with the money Gilbert had given her. As she strolled down Austin Boulevard, she began daydreaming about what it would feel like to have a real job, a nice home, and a nice car. She was trying to visualize herself leading a stable lifestyle. She was so caught up in her fantasy that she didn't notice the old worn-out sedan or the sinister-looking man who'd gotten out of it and was waiting on her.

"Baby girl." The familiar baritone voice startled Veronica. She focused her gaze upon Big Money Chuck. He was a tall and menacing man with brown chocolate skin. His eyes and facial expression had a murderous combination that made her stop and freeze up like a statue. Big Money Chuck approached her, and she noticed how red the whites of his eyes were. It was clear that prison had hardened Chuck up more than he already was. Veronica managed to carve a smile on her face and prepared herself to help ease whatever burdens were on his shoulders.

"I heard that you didn't want to see me," Chuck said as he reached out to caress her cheek. Veronica held the palm of his hand to the side of her face.

"Baby, that's not true," Veronica lied. She removed his hand from her face and kissed the back of it affectionately. "Baby, I'm not settled in anywhere yet. Crazy-ass Bonnie put me out and—"

"Shhh," Chuck silenced her. "I'm not going to hurt you, at least not yet. You and I have business to take care of. Come get in the car with me. You and I need to take a ride," Chuck said. "Come on." He waited for her to start moving.

"You know I'm with you, baby." Veronica kissed him quickly on the lips out of fear and headed toward his sedan.

13

Veronica

Veronica rested her head on Chuck's shoulder and stared out the windshield as they drove down Central Boulevard. Veronica recalled a phrase she'd once heard: *Sometimes, a person will come into your life and bring out the best in you.* Veronica analyzed the phrase and applied it to the relationship she and Chuck had. She couldn't deny that she and Chuck had a romantic yet complicated relationship. She cared for Chuck, and somewhere beneath his harsh exterior, she knew that he cared for her just as much. Even though at times he'd put his foot in her behind and beat on her. She always felt that his hits were out of love for her. Just as Joyce, her mother, felt that Fred's beatings were done out of love. Their romantic relationship was complicated by what they both enjoyed doing for a living. If stealing were a drug, then Chuck would be her drug dealer. Veronica couldn't deny how much she enjoyed it. Being a thief gave her an incredible rush. She enjoyed sneaking around and searching for her next opportunity. In her mind, she was doing what she had to do in order to make it. When she began stealing on her own, it offered her small short-lived thrills. But when

Chuck came into her life, he was able to take her high to new levels, and that both frightened and thrilled her. Chuck didn't have limits, boundaries, or even fear of being caught. Whenever Veronica hesitated about doing a job, Chuck had the ability to seduce her into submission. He was a powerful man. Veronica's biggest fear was that one of Chuck's assignments would somehow destroy her. For that reason, she tried to distance herself from Chuck, but deep inside, she knew that he'd come for her, and in a peculiar and strange sort of way, she was glad that he did.

"I don't have your money, Chuck," Veronica informed him, and then shut her eyes tightly, fearing that Chuck would growl at her about it.

"Do you think that's why I've been looking for you?" Chuck laughed. "Veronica, I've been gone for close to two years. I know that you don't have money," Chuck said as he made a right turn onto Chicago Avenue. "I came looking for you for two reasons," he said. Chuck wasn't the type of man who spent a lot of time talking about his intentions or feelings. He only said what he thought needed to be heard and that was it. It was up to Veronica to decode any additional messages that were tucked away beneath his words. Veronica concluded that Chuck was also expressing how much he'd missed her. She snuggled up closer to him, knowing that he'd enjoy the warmth of her body. She was thankful that his mind wasn't set on whipping her ass. At least it wasn't at this particular moment. They were silent as they drove along. There was no music, no words, just the constant rumbling of the sedan's motor. Chuck stopped for a traffic signal at the corner of Chicago Avenue and Division. Veronica pulled away from him for a moment and studied her urban surroundings. She focused on a gated storefront window, which had the word PAWNSHOP spelled out in large black letters. She turned her head away from the window and focused on a newspaperman standing in the middle of the street trying to sell a few of his newspapers to motorists passing by. She blinked her eyes slowly as the image in her mind changed. She recalled what the morning newspaper headline had read the day after Chuck was arrested. She'd read the article so many times that she knew it word for word.

PROPERTY CRIME UNIT RAIDS WESTSIDE PAWNSHOP

The party is over for members of an alleged Westside burglary ring that fenced hundreds of thousands of dollars' worth of stolen property to support a lifestyle of drugs and wild parties, according to crime-unit detectives. The bust was the result of a four-month-long effort by the property crime task force. The work of the unit led to thirty-five arrests and the recovery of five hundred stolen items worth an estimated $290,000, said crime-unit detectives.

Crime-unit detective Guy Smith said that dozens more could face charges as the investigation continues. Detective Smith said the suspects struck all areas of the city and its surrounding areas, mainly burglarizing homes, sometimes in broad daylight.

"If the suspects were caught on the property, they would pose as landscapers," said Detective Smith. "They're brazen and skilled criminals," he added. The suspects would take the stolen property to a Westside pawnshop owned and operated by Chuck King, known on the streets as "Big Money Chuck." He'd pay the thieves who took the quick cash to support their drug addiction. "Chuck King was the mastermind behind a very lucrative operation," said Detective Smith. "He had an extremely large network and was using his business as a front to traffic hundreds of thousands of dollars in stolen property."

Wearing a hidden microphone and pretending to be a heroin addict, an undercover detective penetrated the crime ring and made a dozen covert deals aimed at dismantling the fencing ring. The property crime unit was painstakingly building a case against Chuck King, who had a well-known street reputation of intimidation and physical violence against any crew member who betrayed him. Over several months, thieves within Chuck's tightly woven circle gave the undercover detective lists of desired items, which included laptop computers; MP3 players; valuable clothing, such as fur coats; jewelry; and even high-priced gym shoes. Other items included digital cameras, camcorders, stereos, and home theater systems. Within days of each request, the undercover detective returned to Chuck's pawnshop with the goods.

When police raided Chuck's pawnshop, detectives said they found boxes stuffed with stolen electronics waiting to be shipped around the country and overseas to under-developed countries. Court documents and videotaped interviews provided a window into how fences have evolved, growing more sophisticated and no longer relying on the walk-in traffic of burglars. Fences hand out "shopping lists" to thieves, give tours of target neighborhoods, explain how to defeat antitheft systems, and pull merchandise from burglaries and major retail stores across the Chicago area.

Fencing stolen items is nothing new. However, masterminds like Big Money Chuck are disciplined and precise in their dealings. "If large theft rings like Chuck's were sloppy, law enforcement wouldn't have to put so much effort into taking them down," said Detective Smith. According to crime-unit officials, more indictments are forthcoming.

Veronica slowly blinked her eyes once again to change the image in her mind from the newspaper article to the day she saw officers escorting Chuck to a squad car after their raid. Chuck looked so shocked and appeared to be trying to determine in his mind which crew member had screwed him over. She was so thankful that she wasn't with him in the shop that morning.

Veronica hardened her nerves when she entered the criminal

courts building on Twenty-Sixth and California streets to watch the conclusion of Chuck's trial. The prosecution presented its final argument, painting a picture of Chuck as a shady businessman with violent tendencies. His defense lawyer painted a different picture, trying to explain that Chuck was an honest businessman who made a bad error in judgment. The jury went into deliberations, and when they returned, they found Chuck guilty. Veronica sat in the courtroom trying to hold back her tears but couldn't prevent them from falling, so she left the courtroom before she made a scene.

"Where are we going?" Veronica asked as she nestled up against Chuck once again.

"We're going someplace where we can talk about business," answered Chuck.

"What type of business?" Veronica asked as she inhaled his masculine scent.

"The type where we discuss how you're going to repay the money you owe me," Chuck said.

"But I already told you, I don't have it." Veronica's heart began to race.

"I know, but you're going to get it for me."

"Chuck, baby, I just got off probation. I'm not as young as I once was and—"

"Veronica," Chuck barked at her, "stop giving me excuses. You owe me four thousand dollars, and you're going to get it back for me. I'm starting up the operation again, but this time things are going to be different. This time I'm going to use the Internet. Some of my most loyal clients want to place orders with me, but I need some start-up cash. One client wants a nice fur coat, so we're making a quick stop downtown at one of the department stores on State Street to check things out. When we boost the coat, I'll sell it and have a little more cash to work with."

"We don't have to go downtown," Veronica said as she hugged him tighter and closed her eyes. "I know where I can get a fur coat that's worth about six thousand dollars."

14

Tabetha

Tabetha had a taste for something sweet, which had to be satisfied. She knew that it was getting close to her time of the month because she wanted some brownies with walnuts smothered with hot chocolate fudge. She got up from the recliner that she was lounging on and went into the kitchen. She opened the refrigerator and removed the ingredients she needed to make her walnut brownies. She turned on the oven, pulled the brownie pan out, and began preparing her dessert.

"Oooh, some chocolate ice cream with this would be fantastic," Tabetha said to herself. She went over to the freezer and pulled down what she thought would be a full container of her favorite ice cream. When she opened it up, she discovered that there was only a small morsel of ice cream stuck to the bottom of the container.

"Rick and Gilbert!" she yelled their names. When neither one responded, she walked up the stairs and barged into Rick's room.

"Dang, Mom. Could you at least knock before you come barging in here?"

"Did you eat all of my ice cream?" She held up her container as if it was proof of his guilt.

"No, I didn't touch it. You chewed my head off the last time I ate it," Rick answered, then turned to continue watching his mindless music video where young women were shaking their behinds all over the television screen.

"Boy, turn that crap off," she commanded him, and then waited for him to follow her order. Rick glared at his mother for a long moment before huffing and turning the channel. "I'm sure that you have homework that needs to get done."

"Mom, I did all of my schoolwork," Rick informed her.

"Then read a book or something!" Tabetha said. She heard the sound of the garage door opening and went to meet Gilbert so that she could blast him out about her missing dessert.

"Gilbert!" Tabetha howled out his name. "I had my mouth all set for some damn ice cream, and now I don't have any because once again you were inconsiderate and ate it all," Tabetha said, ready to start a fight.

"Baby, calm down. You're getting yourself worked up over nothing."

"What do you mean worked up over nothing? It's important to me, Gilbert, or I wouldn't bring it up. I'm so tired of you and Rick eating up stuff that I buy specifically for me. If you wanted chocolate ice cream, you should have bought some when we went to the grocery store. But no, you were too busy worrying about spending an extra twenty cents. Now I have to put on some clothes, drive all the way to the grocery store, and stand in a long-ass line for one lousy container of ice cream."

"Are you done yet?" Gilbert asked. When Tabetha didn't respond, Gilbert assumed that she'd said her piece. "I went to the local quick mart and replaced your ice cream. It's right here on the backseat of the car," Gilbert informed her.

"Well why didn't you say something? You got me over here acting all crazy." Tabetha came over to the car and grabbed the bag that was on the backseat.

"Do I get an apology?" Gilbert asked.

"No, because you shouldn't have eaten it in the first place," Tabetha said as she walked back inside the house.

Gilbert swung his head disapprovingly. *What a nutcase,* he thought to himself.

Later that evening, Tabetha was once again lounging in the family room reading the newspaper. Gilbert came and joined her. He'd prepared himself a hot cup of tea. He sat the tea down on one of the coasters.

"Do you want me to rub your feet for you?" Gilbert asked.

"That would be so nice," Tabetha said, feeling slightly better than she had earlier that day. Gilbert went into the bathroom to retrieve lotion and a bath towel. When he returned, he sat down on the sofa where Tabetha was. He placed the towel across his lap and then had her place her feet on top of the towel. Gilbert began to rub her feet.

"That feels so good," Tabetha admitted.

Gilbert smiled. "You have some of the softest feet," he said to her as his thumbs massaged the soles of her feet.

Tabetha cooed at the sensation. "Crack my toes for me," Tabetha directed him.

Gilbert fulfilled her request and placed just the right amount of pressure on her toes.

"We need to really talk, Tabetha," Gilbert said.

"About what?"

"Us," Gilbert said. "What is happening to us?"

"I'm not sure what you mean, Gilbert."

"Tabetha, I really want to have a baby. But every time I bring the subject up, we get into a nasty argument. I'm not trying to argue with you. I'm just trying to understand why we can't at least try."

Tabetha pulled her foot from his hand. She didn't want to have this conversation.

"Don't run away from this conversation, Tabetha. Talk to

me. What's the real reason behind you not wanting to have a baby with me?"

"Gilbert, I don't want to argue about this either." Tabetha decided not to turn her back on the conversation this time. She decided to face it head-on and put an end to it forever.

"When we got married, you said that if the situation was right, you'd be willing to have another baby. I've been trying my best to make it right," Gilbert said. "I've been thinking that we could move the upstairs office down into the basement. That way the baby's room would be directly across the hall from us. I could repaint the room to brighten it up a little. We could get some baby furniture now so that when the baby arrived we wouldn't be so strapped for cash."

"Gilbert, I don't know an easy way to say this without upsetting you."

"Tabetha, we're a happily married couple. We're both healthy and able to have a child. Doesn't having a baby excite you at all? Don't you want to nurture a baby with me? Don't you want to watch it grow and take its first steps?"

"Gilbert, you're not listening to me."

"Okay," Gilbert said, "I'll be quiet. You talk."

Tabetha exhaled before she spoke. She paused in thought as she attempted to pull together the right words that would alter Gilbert's position about having another child. "This may sound selfish, but it's the truth. I'm done, Gilbert. I don't want any more children. I refuse to get pregnant and go back to changing diapers, finding day care, and going through grade school again. I'm just not into having a baby. Besides, it would cripple us financially."

"What do you mean cripple?" Gilbert didn't like the sound of the word.

"See, there you go. You're about to get upset," Tabetha said, not wanting to continue.

"No, I'm not getting upset. I want to know what you mean by cripple." Gilbert tried to keep his tone even.

"Gilbert, the truth is I'd have to stop working. I'd have to give up my career, which I don't want to do. Even if I did, I'd have to be a stay-at-home mom for at least two years. We wouldn't survive on your salary. We'd struggle, Gilbert, and I don't want to do that."

"So you're saying that I'm not good enough." Gilbert's words were edgy, defensive, and filled with insecurities.

"No, I'm not saying that. I'm saying that we have to face reality. Having a baby is expensive."

"I think if we planned it out, we could handle it."

"Gilbert, you don't even believe that. We have a mortgage, two car notes, and credit card debt."

"People have raised children on far less than what we have, Tabetha. Sure it may be a struggle, but I'm willing to do what it takes. I'll take a second job."

"Gilbert, that's not the point. Why can't you see it? I don't want to bring a baby into this world and struggle with it. That shit is for the ghetto fabulous idiots who don't have good sense."

"Oh, so now you're saying that my idea is ghetto fabulous?"

"Gilbert, you're personalizing this. I'm not attacking you."

"Yes, you are, Tabetha. You're pretty much saying that I'm not good enough for you to even consider having a baby with. How long have you felt this way about me?"

"I've hurt your feelings, Gilbert. I didn't want to do that. We need to stop talking before we both say something we'll regret."

"Too late, Tabetha." Gilbert got up from the sofa. "Thanks for cutting me down. I bet if Marlon asked you to have a baby with him, your legs would fly open." Gilbert wanted his words to cut her as deeply as hers had cut him.

"Fuck you, Gilbert! That was uncalled for."

"Oh, really now? The motherfucker is giving you money as if you've been giving up some ass."

"Gilbert, you're going way too far." Tabetha got up from the sofa. "You shouldn't have said that shit to me." Her voice was filled with contempt. "Don't talk to me as if I'm some whorish wife."

"Well, if the shoe fits—" Gilbert wanted to take his words back, but it was too late. Tabetha walked out of the room without saying anything more. *Damn, why did I say that?* Gilbert asked himself. At that moment, the phone rang and Gilbert answered it. Tabetha walked back upstairs to the bedroom feeling deeply hurt by Gilbert's words.

I can't believe he said that to me. Tabetha paced the floor. *Is that the way he really feels about me?* she thought to herself. *Does he really think that I'm some type of self-centered and unfaithful wife? I have been nothing but good to him.* As Tabetha processed her thoughts, she became more angry. *I'm not about to allow him to get away with this,* Tabetha thought, and then marched out of her room and back downstairs to where he was.

"I don't appreciate you calling me a whore!" Tabetha unloaded on him.

"I didn't call you a whore," Gilbert argued back.

"Yes, you did, Gilbert. In so many words that's what you called me, and that shit hurts."

"And you think that I'm not equally as hurt? How do you think it makes me feel to know that my devoted wife thinks that I'm a poor provider?"

"I never said that you weren't a good provider," Tabetha countered.

"Yes, you did. In so many words." Gilbert used her own phrase against her.

"You know what? Don't talk to me anymore, because you can't handle hearing the truth."

"You guys are at it again?" Rick came into the family room to find out what all of the loud ruckus was about.

"You're skating on thin ice again, Rick. Now is not the time."

"Rick, go back to your room. Our conversation does not concern you."

Rick followed his mother's orders and went back to his room.

"Have you ever stopped to think about how you treat him?" Tabetha asked.

"Every time he comes around to see what's going on, you look at him as if you want to murder him or something. What's that about, Gilbert?"

"He just needs to learn how to respect grown folks' business, that's all."

"No, I think it's much more than that. I honestly do. I think you actually resent the boy because he's not yours."

"That's bullshit, Tabetha. I wouldn't harm that boy, and you know it."

"Maybe not physically, but emotionally, Gilbert. I think that if we had a child together, you'd make such a huge distinction between your child and Rick. That could be abusive. Making one child seem better than the other one."

"I would never do that, and you know it."

"No, I don't know it." Tabetha's voice was earsplitting. She studied the anger in Gilbert's eyes, but she matched his angry glares with some of her own. There was silence between the two of them for a moment as they trapped each other's gaze, neither one willing to let it go first. Both Gilbert and Tabetha wanted to be right. They both wanted to have the upper hand in this vicious round of arguments.

"The next time you accuse me of being some type of whore, it will be your last time," Tabetha threatened Gilbert with an unknown act of retaliation.

"All I know is that you'd better start being more of a wife to me and stop walking all over my love for you. I love you so much, Tabetha, but you are really making it hard on me. It's not easy competing with your past."

"Gilbert, what are you talking about?"

"It's not easy, Tabetha. Marlon walked out on you, but somewhere in my gut, I feel as if you still want to be with him."

"Gilbert, that is so ridiculous. If I wanted to be with Marlon, I would have left a long time ago."

"That's my point, Tabetha. You may not have left this house physically, but emotionally you're not here with me. You're not willing to bond our marriage with a child, and I have a problem with that. I think you're pushing our bond aside in order to make room for Marlon in case he wants you back in his life. After all this time, Tabetha, I honestly think you never got over him."

Gilbert's words made Tabetha feel as if he'd punched her in the stomach. It took the breath out of her. She wanted to deny his claim, but something wouldn't let her speak. Some unknown emotion had caged her voice and wouldn't free it.

"So that is it," Gilbert concluded. He lost the energy to stand, so he sat down. He was emotionally exhausted. He felt as if he'd been fighting with a wild animal and was completely drained.

"No." Tabetha finally freed her words. "That's not the truth, Gilbert. I am so sorry that you feel as if you're competing with him. I'm so sorry that you feel my unwillingness to have a baby with you is because of some unresolved issue with Marlon. I need to get away from you." Tabetha felt tears swelling up within her. "We're at some type of impasse, and I don't know how to move us past it."

"All I want from you is to give me a child of our own. I am a man who wants a son or daughter with you, Tabetha. What's so wrong about that?"

"And I am a woman who has reached a point in her life where I'd rather be taking tropical vacations and living off of room service rather than going back to square one. I just can't see myself doing that, Gilbert."

"So what am I supposed to do about my wants and needs?" Gilbert tried not to sound furious, but Tabetha could tell that he was. His anger was floating beneath his words.

"I don't know. Maybe we can become foster parents or something so that your need is met."

"Tabetha, I don't want to be someone's foster parent. I want to be someone's dad."

"You are already. You're a father to Rick."

"It's not the same, Tabetha. I don't know how much longer I can go on like this," Gilbert admitted.

"Neither do I, Gilbert. Neither do I."

15

Gilbert

Gilbert awoke the next morning with a bad cramp in his neck from sleeping on the sofa all night.

"Man," he groaned as he massaged his neck in an attempt to ease his muscle tension. He decided that he didn't want to be around when Tabetha woke up, so he freshened up, put on some clean clothes, and left the house. He drove to a local fast-food restaurant and ordered himself a value breakfast meal to go. He then drove to Thirty-Ninth Street and Lake Shore Drive and parked his car. Gilbert took in the serene view of the frozen Lake Michigan water as he turned the dial on the car stereo. He found an easy-listening station, opened his food, and began to eat and reflect.

Gilbert wasn't the type of man who believed in cheating on his wife or having an affair to satisfy needs that weren't being met at home. He believed every problem or situation could be worked out no matter how difficult. However, Tabetha was putting his convictions to the test. From his point of view, Tabetha seemed to be pushing him toward infidelity and that perplexed Gilbert. As he mulled over the history of their marriage, he began to wonder if she was really ever fully committed to him, or if he was just filling some void in her life at the time. He thought about their courtship and the happier times they used to share. He thought about how he enjoyed making her laugh and spending time with her and Rick. They used to do fun things, simple things, together that didn't require much effort or money. Gilbert enjoyed packing them up on a Sunday morning to take a long drive to the country. They'd explore small-town communities and shop at small mom-and-pop stores. Some days they'd go to the local water parks and spend hours speeding down the giant water slides and playing in man-made wave pools. Gilbert exhaled a depressed sigh. Those were the happier times before and shortly after they were married and became a family. Somewhere during their years of marriage, Tabetha's career took off, which left her with little free time, and Rick seemed to just grow up overnight. It was as if one day Rick woke up and was this new person who seemed to have a personal vendetta against him. Gilbert once again exhaled in frustration because he and Rick used to get along much better than they did now.

"Then there is Marlon," Gilbert said aloud with his mouth filled with food. He didn't care for the man, because he couldn't measure up to his financial wealth.

"I really don't care about the money he has, because I have Tabetha's heart," Gilbert told himself. "Or at least I thought I did." Gilbert suddenly wasn't so confident. He lost his appetite, and his stomach was turning sour with overflowing anxiety. He reclined the seat all the way back and closed his eyes for a moment.

"Why does loving someone take you through so many changes?" Gilbert whispered to himself. At that moment, his cell phone rang. Before he flipped open the phone to see who was calling, he hoped it was Tabetha phoning him to discuss the status of their relationship and the direction it was going. When he viewed the display screen on his phone, he saw that it was Lenny Gray.

"Hello?" Gilbert answered.

"I can't deal with her, Gilbert. She has got to go." Gilbert could tell by the uneasiness of her voice that she was extremely upset.

"Lenny, what's wrong? What happened?"

"Just come get her, Gilbert, before I call the police. She's left the house for now, but I don't want to let her back in."

"All right, I'll be right over," said Gilbert, then he disconnected the phone. "Damn. If it's not one thing, it's another," Gilbert grumbled as he brought his seat back to the upright position, started his car, and headed over to Lenny Gray's house.

16

Veronica

Veronica kissed Big Money Chuck, then exited his car. He'd dropped her back off at Lenny Gray's house and said he'd come back to see her after he met up with some of his associates to plan out how they were going to set up their new theft ring. Veronica shuffled up the steps to Lenny's house and let herself in. To her surprise, two officers were sitting in her living room taking down a report of some type.

"What's going on?" Veronica suddenly began to panic.

"That's her right there, Officer. That's Veronica." Lenny pointed her out to the officer who was taking the report.

"Ma'am, are you Veronica Vaughn?" asked the officer.

"Yeah, what's going on?" Veronica asked, uncertain of what circumstance forced Lenny Gray to phone the police. "Lenny, did something happen to you?" Veronica asked, concerned that Lenny had been snooping around and had located her stash of illegal drugs.

"Yeah, child. You are what happened." Lenny's words were clear and direct.

"Ma'am," said the officer taking the report, "my partner is going to escort you into the basement area where your personal belongings are. You are being asked to pack up what you can and bring it with you."

"What, am I under arrest or something? What the hell is going on?" Veronica demanded an explanation.

"You haven't learned a damn thing, Veronica," said Lenny. "I'm cutting through the bullshit. You've got to go."

"Lenny, I didn't do anything to you," Veronica countered.

"Ms. Vaughn, would you please come with me to gather your belongings?" said the officer who was instructed to escort her.

"No, wait one minute." Veronica raised her voice because she didn't have anyplace to go and wanted to at least know why she was being forced to leave. "Just tell me why, Lenny, and then I'll go."

"I told you that I wasn't no fool, child," Lenny Gray boldly stated. "I told you that you could stay if you planned on getting yourself together."

"Lenny, that's what I'm trying to do," Veronica said.

"No, you're not. The company you're keeping, Veronica. You're hanging around bad people again. I noticed who has been around here picking you up and taking you places. That man is bad news for you."

"Lenny, that's just my friend. That's all," Veronica lied.

"Friend or not. I know who he is, and I know what he does. I've told you, I may be old, but I'm not crazy. I'm not going to give you the chance to come around here and take what little I've got." Lenny Gray's voice betrayed her by trembling with untamed emotions. "It's only a matter of time before you slip back and start doing the things that got you in trouble the first time."

"You don't know what I'm doing." Veronica became indignant. "This isn't right, Lenny Gray, and you know it."

"Ma'am, I'm only going to ask you once more to follow me. If you refuse, you will leave without anything."

"Fine." Veronica glared at Lenny Gray with contempt as she marched off toward the kitchen and down the stairs to the basement.

When Gilbert arrived at Lenny's house, he saw Veronica walking down the front steps with a large suitcase. He quickly got out of his car to find out what was going on with the officers and his sister.

"Hold up. What's going on here? I'm her brother. Veronica, what happened?" Gilbert asked as he approached the officers.

"Ms. Vaughn has been asked to leave the premises," said the stout officer, who paused in thought for a moment as he studied Gilbert's features. "Don't I know you?" asked the officer.

Gilbert studied the officer and then read his name badge. "Officer Thomas." Gilbert thought for a moment, then popped his fingers. "You were the Chicago Transit Authority officer assigned to my bus route. You rode the bus with me several times. I remember you," said Gilbert.

"Lenny put me out, Gilbert," said Veronica with frustration in her voice.

"What do you mean put you out? Why?" Gilbert asked, trying to understand.

"Apparently she doesn't like my friend. Somehow she got some crazy idea in her head that I was going to do something to her."

"Let me go talk to her," said Gilbert, and he began heading in to see Lenny Gray.

"Sir." Officer Thomas stopped him. "Let me talk to you for a second, man," he said, and stepped off to the side with Gilbert. "Look, here is the situation. Miss Lenny doesn't understand how the law works. She just wants Ms. Vaughn out of her home. She called the police department claiming that there was a disturbance here. When we arrived, there was no disturbance, only an upset and frightened elderly woman. She wanted to file a restraining and harassment order against Ms. Vaughn, who has done nothing wrong to warrant a restraining order. But it was clear that Ms. Lenny doesn't want her on the premises."

"Yeah, man, I know. She called me and told me," Gilbert admitted.

"I'm just trying to prevent something bad from happening here. We could have just summed this up as a prank call and allowed Ms. Lenny and Ms. Vaughn to go at it, but then I'd return and two lives may be beyond repair. All I'm asking Ms. Vaughn to do is perhaps leave for a few hours or perhaps a few days to allow Miss Lenny to cool down. Do you understand where I'm coming from?" asked Officer Thomas.

"I understand," answered Gilbert, releasing another defeated exhale. "To hell with it. I have space at my house. I'll let my sister crash with me for a few days until we can work something out."

"Now that's cool, man. Family is important, and sometimes you have to do things to save people from themselves. You know what I mean?" Officer Thomas chuckled.

"All too well," Gilbert admitted.

Gilbert decided not to disturb Lenny Gray for now with the idea of allowing Veronica to remain. Instead, he thought that it would be best if he worked with Veronica to sign up with the emergency housing and job agencies to assist her with locating a home and finding employment.

"So what's that uppity wife of yours going to say about me staying at your house?" asked Veronica, who was still fuming about Lenny tossing her out onto the street.

"I'll smooth things over with her," answered Gilbert, knowing full well that Tabetha was going to have a fit.

"My big brother," Veronica huffed. "Always there when I need him. I could have gone to a male friend's place, but staying with him could lead to trouble, and I know you don't want me getting into any more trouble." Veronica was building a strong case for remaining at Gilbert's home, although she had her own hidden agenda as to why she preferred to stay with her brother.

"Your big brother is going to help you get on your feet," said Gilbert. "I'm not going to just let you sit on your behind," he said as he accelerated down the on-ramp of the expressway.

"Are you sure you have space for me?" asked Veronica. "I don't want a room across the hall from you and Tabetha."

"I'll set you up in the basement. There is a sleeper sofa down there that you can crash out on."

"It sounds cozy," Veronica uttered.

"Tell me, Veronica. What did you really do to Lenny Gray? And don't lie to me."

"Nothing, Gilbert. Not a thing. But you probably don't believe me. No one has ever believed me when I told the truth. People would rather believe a bald-faced lie than the bare-naked truth."

"If you claim that you didn't do anything, Veronica, then I believe you. Just don't make a fool of me."

"I wouldn't do that. You're always in my corner, aren't you, Gilbert?" Veronica stated. "Even though I've been to jail, you're still keeping faith in me."

"Veronica, sometimes faith is all that a person has."

"Well let's just hope that's all we need to convince Miss Tabetha to allow me to stay for a while," Veronica said. *Or at least long enough to do what I have to do,* Veronica thought to herself. *Chuck will be pleased that I've snatched up this opportunity to get into Gilbert's home.*

17

Tabetha

Tabetha arrived at Evanston High School and entered the building through the gymnasium doors. She located the indoor track and searched for Rick. She spotted him sitting in the bleachers on the other side of the track. She walked around the perimeter of the track to his location.

"Hello," Tabetha greeted her son.

"Hey, Mom," Rick said as he stood up to hug her. "I'm glad you could make it."

"I told you that I would," Tabetha said.

"Is Gilbert coming?" Rick asked.

"I don't think so," said Tabetha. "Or at least he didn't tell me that he was coming. Why are you asking?" Tabetha asked curiously.

"Well, I sort of invited my dad. My real dad, I mean."

Tabetha noticed the strange look on her son's face. She knew Rick well and knew that he wasn't telling her everything.

"And what else, Rick?" Tabetha eyed him suspiciously.

"We've been talking a lot, you know—"

"No, I don't know. What have you been talking to him about?"

"You and Gilbert," Rick said.

"What about us?" Tabetha didn't like having to pull answers out of Rick.

"He asks about you, and I tell him that you're doing well when you're not fighting with Gilbert about money or children."

"You told Marlon that?" Tabetha's voice carried, and it made Rick nervous.

"How much did you tell him?" Tabetha asked abruptly, because she was feeling exposed.

"Not everything. I just told him that I think you guys are having some problems that there may be no solution to."

"Rick." Tabetha tried not to get upset with him. "Marlon doesn't need to know what is going on between Gilbert and me. Do you understand me?" Tabetha spoke to Rick as if he were a two-year-old. "That's like me going around telling all of your friends that you enjoy flexing your puny chest muscles and dancing naked in front of the bathroom mirror after you get out of the shower."

"You know about that?" Rick asked, surprised.

"I'm your mother, Rick. I know you better than you know yourself."

"There is one other minor thing," Rick said.

"What?"

"I sort of invited him to this track meet. I thought that perhaps you guys may have wanted to talk or . . . man, I don't know. I just wanted you guys to talk a little more. Whenever you talk to him, you don't argue. Or at least not as much."

"Rick, your father is too busy counting his money. Chances are very high that he isn't going to show up."

"No. He promised me. I even called to confirm it with him."

"I've heard that one before," Tabetha said sarcastically.

"What's that supposed to mean?"

Tabetha studied Rick's eyes and could see that he was confused about what she meant. "Rick, don't try to play match-maker anymore, okay?"

"I was only trying to help. I mean, Gilbert is okay. He's just been acting as if he's going to hurt you."

"Gilbert isn't going to hurt me, Rick. How did you even get all of that in your head?"

"I don't know. It's just there. I feel like I need to protect you or something."

"That's noble of you, but I can handle myself, okay?"

"Okay."

"Now go warm up and focus on what you need to do." Tabetha sent Rick off to ready himself for competition.

Fifteen minutes later, Rick came rushing back up to Tabetha, who was sitting in the bleachers observing the long-jump com-petition.

"Kevin, our neighbor, is a really good long jumper. I'm sur-prised his parents aren't here supporting his efforts," Tabetha mentioned to Rick before he could say anything to her.

"Yeah, he's all right," Rick said, not falling into his mother's hype about his friend. "He's here, Mom," Rick announced. "He's parking his car."

"Who is here?" Tabetha asked as she focused on Kevin speeding down the runway.

"My dad," Rick said. Tabetha turned to look at him and no-ticed how wide his smile was. "See, I told you he would come."

"Boy, you're really pushing it. What would you have done if Gilbert was here? Then what?"

"Mom, I knew Gilbert couldn't make it. I checked with him beforehand."

"I'm going to say this to you one more time. Stay out of my business."

"Okay, I get your point. Can you at least be nice to him?" Rick asked as more of a plea than a demand.

"Yeah. Now go finish getting ready for your event."

"Thank you, Mom," Rick said, and then rushed off.

"Hey, there," Marlon said as he sat next to Tabetha. "Where is your husband at?" he inquired.

"He wasn't able to make it this time," Tabetha answered him. Marlon nodded his head and let the issue rest.

"What events is he running today?" asked Marlon.

"The fifty-yard dash and the four-lap relay," Tabetha answered.

"It's good to see you, Tabetha," said Marlon as he leaned forward and rested his elbows on his knees. Like Tabetha, he sat quietly and observed the clusters of runners jogging around the indoor track.

"It's good to see you as well," Tabetha responded. She had decided not to get into any ugly confrontations with Marlon like they'd had at the restaurant. Especially since she and Gilbert had had an ugly spat the night before. "Why are you studying the runners so hard?" Tabetha asked.

"Hell, I'm thinking about my track-and-field days," Marlon admitted.

"They're long gone." Tabetha chuckled because she found her own comment to be amusing.

"They may be long gone, but being here sort of rekindles the old fire that I once had."

"Oh Lord," Tabetha said, laughing again. "Don't tell me that you're going to be one of those old men running around trying to recapture the youth he once had."

"No, I'm not going to be like that," Marlon corrected her perception of him. "But I do wish to some degree that things were different." Marlon swiveled his head to the right and met Tabetha's gaze.

"Well, it's too late to change things now, isn't it? You'll never have the body of a seventeen-year-old," Tabetha said.

"That's not what I meant," Marlon once again corrected her.

Marlon turned his attention to Rick, who was loading himself onto the starting blocks for his race.

"What did you mean then?" Tabetha decided to pursue Marlon's comment.

Marlon stood up to watch the race more closely. "Look, there is Rick," he pointed out.

Tabetha looked in the direction that Marlon pointed. Her nerves were buzzing with anticipation as the starter directed six young men to get on their mark. The starter held the boys in the set position for what seemed like a long time before he fired the starter's pistol. Out of the corner of her eye, Tabetha noticed how Marlon twitched as if he was running the race himself. She watched Rick get off to a slow start but pick up speed as he raced toward the finish line.

"Come on, Rick!" Marlon yelled out excitedly. Rick was mixed in with the pack of runners but wasn't able to pull in front of them to establish himself as the quickest man. When the competitors zoomed through the finish line, Marlon turned to Tabetha, who had been watching the competition with as much enthusiasm as he had been.

"I couldn't tell who won the race," said Marlon. "Rick should have leaned forward at the finish line. I think I've mentioned that to him before," he said. A few moments later, Rick came trotting over to Marlon and Tabetha.

"What place did you take?" Marlon quickly asked.

"I took second place," Rick said. "The guy from the other school nipped me at the finish line."

"Oh." Marlon reacted to the second-place finish. "We've got to work on getting you off the starting blocks quicker," Marlon said, eager to offer some coaching tips.

"I know. My starts are slow, but once I get going I'm good."

"You'd do even better if you were able to get off the starting blocks quicker," Marlon explained.

"Well, I think that you did a fantastic job," Tabetha praised him.

"Yeah, I think you did a good job as well," Marlon said,

agreeing with Tabetha. "But winning is what you want to do, son. You don't want to settle for second place. In fact, push settling for second place out of your mind. It's either finish first or don't finish at all." Marlon's competitive nature was driving his comments. "Even in business. Don't settle for less than number one because your competitors aren't looking to be number two—"

"All right, Marlon," Tabetha interrupted him. "The boy is only a junior in high school."

Marlon swallowed his zealousness and let it go.

"I have to go prepare for the four-lap relay," Rick said, and rushed off.

"You should let me take him, Tabetha," Marlon said as he sat back down. "I can do so much for him."

"I'm not about to allow you to take my baby from me. Are you crazy?" Tabetha said.

"Tabetha, Rick hasn't been a baby for some time now. He's a young man, and he needs guidance."

"He already has a man in his life," Tabetha countered.

Once again, Marlon swallowed his immediate words and searched for better ones. "What is so wrong with him moving in with me? He's stayed with me before, Tabetha. It's not like I live in another state. You can come see him at any time. Or he can come to see you at any time. Let him come stay with me."

"For what? So that you can teach him how to gallivant around and be a player, something like that?" Tabetha had preconceived notions about Marlon and his lifestyle.

"Tabetha, I'm not a monster. And I'm not surrounded by a harem of women. I've changed that part of my life. I've gotten older and have come to realize that not every woman has my best interests in mind."

"Yeah, right. I bet if I went to your house, it would look like some rich playboy's paradise."

"Okay," Marlon said. "If that's what you believe, why don't you and Rick come by my home today. Rick has been there before, but you haven't. I'd love for you to see it."

"Stop lying. You're not going to let me come into your house. You never have."

"You never asked to either."

Tabetha studied Marlon's eyes for a moment, searching for some hidden treachery.

"Seriously. Come on by. I would love for you to see my place," Marlon encouraged her.

"Hey, guys. Are you two getting along okay?" Rick came back over and asked for his duffel bag. Tabetha handed it to him.

"I've got a few track spikes that need to be tightened up," Rick informed them.

"Rick, don't you think your mother would love to see my house?" Marlon asked. He was looking to get Rick on his side.

"Oh man, Mom. You should see his house." Rick's voice went up several octaves. "Dad's place is the bomb!"

Tabetha looked into her son's eyes and saw them dancing with excitement.

"I've invited you and your mother over to my house after the meet," Marlon said. "If you want a few of your teammates to tag along, that's cool too," Marlon said.

"Yeah, I've been telling Kevin all about your home in Wilmette. I know that he'd love to see it. Can we go, Mom?"

Tabetha thought about it for a moment. She really did want to see Marlon's home; her curiosity was killing her.

"You'll be okay," Marlon said. "You're just visiting. Nothing more."

"Okay," Tabetha gave in. "But only for an hour or so, then we'll have to leave."

"Cool," Rick howled out. "I'm going to let Kevin know."

"Tell him to ask his parents if it's okay, Rick," Tabetha said to him before he rushed off.

After the track meet, Marlon, Tabetha, Rick, and Kevin exited the gymnasium and headed to the parking lot where their cars were.

"Dad, where is your limo driver?" Rick asked.

"I drove myself today, Rick," Marlon answered.

"Which car did you drive?"

"The Dodge Viper," Marlon said, and pointed to it.

"Wow!" Kevin blurted out. "That's a sweet ride."

"Here you go." Marlon handed the keys to Rick. "This button opens the door," he instructed his son, who quickly snatched the car keys and jetted off with his friend toward the car.

"You really shouldn't encourage him like that," Tabetha warned. "You know that he has a fondness for luxury cars."

"He's a young man, Tabetha. He'll be eighteen soon. He's supposed to be into luxury and hot-rod cars. That's just part of being a boy."

"I don't want him going out and killing himself trying to impress his friends by showboating in a hot rod," Tabetha countered.

"He'll be fine," Marlon answered her without concern. They made it over to his car, and Rick had turned the sound system all the way up. The rapping voice of a hot new artist named Chump Change came blaring from Marlon's car. Tabetha was about to yell at Rick to turn down the music but was caught off guard when Marlon started grooving to the music. Tabetha laughed at his dance moves.

"Oh my God." Tabetha stopped in her path and began laughing uncontrollably.

"What?" Marlon asked, wondering what she'd found so humorous. "That's Chump Change."

"What I'm laughing at has nothing to do with Chump Change. You still doing the same dance move that you did back in junior high school." Tabetha continued to laugh at him. "Nobody dances like that anymore." Tabetha wiped away a tear of laughter. "You shouldn't move like that in public."

"Whatever," Marlon said jokingly as he continued to his car.

"Man, Dad," Rick said. "You've got to let me drive this to

prom. All the honeys would want to hook up with this brother if I told them I would be rolling like this on prom night."

"I tell you what. If you pull off all As on your next report card, I'll let you roll like this on prom night."

"Yeah!" Rick said as he gripped the steering wheel.

"This baby does two hundred twenty mph," said Kevin.

"Don't you think that this car may be a little too powerful for him?" Tabetha asked. "Gilbert was going to let him drive his Excalibur."

"I don't want to drive that old thing," Rick quickly answered. "I want to ride in this Viper. Wahoo! I can see it now! I'll be all decked out in my tuxedo, with the finest honey in school rolling with me. No, bump that. The finest honey in the entire state. I'd burn me a CD with all the jamming hits and would look cool." Rick couldn't contain his excitement.

"See, my son wants to ride in style," Marlon pointed out.

"Yeah, and possibly get some girl pregnant on prom night."

"Well, one thing is for sure. He can't get any action in this car. It's way too small."

"Mom, if I was going to get some action in a car, I'd get a minivan or something like that."

"I know that's right," Kevin agreed with Rick.

Tabetha glanced at Rick and then Marlon suspiciously, as if they had already determined what they were going to do. "I don't know. I'll have to think about allowing you to drive a car like this on prom night."

"Man," Kevin groaned. "I wish I could go with you guys, but my mom said no." Kevin got out of the car with Rick. "I'll catch you later, Rick," Kevin said as he headed back to the gym.

"Yo. I'll holla at you later on tonight," Rick shouted out to his friend.

"Come on. Let's get this over with. Should I follow you to your house?" Tabetha asked.

"Yeah," Marlon answered.

"Mom, I'm going to roll with Dad. Is that cool with you?"

"Yes, that's fine with me."

Tabetha was certain that by some measure she'd be unimpressed with Marlon's home. She was certain that she'd find some defect that she could quickly point out. However, when she arrived at Marlon's, she didn't anticipate her heart betraying her. Tabetha would have never thought that she'd be taking a tour of his home and imagining herself in every room.

"This room over here is my home office and library." Marlon pushed open the French doors and allowed Tabetha and Rick to enter.

"Check it out, check it out." Rick rushed over to the television, which was embedded in the wall. "Dad, where is the remote to it?"

"It's sitting over there. On the table near the fireplace."

Tabetha took in everything about the room. The high ceilings, the mahogany decor, the custom-made bookshelf. She studied his large desk that had a few folders and a laptop computer sitting on top of it. She eyed the bookshelf for a moment, then moved over toward the fireplace.

"Is this a wood-burning fireplace?" Tabetha asked.

"No," Marlon replied. "Well, actually, it was wood-burning when I purchased the home, but I had it converted to gas because I didn't want to dump ashes all the time."

"Very nice," Tabetha said as she mentally pictured how she'd change the room to fit her tastes. She felt that the wood paneling was a bit too dark. "You need some artwork in here," she said. "It would help give the room a more comfortable feeling."

Rick clicked on the television and flipped through the channels until he found the music video channel.

"Go on and finish taking a look around, Mom," Rick said. "I'm going to chill right here."

"Don't get too comfortable, boy. We are not staying long,"

Tabetha said. Rick didn't respond to her, so she restated what she'd said. "Did you hear what I said?"

"Yeah, Mom. I heard you." Rick refused to take his eyes off of some young female singer who was dancing very seductively.

"Well act like it then. Don't make me repeat myself." Tabetha quickly became annoyed with her son.

"He'll be okay," Marlon said. "Follow me." Marlon walked her through the library and over to the glass patio door. He slid the door open, stepped through it, and entered an enclosed patio deck.

"Oh my," Tabetha said, completely overtaken by the beauty. The deck was enclosed with high glass ceilings that provided excellent sunlight. There was an oversized inground hot tub that featured two waterfalls. Tabetha observed Marlon as he walked over to a wall and pressed a button.

"See," Marlon said, pointing back to the water. "I've turned on the underwater jets." It was clear to Tabetha that Marlon was very proud of his home.

"I see," Tabetha said, noticing how the large pool of water was bursting with bubbles.

"Do you want to try it out?" Marlon asked with a sly smile on his face. Tabetha could tell that his eyes and mind were under her clothing.

"It's time for me to go, Marlon," she said. "You have a nice home." Tabetha walked back inside to where Rick was.

"Let's go, Rick." Tabetha said as she entered.

"Mom, we just got here. You haven't even looked at the rest of the place yet."

"Let's go, Rick," Tabetha said more forcefully.

"Are you sure you must go?" Marlon entered the study.

Tabetha caught his gaze and held it for a moment. She was feeling something that she didn't understand. She didn't understand why her heart and emotions were betraying her. She didn't understand why her feelings for Marlon were still strong even after all that he'd put her through. As much as the sexual goddess inside of her wanted to jump into the hot tub, strip naked, and have a grand time, she had to stop herself. She couldn't let Marlon's house, wealth, and pride seduce her.

"All right, Dad." Rick got up from the sofa. "I'll see you later."

Tabetha waited for Rick to exit the room so that she could follow him.

"Are you sure you want to go?" Marlon asked from the other side of the room.

"Yes. I have a wonderful husband and a house of my own to return to." Tabetha wanted her words to sting Marlon.

"Well, if you say so." Marlon's words had a double meaning, and Tabetha knew it.

"Yes, I say so."

"Tabetha. When you have some free time, I'd really like to discuss something with you."

"What?"

"It's a private matter. Just let me know when you have a little time."

Tabetha studied his gaze a little longer than necessary before saying her final good-bye.

18

Gilbert

When Gilbert arrived back home, he was happy to see that Tabetha had not returned yet. He knew that having Veronica as a guest in the house without obtaining her consent would be viewed unfavorably. Gilbert wasn't looking forward to the massive confrontation that was forthcoming.

Veronica wheeled her suitcase into Gilbert's family room and waited for him to come inside. She looked around her brother's home, noticing the new home entertainment system, the fireplace, and the nice patio deck outside the glass patio door.

"This looks nice," Veronica said as she tried to lasso her jealousy.

"Tabetha is always working on the house. She's not much of a bargain shopper, though. She'll pay full price before she'll hustle around for the best deal."

"I don't know what she has to work on," Veronica commented as she continued to survey her brother's home.

"You can have a home as well, Veronica," Gilbert said, hoping that his words would inspire her in some fashion. He trapped her gaze for a moment before she broke eye contact. "Follow me," Gilbert directed as he escorted her into the basement.

"All you have to do is believe that you can do it. Just have a little bit of faith and be willing to work hard. The rest will come. Everything may not happen when you want it to or the way you want it to, but it will happen," Gilbert said as he opened a closet door. "You can place your suitcase in here for now."

Veronica wheeled her suitcase inside the closet and left it there.

"This sofa here has a bed in it. It's not the most comfortable bed in the world, but I think you'll find it to be cozy."

"Cozy is fine by me," Veronica said, waving off his words of uncertainty. "That's more than enough. You know me. I don't need much. Just a place to rest my head at night."

"But you should want much more than that, Veronica." Gilbert exhaled loudly before speaking again. "Come on. Let me give you a quick tour."

"So when did you move into this house?" Veronica asked.

"When you were away," Gilbert answered.

Veronica still couldn't get over the fact that after all this time, Gilbert still had trouble allowing himself to believe that she'd actually spent time in jail. Veronica and Gilbert walked back up the basement stairs and entered the kitchen. Veronica took note of all the countertop space and all of the different containers. They made a right turn and entered the dining room.

"That's a nice dinette set," said Veronica as she studied the wooden table and the rug on the floor, which matched the pattern of the chairs perfectly.

"Man, how much did that nice throw rug hit you for?" Veronica asked.

"I don't know," Gilbert answered. "I don't do the decorating, Tabetha does. She's really attached to this house. When she walked in it for the first time, she knew that this was the home she wanted. With regard to the rug"—Gilbert shrugged his shoulders—"knowing her, she paid a high price for it." Gilbert chuckled nervously to himself as the thought of how he was going to present Veronica's situation to Tabetha entered his mind.

"Damn, I didn't even call her to let her know about this," Gilbert mumbled to himself. "This is the second time I've done this to her."

"Did you say something?" Veronica asked as she studied the artwork on the wall.

"No," Gilbert mumbled his reply.

Veronica looked at the chandelier hovering above the dinette table. "That's a nice fixture. I like the design of it," Veronica said, nodding her head approvingly. She couldn't help herself. It was a bad habit of hers. She just automatically began adding up the price of items in her mind. She was always thinking about resale value. Veronica focused on the china cabinet with decorative plates situated nicely on the shelves. She walked over to the cabinet to take a closer look at the dishes.

"Oh, these are nice too." Veronica smiled as she inspected the china more carefully.

"Those dishes have been in Tabetha's family for years. Her grandmother originally bought them but then passed them on to Tabetha's parents."

"Has she ever had this dishware appraised?" Veronica asked. "Stuff like this could fetch a pretty penny at an auction or an antique shop. Hell, even antique doorknobs can be sold for a nice chunk of change."

"I don't know," Gilbert said. "I'm not into all that stuff. To me they're just dishes on a shelf."

"It's a shame that that's all you see," Veronica muttered under her breath. She thought for sure that all of her inquiries would trigger some type of concern in her brother's mind, but it didn't.

"Come this way," said Gilbert.

Veronica trailed behind him around the corner and into the living room.

Veronica took note of the nice furniture that complemented the decor of the home. Gilbert escorted her to the front door and up the staircase.

"Up here are the bedrooms and the office," Gilbert said. "Here is the office." He pointed to a door on his left. Veronica peeped her head inside and focused on the nice computer. *I can get at least a few hundred dollars on the street for that,* she thought. "This is Rick's room." Gilbert pointed to a room on his right as he continued down the corridor. Veronica peeped inside of his room and saw yet another computer. *Oh yeah,* she thought to herself, thinking that she could pay back Big Money Chuck, and maybe have enough left over for herself. *My goodness, Gilbert,* she thought as he rambled on about how Tabetha had located the house and just had to have it. *You're so—* Veronica searched her mind for the right word—*trusting.*

"Here is the bathroom," said Gilbert. "There is nothing spectacular about that room. And finally, here is the master bedroom."

Veronica stepped inside the master bedroom but stopped in her tracks when she spotted Tabetha's fur hanging up in the closet.

"Is that her fur coat?" Veronica asked as she stepped toward the closet.

Gilbert looked at the coat and answered, "Yeah that's it."

Veronica touched the fur coat and lost herself in the idea of wearing it.

"Can I try it on, Gilbert?" Veronica asked as if she was some moonstruck young girl.

"No, Veronica. Leave the coat alone," Gilbert said. "A fur coat should be the last thing on your mind."

"Yeah, you're right, Gilbert," Veronica agreed with him.

"But hey, it doesn't hurt to dream about having one now, does it?'

"No, I suppose not," Gilbert replied. "Come on. Let's go sit down and have a talk."

My brother, Gilbert, Veronica thought. *You're so blind.*

Veronica and Gilbert went back down to the kitchen. Gilbert asked Veronica to have a seat at the kitchen table while he prepared some coffee.

"So what is Tabetha going to say about me staying here?" Veronica asked, sensing that Gilbert was in an odd position. She watched as he stopped making coffee for a moment.

"Are you okay?" Veronica asked. "I mean, if it is going to be a real hassle, I can go to a homeless shelter." She knew that Gilbert wouldn't allow her to leave for a homeless shelter.

"Veronica, I don't want you in a homeless shelter," Gilbert said. "I'm trying to help you out. Do you understand?"

Veronica noticed how Gilbert's voice was filled with conviction.

"Do you really want to help me?" Veronica asked.

"Yes," Gilbert said.

"Okay. I'm going to be straight with you," Veronica said. "I'm in a bad situation right now."

"I know that, Veronica," Gilbert said sarcastically.

"No, you don't understand, Gilbert. I owe money to somebody who wants it back."

Gilbert rubbed his temples with his forefingers. He closed his eyes for a moment to allow his anxiety to pass. "How much do you owe?" Gilbert asked.

"Just a few thousand dollars. That's all."

"A few thousand?" Gilbert's reaction was loud and a bit explosive.

"Yeah, shit. It's not that much. I could make it back in a minute if I had a little start-up cash."

"Make it back doing what, Veronica?" Gilbert asked, even

though he didn't want to know the answer to his question. He was hoping that she'd come up with something other than some street con.

"Hustling, Gilbert." Veronica saw Gilbert's head drop and knew that she'd lost him. "Wait, before you get upset and say no, hear me out. All I need you to do is take out a loan against this house. Or if that doesn't work, perhaps you can withdraw money from your retirement plan. Then I could pay off Big Money Chuck and have a little extra something for myself. Now doesn't that sound good? Doesn't that sound like a good plan?" Veronica said, believing that the flimsy suggestion she'd presented to Gilbert was the most excellent plan for her situation.

"Veronica, no," Gilbert answered sternly. "Your plan sounds like a desperate move to get some quick cash to run away with."

"Gilbert, come on. You're my big brother." Veronica wasn't willing to give up. She'd persuaded Gilbert before and was still searching for the right words or catchphrase that would convince him. "You're the man. I know that you have money saved up that you can loan me. I'm thinking about starting my own business."

"And what business would that be?" Gilbert asked, feeling for the first time that allowing Veronica to stay with him was perhaps a bad decision.

"I don't know, man." Veronica became irritated. She didn't want to work so hard to convince Gilbert. She just wanted him to freely provide her with money.

Gilbert tried another approach. "Veronica, you have been behaving this way since we were children, and it has got to stop. You've gotten too old for this type of behavior."

"Gilbert, I don't have the nice things that you do," Veronica countered. "And I never will. The only thing that I've got in this world is myself, and the only things I know how to do are done underground and below radar."

"Veronica, all you have to do is use your brain. Take some of the energy you're wasting on helping that criminal you're messing with and get your shit in order." Gilbert's tone was abrasive. "Hard work isn't going to kill you," he added.

"Okay," Veronica said, backing off for the moment. The last thing she wanted at that point was for Gilbert to think that he was wasting his time with her. "We'll try things your way."

"Good," Gilbert said, feeling as if he'd finally reached her.

"So, what do you have in mind? What do you think I should do?" Veronica asked, wanting Gilbert to make the decisions for her. In her mind, it would make Gilbert feel empowered, and she figured that he'd like that. She figured that he would feel a certain amount of pride if she was to come to him for the answers to all of her questions and problems. If Gilbert wanted to act like Mr. Know It All, she was going to make sure he felt that way.

"First thing we need to do is work on a resume. Then we'll sit down, go through the Sunday paper, and search for a job. Once we locate a job for you, then we'll find an affordable apartment."

"Is it really that simple, Gilbert?" Veronica asked, trying to sound pitiful and helpless.

"Yes. The only thing we're doing here is scratching out a decent living for you." At that moment, Gilbert heard the garage door open.

"Why are looking like that, Gilbert?" Veronica asked, sensing an enormous amount of tension in the air.

"Tabetha's home," Gilbert said. "This is going to be a surprise to her."

"Well, you're the man of the house, Gilbert," Veronica said, adding fuel to a building flame of tension. "Make her understand. Make her see that you're a caring and loving brother who is willing to go the extra mile for family."

"That may not be enough," Gilbert said. "This situation isn't going to go over well."

"Do you want me to talk to her? I mean, I could speak for myself, you know," Veronica offered.

"No," Gilbert said. He walked into the family room and opened the garage door. "Tabetha and I are going to take a short drive to discuss this. Rick will keep you company until we return," Gilbert said as he stepped through the door and into the garage. He shut the garage door so that she couldn't hear what was being said.

Veronica leaned back in the seat and smiled. She couldn't wait to tell Big Money Chuck that it would be only a matter of time before she was able to pay him off.

19

Veronica

Veronica didn't think Gilbert could hold his ground during the massive confrontation he and Tabetha would have when he told her that she'd be staying for a while. So Veronica determined that she would have to pull Rick over to her side and turn Tabetha's house completely against her, and she knew just how to do it.

Most individuals would feel uneasy about being the cause or the center of controversy but not Veronica. The idea of conflict and drama excited her. It was like a drug to her, and she got high off of it whenever she could. Veronica knew that all hell was about to break loose by the ugly look Tabetha gave her when she walked inside the house and found Veronica sitting in her family room after she and Gilbert had returned.

"Veronica." Tabetha's voice carried a certain type of meanness beneath it. "What are you doing?"

"Hanging out," Veronica answered Tabetha with an awkward smile.

"Oh really." Tabetha turned and looked at Gilbert contemptuously.

"You don't have to give him an ugly glance," Veronica said, willing to challenge Tabetha in her own house.

"Veronica, I'll handle this," Gilbert quickly said before Tabetha snapped back in a vicious way. Gilbert could manage the battle between him and Tabetha on his own.

"Hey, I'm just trying to help her understand things," Veronica added.

"Understand what things?" Tabetha's voice tightened with explosive tension. It was difficult for her to remain calm. She didn't like the fact she was being forced to share her home.

"Are you a God-fearing Christian woman, Tabetha?" Veronica asked. Tabetha didn't answer the question. "Never mind. I know that you are. Look deep into your heart. I'm sure you'll find a little room for me."

"Gilbert, you've just committed an act of marital warfare," Tabetha said, and walked away.

"It's only temporary, Tabetha," Gilbert said as he followed her up the stairs.

"I don't give a damn! She's not staying in my damn house, Gilbert," Veronica heard Tabetha bark. A short moment later, the bedroom door slammed so hard that the entire house vibrated.

"Well that didn't go over too well," Veronica said with a slight laugh to Rick. "What's wrong with you, boy? You act as if you're afraid to come inside your own home."

Rick didn't answer.

Veronica noticed right away how his attention was focused on the loud voices coming from upstairs.

"Don't worry about them," Veronica said, trying to smooth over Rick's uneasiness. "That's what married people do. They argue. They'll be fine."

"What's this all about, Veronica?" asked Rick.

"It ain't about nothing, handsome," Veronica said, attempting to win Rick over.

"I worry about them," Rick admitted. "Things haven't been going well for them, and you being here isn't going to go over very well." Rick became edgy and began pacing the floor as the loud voices above became more spirited.

"How in the hell are you going to justify letting a known thief into the house?" Tabetha's voice was so clear that it sounded as if she was in the room with Veronica.

"She just needs a little help, Tabetha. Some direction. She deserves a chance to get herself together!" Gilbert countered.

"Gilbert, if she stays in my house, I swear I will make you regret it," Tabetha barked.

"I'm not turning my back on my sister. I owe her this," Gilbert howled back.

"I should go up there before this gets out of hand," Rick said. He was about to head upstairs, but Veronica got in his path.

"Rick." Veronica smiled at him. "It's okay. You have to let them work that out. If you go rushing up in there right now, you'll only make it worse."

"You don't understand, Veronica. I've seen the look that Gilbert has in his eyes when he's run out of words. He wants to hit her, and I can't let him do that."

"Has he ever hit her before?" Veronica wanted to know.

"No," Rick answered.

"I don't think he's going to start now. Come on." Veronica grabbed his arm. "Let me get my coat so we can take a walk." Veronica knew that she needed to get Rick pulled over to her side, which would aid in persuading Tabetha to allow her to stay. Rick reluctantly left the house with Veronica for a brisk walk around the neighborhood.

The winter air was cold, but it wasn't bad enough to send either of them running back into the house for warmth.

"So, do you have a girlfriend?" Veronica asked Rick.

"No," Rick answered.

Veronica could tell by his direct answers that his mind was still back at the house. She had to think of something else for him to focus on besides his mother. She had to offer Rick something he was searching for and show him that there was an added benefit to allowing her to remain in the house.

"Are you kidding me? A handsome young man like yourself should have girls falling all over him." Veronica stroked his ego. She was hunting in the dark for something to use to her advantage and figured sex was a good place to start.

"Girls hardly pay attention to guys like me," Rick admitted. "They don't notice me."

"Why do you think that is?" Veronica asked.

"Hell if I know."

"Have you ever kissed a girl?" Veronica asked. She noticed how Rick hesitated to answer her question. "Come on, tell me. It's okay. I know that we're not really cool like that, but it would be nice to talk to a woman who is cool. Don't you think?" Veronica asked, attempting to persuade him. "Come on. You can talk freely. You can even motherfucking curse if you want to. This is me." Veronica patted herself on the chest a few times with the palm of her hand. "You can call me Miss V. We can talk," she added.

"Yeah, I've kissed a girl before," Rick said, still reluctant to open up fully.

"Well, did you like it?" Veronica asked.

"Yeah, it was cool."

"Did you get any tongue with the kiss?" Veronica boldly asked.

Rick laughed. "You just come right out with it, don't you."

"That's the way it should be. Don't you think?"

"Yeah, I suppose," Rick said uneasily.

"Do you like boys, Rick?" Veronica asked, thinking that perhaps Rick was struggling with some sexuality issues.

"Oh no. It's not even like that." Rick quickly made his position known.

"Okay, just checking," Veronica said as they came upon a small neighborhood playground. "Let's go over there and sit on the bench for a minute," she suggested. Once they got situated, Veronica positioned herself to face him. Rick focused his gaze on the ground before him.

"Are you a virgin, Rick?" Veronica asked as she studied his young sexy lips.

Rick laughed. "I don't believe I'm talking to you like this," he said.

"Like what?" Veronica asked, as if everything was totally normal.

"I mean, all hell is breaking loose back at the house, and you're not even concerned about it. Instead, you're out here talking to me about, you know. Stuff."

"Don't tell me you afraid to talk about fucking." Veronica chuckled this time. "Doesn't Gilbert talk to you?"

"Well, Gilbert"—Rick paused in thought—"I mean . . . no, I don't talk to him like that. I talk to my dad sometimes, but it's not easy talking about that sort of thing with him. I mean, if I have a question, he'll answer it, but he always tells me to make sure that I don't get some girl knocked up. And my mother. Whew. We talk but it's not the same. I mean, it's my mom. I can't talk about my erections with her."

"It must be tough." Veronica sympathized with him in an effort to gain more of his trust. "I'll bet you're hard all day long, aren't you? I'll bet that you're dying to know what it feels like to be inside of a woman," Veronica said as she allowed her gaze to drop and study what appeared to be a growing erection.

Rick laughed again, feeling embarrassed.

Veronica noticed how he leaned forward to conceal his growing pride. "How far have you gotten with a girl, Rick?" Veronica asked.

"You know. I felt a girl up before." Rick paused.

"Have you been inside of a girl's panties yet?" Veronica asked.

"Whew." Rick exhaled.

Veronica knew that she had him. She was enjoying toying with him and manipulating him.

"Every time I make my move, you know, they squirm away. Or move my hand."

"Has a girl ever touched your dick before?"

"God, I wish," Rick said. "Whenever I put their hand on it, they just squeeze it. You know what I'm saying. It's like they're trying to choke it or something."

"So let me get this straight. You've only felt a few tits. Never been inside the panties or touched a pussy and never had a girl even give you a good hand job."

"Yeah, that's about right," Rick said.

"You poor baby," Veronica said, placing her hand on his lap. She thought Rick would move it, but he didn't, so she took it as an invitation to do a little more. She decided to be bold and risqué. She leaned toward him, put her lips by his ear, and spoke softly. "I can teach you," she said, rubbing her hand up and down his thigh. "And if you help convince your mother to allow me to stay for a little while, I'll show you paradise."

"Whoa," Rick said, and sprang to his feet. Veronica noticed that his pride was eager to be set free.

"Are you okay?" Veronica asked, knowing full well that Rick was losing the battle against his undiscovered lust.

"I mean, you're like a vet—I mean, a grown woman," Rick said. "I've heard stories about guys getting down with an older woman their first time but never thought anything like that would happen to me. Wait. We're not related, right?" Rick had to stop and think for a moment.

"Not at all," Veronica said. "At least not through bloodlines." Veronica's womanhood began buzzing at the suggestion of having sex with Rick.

"Help me stay for a little while," Veronica said. "And I'll make sure that a wild pony like yourself gets broken in. I'm not all that much older than you. Do I look bad to you?"

"No," Rick quickly answered. "I wouldn't kick you out of bed.

"Good. Because I wouldn't want you to, especially if you got the chance to creep down into the basement during the night." Veronica was putting ideas in his head.

"Man, I don't believe this is happening to me. I sit in my room all the time hoping that a girl would want to get down with me."

"Stop looking," Veronica said. "Come sit next to me." Rick sat down next to Veronica. "Give me your hand," Veronica said. Rick placed his hand on top of hers. Veronica flipped his hand over, placed it on her thigh, and guided it toward her warm and ready paradise.

"Do you feel it?" Veronica whispered in his ear. "Do you feel how warm it is up there through my jeans even though we're out here in the cold?"

"Yes," Rick answered with a quivering voice.

"Just imagine what it would feel like to be inside of something so warm and soft." Veronica spoke purposefully in his ear and then traced the shape of his ear with the tip of her tongue.

"Wooo." Rick quivered with unbridled excitement.

"Are you going to help me stay?" Veronica asked.

"Hell yeah. I'll help you."

"I need you to trust me," Veronica added. "I need to know that you're on my side."

"I'm on your side," Rick said eagerly.

"How do I know that? Can you prove it to me?"

"How?" Rick asked.

Veronica cooed and made a sexual sound in his ear. At the same time, she ran her hand up and down his manhood through his clothing. "Information," Veronica whispered. "I need a little important information. If you get it for me, I'll drain this weapon of mass destruction you have between your legs." Veronica ran the tip of her tongue around his earlobe more passionately. She then clenched her teeth and pulled at his ear.

"I won't get in trouble will I?" Rick asked.

"Baby, I wouldn't get you into trouble. You can trust me." Veronica was laughing on the inside. She whispered what she wanted to Rick.

"Yes," answered Rick, who was completely caught up in her web of lust. "I can get that for you."

"That's what I'm talking about, Boo," Veronica said, feeling a new type of excitement flowing through her.

"I just need a place to stay for a minute," she explained. "I'm just looking to get a second chance, you know. I just want a fresh start. Can you tell your mother that for me?"

"Yeah, I'll tell her," Rick answered.

"Good. When we go back inside that house, you make sure you stand your ground for me, okay?"

"Okay," Rick said.

When they arrived back at the house, Tabetha and Gilbert's argument had subsided some.

"Boy, where in the hell have you been?" Tabetha shouted at her son.

"Nowhere," Rick answered. "I was just taking a walk with Veronica."

"I don't want you going anywhere with her. Do you hear me?" Tabetha said with a demanding voice.

"Mom, I think you're overreacting."

Tabetha didn't like the tone of Rick's voice.

"I think you have Veronica all wrong. She's just looking to start over. Give her a chance."

Tabetha darted her eyes over to Veronica and met her gaze. Veronica had a smug look on her face that Tabetha didn't like. She looked back at her son and wondered why he was suddenly siding with Veronica.

"Mom, seriously. I think you should give her chance," Rick repeated himself.

"How can you stand here and say that to me?" Tabetha looked at Rick as if he'd betrayed her. She felt as if he was putting Veronica's interest above hers, and she had a problem with that.

"See there, Tabetha," Gilbert said as he entered the family room where everyone was. "Even Rick understands that everyone deserves a second chance."

"Well, I'm going back to my room," Veronica said. "I'll be downstairs if anyone needs me." Veronica moved past Tabetha, who was stunned.

"I'll be down to hang out with you, Veronica," Rick said before heading upstairs to his room.

"It will be okay." Gilbert continued to ease Tabetha's concerns about Veronica's situation.

"The hell it will," Tabetha snarled. She looked Gilbert directly in the eyes. "Gilbert, I don't know if we're going to make it."

Veronica awoke from a restful night's sleep and focused her gaze upon some artwork displayed on a nearby wall. The painting was of a woman sitting on the side of a bed with her head hanging down between her shoulders. The picture touched Veronica, because she identified with the hidden emotion embedded in the painting. The scent of fresh bedsheets and the comfort of soft pillows was enough to make her never want to budge an inch from the sofa bed she'd slept on. *Oh, this is so much better than Lenny Gray's house,* she thought as she stretched out her body. Veronica had been turned off by the stale odor that was constantly wafting through the air at Lenny Gray's place. Her scalp began to itch, so she began rubbing it with her fingertips to prevent it from itching even more. Once her scalp calmed down, she exhaled and began thinking. As she adjusted her head on the pillow, she felt a presence in the room. Veronica glanced around and saw Tabetha sitting in a chair watching her. Veronica suddenly felt threatened and quickly sat up.

"Let's get one thing straight," Tabetha said, not taking her gaze off Veronica. "This shit here that you're pulling isn't going to last. You may be here for the moment, but don't get too comfortable."

Veronica didn't answer Tabetha. She just glared at her until she finished saying what she had to say.

"I'm going to tell you like I see it. You've gotten yourself involved in some bullshit that you can't handle. And now you're looking for Gilbert to rescue your sorry ass."

"You don't have to talk to me like that," Veronica said, not wanting Tabetha to speak to her in a negative manner.

"Let me be very clear, Veronica. I'm going to say it so that even you can understand it. I don't trust your ass the way that Gilbert does. In my mind, once a thief, always a thief. The minute you fuck up and step out of line, out the door your sneaky ass goes."

Veronica inhaled and then exhaled loudly as if Tabetha was boring her to death.

"Oh, am I boring you?" Tabetha asked, wanting to get into a physical confrontation with Veronica.

"No," Veronica answered.

"Listen up, ghetto queen. Your days are numbered."

"Who are you calling ghetto queen?" Veronica snapped at her.

"I'm talking to you," Tabetha said.

"No, I don't think so," Veronica fired back.

"You know what?" Tabetha tried to laugh away her anger. "All you need to know is that everyone in this house punches a clock. When I get up to go punch my eight hours, your ass has to leave."

"What? Where am I supposed to go?"

Tabetha stood up and walked over to the staircase. "The hell if I know. But you're not going to sit around in my house all day doing nothing."

"I'm going to talk to Gilbert about this. You're being unreasonable. It's cold as hell outside, and I don't have money or transportation."

"It sounds to me like you need to hurry up and find a job, now doesn't it."

Veronica didn't respond to her for a moment. Then she said, "I'm not going anywhere unless my brother puts me out." Veronica knew full well that Gilbert would always be there for her.

"I'm his wife. And the wife always wins. One way or another."

"Whatever!" Veronica said, discounting Tabetha's statement.

"Oh, and make sure that you keep your ass well covered. Because if I even think that something unnatural is going on between you and my son, bitch, I'll kill you cemetery dead," Tabetha said as she walked up the stairs.

"Huh," Veronica muttered. She didn't fear her bluff for one moment. It only impassioned her to take Tabetha for all that she could. *She doesn't know me*, Veronica thought. *I'll beat her ass in her own damn house.*

20

Tabetha

"She has got to go, Lynise. I can't take her ass being in my house too much longer." Tabetha paced the kitchen floor at Lynise's home. "Everything about that woman is foul," Tabetha added. "She's been at my house for four weeks, and it feels as if she's been there for one year."

"Tabetha, calm down before you burst a blood vessel or something. Sit down, girl."

"I can't, Lynise. I'm just too wound up about this. Just the thought of Veronica makes my asshole hurt."

"Tabetha, you need to convince Gilbert that she can't stay there. That's all there is to it. You have to tell him that your marriage depends on this."

"Don't you think I've tried that?" Tabetha continued to confide in Lynise. "He won't listen to me. He says that she's just going through a phase and needs a little time to get herself in order. My fear is that a little time is going to turn into six months or more, and I'm just not going to put up with it," Tabetha said, using her hands to express her anger. "I'm just not."

"Well, can you help her?" Lynise asked, trying to offer a solution.

Tabetha shot daggers at Lynise with her eyes. "Lynise, that wench isn't thinking about trying to find a place of her own or getting a nine-to-five or even going back to school for some type of training. I overheard her trying to convince Gilbert to pull money out of his retirement fund to help her start up a pawnshop." Tabetha was so furious that she felt light-headed.

"Wasn't she involved in some pawnshop fencing operation a while back?" Lynise asked, vaguely recalling Tabetha mentioning something about it to her.

"She was involved with some shady character who got arrested for it. But she got caught up on damn identity theft," Tabetha said. "Why she wasn't arrested during the pawnshop raid is beyond me. Her black ass was right there with the criminals."

"Oooh," Lynise replied, suddenly understanding Tabetha's rage. "Yeah, she has to go. I agree with you on that point. Do you want me to talk with Gilbert?" Lynise offered.

"Girl, no," Tabetha said, finally taking a seat. "I just have to work through this. I just don't know how all of this is going to play out."

"What does she do all day while everyone is gone?" Lynise asked.

"I told her that she couldn't stay in my house. Gilbert says that he drives her back into the city and drops her off at the godmother's house where she is supposedly spending the day searching the newspaper for a job. I keep hoping that Gilbert leaves her ass over there but he doesn't. After work he drives over there to pick her wayward ass right back up."

"Well, why isn't she staying with her godmother?" Lynise asked.

"Huh. That old woman put her ass out," Tabetha answered. "She didn't trust her."

"If she put her out, then why is she allowing her to come back in?"

"Honey, your guess is just as good as mine. Personally, I don't think she's staying there all day like she claims. I think she's running around doing other shit. But that's just my gut feeling. You know what I'm saying?"

"Whew." Lynise stood up from the table, got a glass from the dish rack, and filled it with ice from her refrigerator door. She then opened it up and pulled out a container of lemonade she'd mixed.

"Would you like some?" she offered Tabetha.

"No, thanks." Tabetha paused in thought. "Then get this shit. She had the nerve to step to me one evening and ask me if I had a problem making babies."

"What?" Lynise shouted louder than she intended to.

"Girl, she presented me with a sideways conversation about having a baby for Gilbert."

"Tabetha, stop lying." Lynise couldn't believe what she was hearing.

"Lynise, I'm not lying. I was sitting at the dining room table reading my mail when she sat her plump ass down and started talking. She got to saying that it's not right for me not to give her big brother a child, that he really wants a baby of his own. Lynise, I'm telling you, I was two seconds from catching a criminal case. She thought I was going to share my damn medical history with her ass."

"Girl, I can't imagine what all of this must be like for you," Lynise said, swiveling her head from side to side.

"It hurts, Lynise. Shit." Tabetha paused as she sorted out her feelings. "I like that Gilbert is a family man, I really do, but this is going overboard in my opinion. I feel as if he is on some crusade to save his sister and start a family that I don't want to have at this point in my life. Something has got to give because if it doesn't, Gilbert and I aren't going to make it."

"Don't say that, Tabetha. You don't mean that."

"The hell I don't. Besides, Marlon—" Tabetha stopped talking because she didn't intend to utter Marlon's name.

"Marlon?" Lynise raised her voice. "What's going on with you and Marlon?"

"I don't know yet, but he wants to talk."

"Do you have any clue about what?"

"No, but I wish that I did," Tabetha said as she reflected on how she felt when she was at his home a few weeks ago. Tabetha was once again visualizing what it would be like to live so lavishly.

21

Gilbert

Gilbert was sitting up in bed, engrossed in a slice-of-life news program with his favorite journalist, Angela Rivers. Ms. Rivers was presenting an exclusive special segment about a husband's crusade to help his wife recover from drug addiction and a life of petty theft.

"It was embarrassing," said the husband, who was sitting with his wife and speaking candidly about the problems they had gone through. "I would have to call friends and family to help me come up with bail money for my wife. They all told me to just give up on her. They said that trying to save her was a lost cause. I refused to believe them. I knew in my heart that she was a good person, even though I was very ashamed of her at the time."

"What was the lowest point for you?" asked Angela, who wasn't afraid to ask a tough question.

"Oh God." The woman exhaled.

Gilbert was on edge waiting for her response. He was happy that the couple had worked through their problem, but he was equally interested in the road they'd traveled.

"I would have to say it was when I checked myself out of the rehabilitation center and came back to the house while Michael and the kids were gone. I broke a small basement window and entered the house to steal," said the woman. "I was looking for anything that I could sell quickly to get money to support my addiction. I took money from my children's piggy bank and stole their computer. I was crazy. I was out of my mind. I hated myself for what I was doing, but I felt as if I couldn't control the urge," the wife said as she lost control over her emotions and began sobbing. After a brief moment, she pulled herself together again. "I took the computer to a sleazy pawnshop called Big Money Pawnshop. I was part of a large theft ring at the time," the woman admitted. "Eventually I was arrested in connection with Big Money's operation."

"How did you handle that?" Angela asked the husband.

Gilbert felt the pain that the man was going through. *This is similar to what I'm trying to do for Veronica,* Gilbert concluded.

"Through prayer, patience, and understanding," said the husband. "There were days when I wanted to give up on her, but I just couldn't."

"What was the turning point for you?" Angela asked the wife.

"My own mother turned her back on me. And that hurt me. But Michael didn't, he told me that if I was willing to meet him halfway, we'd get through this together. I'm blessed to have a man like him. During my darkest hour, he guided me through, and I love him for that."

"Oh wow," Gilbert said, feeling the emotion behind her words. At that moment, Tabetha entered the bedroom with her hair tied up in a towel.

"Baby, you're missing a really good program," Gilbert said, wanting Tabetha to watch the conclusion of the program with him. He was hoping that it would spark an adult conversation about why he felt so strongly about Veronica.

"I've been listening to part of it in the bathroom," Tabetha admitted.

"What do you think about it?"

"What do you mean what do I think about it?" Tabetha sat down at the foot of the bed and uncoiled the towel from around her head.

"Don't you think that the husband did the right thing?" Gilbert asked.

"He did what he had to do," Tabetha answered.

"Well, don't you see that I'm trying to do the same thing?"

"Gilbert." Tabetha scooted around to face him. "Baby, I don't want you to take this the wrong way, but that's different. That was the man's wife. I can understand him not wanting to lose the mother of his children to a seedy lifestyle. Our situation isn't like that. You've allowed a grown able-bodied woman to move into our home. You didn't tell me about it. We didn't discuss it, and we didn't agree on it. Had you come to me first, we could have probably worked things out so that she didn't have to move in here like this. But no, Gilbert, you were on some out-of-control crusade, and you didn't give a fuck about me or my feelings on this. I'm sorry. I just have a major problem with a grown-ass woman who is healthy but refuses to take a job. All she wants to do is leech off people, and right now she's leeching off of you." Tabetha said her piece and then turned back around to face the television.

Tabetha's strong opinion hurt Gilbert in a way that he didn't anticipate. Instead of exploding at her, he listened to what she had said. He knew that his marriage was in jeopardy as long as Veronica was in the house. However, he didn't have the heart to put her out, because he knew that she had absolutely no place to go. Well, at least not any place that he wanted her to go. He didn't want her to have a setback. He wanted Veronica to use her time productively and put some type of plan together that would lead to her bettering herself. Gilbert felt as if he had to choose between making his wife happy and putting his sister out on the street.

"Baby, look." Gilbert came up to her and massaged the back

of her shoulders. Tabetha tensed up at first but eventually welcomed his touch. Gilbert kissed her shoulder. "I'm sorry that I didn't consider you when this decision was made. You're right. I was wrong for that. I'm sorry."

"You should be," Tabetha added. "Bringing someone like her up in here was just crazy."

"I know. But I'm going to get things straightened back out. Just give me a little time," Gilbert said.

"Gilbert, the longer she stays, the more irritable I'll get," Tabetha said conclusively. "I don't like sharing my house this way. I don't like having another woman in my house. My position about that is not going to change. Ever," Tabetha stated.

"Okay. Point well taken." Gilbert stopped rubbing her shoulders.

"And another thing, Gilbert. You shouldn't tell Veronica about our personal differences," Tabetha said, looking for a smooth way to bring up the fact that she didn't like it when Veronica asked her why she wouldn't have a baby with him.

"What are you talking about?" Gilbert wasn't following Tabetha.

"I mean, you shouldn't go around telling her that I refuse to have a child for you."

"Oh, here we go," Gilbert said, knowing Tabetha was about to revisit an already raw area of their marriage.

"I don't like her confronting me with the issues of our marriage. It is none of her business why we haven't had children. I don't appreciate you sharing our business with her."

"Tabetha, my sister and I are close, okay? I talk to her. If you have a problem with that, you need to get over it," Gilbert said, feeling as if Tabetha was ready to step over a line that he felt she shouldn't.

"Gilbert," Tabetha whined, "you and Veronica aren't all that close, so don't even go there."

"Tabetha, you don't know shit," Gilbert said, completely irritated with her.

"And you don't know shit either," Tabetha barked back at him. "Do you want to know the truth, Gilbert?" Tabetha asked, even though she was going to tell him her thoughts whether he wanted to hear them or not. "You're doing this just to get back at me."

"What?" Gilbert said, ready to discount her opinion.

"I'm serious. This isn't about helping your sister, it's about getting even with me for not wanting a baby. You're doing this out of a sense of anger. That's what I think."

"Well your thinking is wrong, Tabetha," Gilbert snapped. He got up and headed into the bathroom to get away from her. "You are so wrong," he continued as he shut the bathroom door.

Agh! Tabetha thought to herself. *Gilbert, why can't you see it?* she wondered. She realized that she'd placed her hair rollers in the bathroom that was in the hallway. She stood up and walked over to the door. As she entered the corridor, she stopped in her tracks when she noticed Veronica standing in the hallway peeping inside the bathroom. Tabetha placed an ugly expression on her face as she studied Veronica and her behavior. Veronica was so caught up in what she was peeping at that she didn't even notice Tabetha. As Tabetha studied the situation, she realized that Rick was taking a shower, and Veronica was standing in the doorway watching her son bathe. Tabetha's rage shot sky-high, and before she knew it, she howled out Veronica's name.

"Veronica!"

The sound of Tabetha's voice didn't stun Veronica at all. She turned and caught Tabetha's gaze and smirked at her. Tabetha instantly picked up on the lust in Veronica's eyes.

"What's up?" Veronica answered Tabetha as if she wasn't doing anything wrong.

"What are you doing?" Tabetha asked.

"Nothing." Veronica smiled. "Just looking," Veronica said, peeping in on Rick one more time. Veronica could see the reflection of Rick taking a shower through the mirror on the medicine cabinet. "Lord knows there isn't anything wrong with just looking."

Tabetha marched down the hall toward Veronica and guided her away from the door and down the stairs.

"Have a seat at the table. We have to talk." Tabetha's patience with Veronica had ended. "Bitch, are you crazy? That's my baby in there." Tabetha was trying to restrain herself from going totally ballistic.

"Girl, that boy hasn't been a baby for a long time," Veronica said, not feeling at all threatened by Tabetha's posture and body language.

"Listen here, you wench. You stay away from my boy or I swear I will make you regret it." Tabetha was so angry and upset that the hairs on the back of her neck were raised like sharp chips of glass.

"I'm not the one you have to worry about." Veronica glared at Tabetha. "You tell your boy to stay away from me," Veronica said. She trapped Tabetha's gaze for a moment and held it. The tension and animosity between them hung in the air like thick smoke from an inferno. "He likes looking at me," Veronica said. "He undresses me with his eyes." She smirked at Tabetha. She was getting a real rush feeling all of the tension that was between them.

"If I think that you are corrupting my minor son, you're going to want to run into a burning building rather than deal with me." Tabetha slammed the palm of her hand down on the table so hard that Veronica knew she meant business.

"Okay. I won't touch him. I'll leave him alone," Veronica lied. "But sooner or later, some young girl or woman is going to, well, you know. I don't have to spell it out for you," Veronica said, and stood up. "Is that all?" Veronica asked as if she was in complete control.

Tabetha couldn't stand her arrogance and was looking for the slightest reason to leap around the table and put her foot in Veronica's ass.

"Have a good night." Veronica ended their conversation and headed back downstairs.

Tabetha remained in the kitchen thinking to herself, *Your days are numbered, Veronica.* She heard the shower turn off and decided to go and have a talk with her son. The last thing she wanted was for him to get stupid and have sex with the likes of a tramp like Veronica.

22

Veronica

"I didn't wake you, did I?" Rick asked as he peeped in on Veronica. She sat up on the sofa bed and looked over at Rick, who was walking down the steps.

"This is the track suit that I wear," Rick said, displaying his blue and gold jogging set. "How do I look?"

"You look handsome," Veronica said, smiling at him.

Rick sat down on the edge of the bed. He reached inside one of his pockets and pulled out an envelope. "Here," Rick said, and handed it to her. "I got something for you."

"What did you get for me, baby?" Veronica asked.

"Open it. It's a surprise," Rick said.

Veronica tore open the small envelope and allowed the contents to fall out onto the bed. "Keys," she said.

"Yeah. I figured you didn't have a set of house keys, so I had a set made for you. I'm sorry I took so long, but I wanted to make sure you were going to be staying."

"You are so wonderful," Veronica said, and then hugged him.

"Well, they're not any good without the alarm code," Rick

said. "It's 199900. You should memorize it by thinking about Prince and his song '1999,' and the 00 stands for the year 2000. I know you asked for this information when you first arrived, but I assumed Gilbert gave it to you."

"You are so special, do you know that?" Veronica looked directly into Rick's young and impressionable eyes. She could tell by the look in his eyes that he wanted to be rewarded in some fashion for what he'd done.

"Come here," Veronica said, and scooted over so that Rick could lie beside her. "I watched you take a shower last night," Veronica told him.

"For real?"

Veronica watched as Rick's eyes grew wide with wild excitement. "Yes. I watched you lather yourself up. I saw your ass and your thighs and your dick." Veronica eased closer to him so that her body was touching his. By the stiff way Rick was lying, she knew for sure that he'd really never been so close to a woman. This excited her. She allowed her fingertips to dance around on his stomach just below his belly button.

"You know that you're big, don't you?"

Rick laughed nervously. "Am I really?" he asked.

"Oh yes," she said. "You're a man, Rick. A real strong man." Veronica was getting such a charge out of manipulating Rick. "When the time is right, are you going to give it to me?" Veronica asked.

"I'll give you whatever you want," Rick said with uncontrollable nervousness and excitement.

"Good," Veronica cooed.

"Rick." Veronica heard Tabetha call out his name.

"Shoot," Rick hissed. "Does she have radar or something?" he whispered loudly. "Every time I want to have some fun, she messes it up," Rick complained as he got out of the bed with Veronica.

"Don't worry. We'll have plenty of time to do it all," Veronica said as she winked at him. "Now go on. Get up those stairs before she has a bitch fit." Rick and Veronica laughed as he rushed up the stairs.

Veronica reached under her pillow and removed the cell phone Chuck had given her. She dialed his number and waited for him to pick up.

"Hey, baby," Veronica said as she allowed her head to hit the pillow once again.

"I've got the keys," she whispered, feeling bolts of adrenaline travel through her.

"You are one badass woman," Chuck said.

"I learned from the best," Veronica replied. "Do you have a crew together yet?"

"I will in a few days. Are you sure about this, Veronica? Can you handle this?"

"Don't tell me you're getting all sentimental on me, Chuck."

"I'm just saying. He's the only family you've got."

"If I can steal from my own mama and not feel bad about it, I know damn well I can steal from my brother. He'll be pissed off for a while, but he'll come around. Gilbert is forgiving like that. You let me worry about him," Veronica said.

"I need that merchandise we talked about, Veronica. I have a client who's willing to pay top dollar for it. How soon can you get it?"

"Pick me up at River Oaks Shopping Mall around one PM," Veronica said. "It will not take much time to do what we need to do."

23

Tabetha

Tabetha didn't want to travel down the path she was about to, but felt she had no choice. If she didn't, she felt as if something irreversible and regrettable would happen in her own house, and she had to do everything she could to prevent it. Tabetha called Marlon and asked if he had time to meet with her.

"What's going on?" Marlon asked over the phone.

"I need to see you," Tabetha said, trying not to speak too loudly. The last thing she needed was for Gilbert to overhear her speaking to Marlon. That would really send him through the roof.

"I can have my secretary schedule some time. I'm glad that you finally gave me a call," Marlon said.

"Marlon, this can't wait," Tabetha said. "I want to see you today."

"Okay." Marlon paused in thought. "I have a meeting at my home this afternoon. Why don't you swing by around three PM. You can relax in the coach house for a while until I finish up."

"That's fine, Marlon," Tabetha said, and then hung up the phone.

"It sounds as if you have a date."

Tabetha was startled by Veronica, who must have been listening to her conversation.

"So that's what this is all about," Veronica said as she folded her arms across her chest. "And you have the nerve to accuse me of being up to no good." Veronica's dislike of Tabetha had reached a new level.

"You don't know what you're talking about," Tabetha said as she shot daggers with her eyes at Veronica.

"Oh really," Veronica answered defiantly. "It sounds to me like you're having sex with your ex-husband."

"Veronica. Just do everyone a big favor and grow the fuck up. If you can't do that, then you need to stay the hell out of grown folks' business."

"Is that a threat?" Veronica asked. "Because it would be such a shame if Gilbert were to find out that you're sneaking around with Marlon behind his back." Veronica glared at her. "Perhaps that's the reason why you won't have a child for him. You're still trying to get back with Marlon."

"Listen, bitch!" Tabetha got close to Veronica, and the tension between them was about to explode. "I will kill you."

"Huh." Veronica backed away from her. "Heifer, you don't have the guts to kill a spider crawling up a wall. You don't scare me," Veronica said as she headed back down to the basement.

Tabetha was fuming with anger as she drove over to Marlon's house. She was angry with Gilbert for allowing Veronica to move in. She was angry with him for discounting her point of view about his sister, and she was angry because she couldn't contain Veronica the way she wanted to.

When Tabetha arrived at Marlon's house, one of his servants escorted her out through the garden and into the coach house at the back of his property. Tabetha took a seat on the sofa, crossed one leg over the other, and tried to calm herself down.

"May I get you something to drink, Ms. Murphy?" asked Marlon's servant.

"A glass of wine," Tabetha requested. "Anything will do."

"Certainly, madam," said the woman, who returned a short time later with Tabetha's drink.

"Here you go, madam. Mr. Wayne will join you shortly," she said before leaving to let Tabetha wait for Marlon. Tabetha took a few sips of her wine and then set her glass down atop a coaster on the small cocktail table before her. She tilted her head back and waited for the soothing effects of the wine to work its magic. She massaged her own neck in an extra effort to remove the additional tension that was embedded in her muscles.

"I can take care of that for you," Marlon said as he entered the room.

Tabetha didn't respond to him right away because her mind was still focused on doing harm to Veronica. Marlon took Tabetha's silence as an invitation to touch her and massage her tension away. Tabetha flinched when he began massaging her neck from behind the sofa.

"Sorry," Marlon quickly said. "I thought you wanted me to rub away your stress."

Tabetha decided that no harm could come from him massaging away some tension, so instead of making Marlon feel foolish for crossing a line, she held her neck down and directed him to the area that needed to be worked on.

"Oh, that feels so good," Tabetha said as Marlon worked magic with his fingertips. After a minute or two, Tabetha felt her tension give way to a new feeling of light-headedness.

"Okay, Marlon." Tabetha stopped him before she got too relaxed. Marlon obeyed her request and stopped massaging her. He walked around and sat in a chair that was facing the sofa and her.

"You go first," Marlon said as he got comfortable in his seat.

Tabetha exhaled as she began to pull her thoughts together. "I want Rick to come and stay with you for a little while," Tabetha said. She noticed how Marlon raised his eyebrow at the request.

"Why do you suddenly have a change of heart?" Marlon asked curiously.

"I'm trying to prevent the boy from doing something stupid that could screw up the rest of his life."

"Tabetha." Marlon leaned forward in his seat and brushed his fingers across his lips before speaking. "I don't mind Rick coming to stay with me, but have you thought this through? What about school? How will he get back and forth?"

"Marlon, that should be the least of your worries. He has a driver's license, and you have cars and drivers who can take him any place he needs to go."

"Okay," Marlon agreed. "So what's the real reason you want him to come here? Did that bus driver do something to him?"

"No, but Gilbert has moved his lazy and ignorant-ass sister into our house and refuses to put her out," Tabetha said, feeling the tension in her neck building up again.

"Did you agree with her coming to stay with you?" Marlon asked.

"Hell no," Tabetha answered sharply. "I want the bitch out of my house."

"Then put her out," Marlon said with absolute conviction.

"I would, but he will not turn his back on her," Tabetha admitted. "He has some type of soft spot or weakness for her that I don't understand."

"Now, is this the same sister who was incarcerated a while back?" Marlon asked. "I vaguely remember Rick mentioning to me that Gilbert's sister was arrested."

"Yes," Tabetha answered. "And now that she's in the house, she has her eyes set on having sex with my baby." Tabetha paused. "Our baby, I mean."

"What?" Marlon asked.

"You heard me. Veronica is crazy like that. I caught her watching him take a shower the other night. When I confronted her about it, she was so damn defiant that we almost got into a physical confrontation. So what I'd like to do is have Rick come stay with you for a while until Gilbert and I can work this thing out."

There was a long pause before Marlon spoke. Tabetha studied his eyes and saw that he was processing something. She could tell that some type of major calculation was in progress.

"Marlon?" Tabetha interrupted his thought process.

"Yeah," Marlon answered, brushing his fingers across his lips once again. "Look. I want you to hear me out on something. It's going to sound unconventional, but I want you to consider it." Marlon held Tabetha's gaze for a moment. "What I'm about to tell you is something that should remain confidential for now."

"You look serious, Marlon," Tabetha said as she picked up her glass of wine and took another sip. "Okay. Lay it on me. You've had this on your mind for a while. I can tell."

"Rick and I have been talking," Marlon said. "He has expressed to me that perhaps you and Gilbert aren't exactly happy together."

"And?" Tabetha got defensive.

"Don't get upset," Marlon said. "Kids notice those types of things, Tabetha. I'm not saying that I was the best father, because I know what I did." Marlon gestured with his hands. "Tabetha, if you're not happy there, consider coming back to me."

"What?" Tabetha couldn't believe what she was hearing. "Marlon, we just can't pick up where we left off. That's impossible."

"Do you really think it's that impossible, Tabetha?" Marlon asked.

"Marlon, I'm married, remember?"

"Yeah, but from what I'm hearing, you really don't want to be married to him any longer. I know about the pressure he's putting on you to have a baby. Hell, I don't blame you for not wanting a baby at this stage in your life. Rick will be in college soon, and, hell, who wants to go back to changing diapers?"

"Lord knows that I don't," Tabetha admitted.

"Leave him, Tabetha. Come stay with me. We'll work it out."

"Marlon, it doesn't work that easily."

"Sure it can. What do you need? Money? I've got plenty."

"What's this all about, Marlon? What's in it for you?" Tabetha asked, not really understanding why she was even considering what Marlon wanted. Tabetha studied Marlon's eyes. She was all too familiar with his expressions. "Tell me the truth, Marlon. What's this all about?"

Marlon licked his lips and began speaking. "Okay. Here it is. I had a meeting with some other business leaders today before you arrived. They're very powerful and have influence in political circles. The current state congressman in your district is under fire because of an inappropriate relationship with an underaged girl. I want his slot," Marlon said with absolute certainty. "However, your district has a strong commitment to family values."

"And what's wrong with that?" Tabetha asked.

"Nothing. That's great," Marlon said. "My problem is my public image needs to reflect that I'm a family man as well. What I am offering you, Tabetha, is a chance to live the life you deserve to live. No more money problems. Plenty of social status and respect from the community. You can have it all," Marlon said. "All you have to do is divorce Gilbert and remarry me. I'll have my attorneys draw up the paperwork. It's a good deal, Tabetha."

"Marlon, that's crazy. The media will know you're a fraud. That sounds crazier than what I'm going through with Veronica. What happened? Did everyone wake up one day and say, 'Hey, let's do some crazy shit'?"

"No, they won't!" Marlon answered sharply. "I'm not crazy. I can have all of our marriage records sealed so that the public doesn't have access to them. I'll even pay Gilbert off to disappear and keep his mouth shut while I run for office. We can do this, Tabetha. You know me better than anyone, and I know that you can pull this off. Just think about it. I'll take care of everything."

Tabetha was speechless. She had no idea how to respond to

Marlon. She didn't flat out say no, because somewhere in the back of her mind, something was telling her to welcome the opportunity and the change, even though on the surface the entire plan seemed too crazy for words.

"What if you lose, then what?"

Marlon smiled. "You're stuck with me." Marlon's grin appeared to look rather sinister to Tabetha.

"And what if I leave you afterward?"

"There are conditions to my offer, Tabetha. One of which is you must sign a prenuptial agreement. The other conditions are designed to make sure that neither one of us says or does something that would be damaging to my campaign.

"What about Rick? Where does he fit?"

"He won't be in the spotlight. Minor children are off-limits."

"So basically you're asking me to behave deceptively for money."

"That's the American way, Tabetha."

"I don't think I can handle something like this, Marlon."

"What if I gave you a handsome sum of money up front?" Marlon asked. His offer caught her off guard.

"You must really want to do this," she said.

"Things are not finalized just yet, but I'd be willing to pay for you to come on board. So what's it going to be?"

"I don't know, Marlon. That's a big step. Give me some time to think about it."

"Okay, I can understand that. But don't study it too long."

"Marlon, this isn't easy. I know you too well. I know how dark and mean you can get. I still haven't forgotten how you left Rick and me. I never got over that, and I don't know if I can put myself back in that vulnerable position again."

"Okay, I can respect that. I'm not the easiest person to deal with. Think about it, though. Give it some serious consideration."

24

Gilbert

"Gilbert, where did you put the suitcase?" Tabetha asked as she searched the closet for her luggage.

"Suitcase?" Gilbert asked, puzzled. "Why do you need the suitcase?"

"Because," Tabetha said as she pushed more clothing aside so she could reach the rear of the closet. "Shit, I hate these tight-ass closets!" Tabetha complained.

"Why do you need the suitcase?" Gilbert asked again.

"Because we have a problem, Gilbert." Tabetha came out of the closet and glared at him.

"Oh, now what, Tabetha?" Gilbert's tone was filled with annoyance.

"You know what the damn problem is, Gilbert. That trifling-ass sister of yours."

"I'm working with Veronica, okay? I'm going to get her situated soon," Gilbert added.

"Well it's not soon enough. I can't wait for her to do something that she can't take back."

"Tabetha, what are you talking about? You're not making any sense."

"Rick, Gilbert. She has a thing for my son. I saw her watching him take a shower the other day."

"That's ridiculous. I'll admit, Veronica is not the most sane individual, but she'd never do anything like that."

"Gilbert, you are honestly that blinded by her? What is it with you and her? Why can't you see that she's just using you?"

"Tabetha, she's my sister. She's family. Maybe if you weren't an only child and had a brother or sister, you'd understand my position better," Gilbert offered as an explanation.

Tabetha was upset that Gilbert said that to her. She felt as if her feelings or her viewpoint on the matter weren't strong enough for him to seriously consider. She decided to lash back out at Gilbert in a way that she knew would hurt.

"I'm sending Rick to live with his father," Tabetha said as she moved to the other side of the room to search the other closet.

"Wait." Gilbert trailed her around the room. "What do you mean he's going to live with his father? What about school?"

"Marlon has money and drivers who can make sure that he gets to where he needs to be," Tabetha said, knowing full well that her words would sting him. "It's what Marlon and I want," Tabetha added. "We've agreed on this."

"When did this shit happen?" Gilbert raised his voice at her. The ugly feeling of insecurity had him feeling tense.

"Hold up!" Tabetha began sliding her clothes down the rack. She didn't see her fur coat. An ugly and upset expression embedded itself on her face. She rushed back over to the closet on the opposite side of the room to make sure that she wasn't overreacting. She searched but didn't find it. She stopped moving around and began thinking about the last time she saw it, which was earlier. *It was hanging up in the closet earlier today. I didn't wear it at all today, so where in the hell is it?* Tabetha searched the closet again, and then it hit her.

"Oh no, that bitch didn't!" Tabetha growled like an enraged beast about to strike and kill.

"Now what's wrong?" Gilbert asked.

"Where's Veronica?" Tabetha shot Gilbert a murderous glare.

"She's downstairs. Tabetha, what's wrong? Why are you looking at me like that?"

Tabetha didn't say a word. She couldn't because she was so enraged and about to explode. She flew out of the room and down the stairs. She rushed into the basement, flipped on the light switch, and interrupted everything that was going on between Veronica and Rick.

"We weren't doing anything!" Rick leaped up backward off Veronica. He was still fully clothed and so was she, but the sight was enough to send Tabetha over the edge.

"Rick, shut up!" Tabetha barked so loudly at him he trembled.

"Oh God," Veronica said as she sat up. "Boy, are you going to let her talk to you like that?"

"You know what, bitch?" Tabetha rushed over to the bed. Veronica sprang to her feet in order to defend herself.

"Mom!" Rick called to her.

"Veronica," Gilbert said. "What were you doing?" Gilbert asked.

Veronica could clearly see the hurt in his eyes.

"Nothing really," Veronica answered as if everything they had seen was being taken out of context.

"Rick, go to your room!" Tabetha ordered him out of the basement.

"I don't want to go," Rick said, trying to hold his ground.

"Get your ass out of here," Tabetha exploded at him and shoved him away from her.

"It's okay," Veronica told Rick. "I'll handle this."

When Rick followed Veronica's order to leave, Tabetha was speechless. She couldn't believe that her son had suddenly turned against her.

Veronica grinned at Tabetha. It was fun watching her. *I've turned her son against her,* Veronica thought.

"Do you see what I'm talking about, Gilbert?" Tabetha shot him an ugly glare. "Now do you see?"

"I see it, but I don't believe it," Gilbert answered. "I don't want to believe it."

"Then don't. This entire thing is really being blown out of proportion," Veronica said in her defense. "I wouldn't think of doing something so foul in this house."

"What was just going on in here, Veronica?" Gilbert tried not to raise his voice at her.

"We were wrestling," Veronica answered as if she'd arrived at the perfect explanation for what was going on.

"In the fuckin' dark, bitch? Come up with something original." Tabetha wasn't cutting her any slack.

"You know what, if you call me out of my name one more time, I'm going to show you what a real bitch can do," Veronica threatened Tabetha.

"Who do you think you're talking to?" Tabetha was ready to hurt Veronica.

"I'm talking to you." Veronica glared at her directly, feeling no fear about taking Tabetha to the mat.

"We are not going to be in here fighting like cats and dogs!" Gilbert shouted out, wanting to maintain order in his house. "Veronica, sit the hell down," Gilbert ordered her. "Tabetha, relax. We're going to sit down like adults and talk about this."

Veronica sat down on the edge of the bed and crossed one leg over the other. Tabetha folded her arms across her chest and decided to be patient for the moment, although her sensibility had begged her to slap Veronica at least once.

"Veronica, you can't wrestle with a teenage boy like that. You're too old for that," Gilbert said.

"Gilbert!" Tabetha glared at him as if he was the dumbest man on the planet. "She wasn't wrestling with him. She was trying to fuck him." Tabetha thought that being blunt would remove Gilbert's blinders. "What I want to know, Veronica, is where in the hell is my fur coat?"

"The fuck if I know," Veronica answered.

"No, bitch, you stole my fur coat. It was in this house, and now it's not. I'm going to ask you one more time," Tabetha said as she felt her nerves twitch and tingle with anticipation. "Where is my coat?"

Veronica was about to kick Tabetha in the gut with her next comment, and she knew that it would spark an explosive reaction. But she had to get the attention off of her, and she didn't care how she did it.

"Maybe you left it at Marlon's house. You've been over there with him all day. Perhaps you were over there fucking him in it." That did it. Tabetha cocked her arm back, rushed toward Veronica, and swung at her. Her blow connected with the side of Veronica's face and made a hideous popping sound.

"Tabetha!" Gilbert called her name as he swiftly moved to-ward her. He approached her from behind, grabbed both of her arms, and pulled her away from Veronica, who wasn't about to allow the slap to go unanswered. She swung back at Tabetha and connected with a blow of her own.

"You don't put your damn hands on me," Veronica barked at Tabetha.

At that moment, Rick rushed back into the basement. The first thing he noticed was the way Gilbert was manhandling Tabetha. He assumed that the worst was taking place and thought Gilbert was attacking his mother. Rick rushed over to Gilbert, leaped onto his back, and locked his arm around his neck to place him in a choke hold. Gilbert lost his balance and fell backward onto the floor.

"Let her go!" Rick insisted.

Gilbert released Tabetha, grabbed Rick's arm, and removed it from around his neck with ease. His manly strength outmatched Rick's overzealousness. Gilbert swiftly repositioned himself and got to his feet much quicker than Rick could.

"What the hell is wrong with you, boy?" Gilbert barked at Rick.

"You were attacking my mother." Rick's chest heaved with contempt.

"Have you ever seen me hit or beat on your mother?" Gilbert yelled at him for his stupidity.

"No," Rick answered.

"Then what in the hell makes you think that I'm going to start doing it now? Huh?"

"I don't know," Rick quickly answered. "You guys argue so much I figured that was the next thing that was going to happen."

"Well you thought wrong, boy!" Gilbert howled at him. "And the next time you think you're man enough to jump on me, I will kill you dead." Gilbert's threat vibrated throughout the room. "Don't move from where you're at," Gilbert ordered Rick.

"Gilbert, I'm telling you, this is your last chance—" Tabetha said, full of anger.

"You don't have to say anything. It's clear that we can't get along like adults in here."

"She started it," Veronica quickly said, feeling confident that her brother would side with her as he always had. "And she hit me first. You saw her."

"Mom, you hit Veronica?" Rick asked, stunned.

"Shut up, Rick. I'm pissed at you too!" Tabetha gave him one of her murderous glares. "Now go back upstairs and start packing your things. You're going to stay with your father for a while."

"But I don't want to go," Rick insisted.

"Rick, you're skating on thin ice, boy. Do what I told you." Tabetha wasn't playing with him.

"Veronica, you need to pack your things," Gilbert said.

"What?" Veronica didn't believe what she was hearing.

"You can't stay here anymore," Gilbert said.

"Well it's about damn time you opened your eyes," Tabetha said, feeling some type of satisfaction.

"What do you mean I have to leave?" Veronica asked, believing that Gilbert was toying with her. "I know you are not serious about putting me out."

"Yes, he is," Tabetha said, eager to take another swing and kick at Veronica.

"Tabetha, calm down," Gilbert insisted.

"What in the hell do you mean calm down? She stole my fur coat, and I want it back." Tabetha directed her anger toward Gilbert.

"Veronica, did you take her coat?" Gilbert asked.

Veronica developed an attitude and refused to speak. Instead, she focused her gaze on a spot on the ceiling.

"Veronica, I know you heard me. Did you steal her coat?"

"I don't know what she's talking about," Veronica finally answered.

"My own brother thinks that I'm in his house stealing shit," Veronica said in an effort to make Gilbert feel bad for even asking such a question.

"Tabetha, look, she said that she didn't take your coat." Gilbert looked at Tabetha, feeling as if he'd resolved the issue.

"And you believe her?" Tabetha was now even more upset than she was before. She didn't understand how or why Gilbert was so trusting of Veronica. She wanted Gilbert to be more aggressive and supportive of her claim and not straddle the fence. Tabetha didn't like that about him at that moment. Something inside of her fell and shattered. She checked her feelings to see what it was. It was her respect for Gilbert.

"She probably left it over there with Marlon." Veronica refused to let the issue die. "Gilbert, listen to me." Veronica pointed at Tabetha. "I heard her on the phone whispering to Marlon about hooking up with him. She's so concerned about me being a backstabber, and she's off sneaking around with Marlon. I'll bet you a thousand dollars that's where the coat is," Veronica boldly stated. "He probably took it back, since he is the one who bought it." Veronica glared directly at Tabetha as she expressed her dislike of her. "Think about it, Gilbert." Veronica was appealing to Gilbert's jealousy and insecurity. "What man do you know just gives up his money freely and doesn't expect any ass in return?" That did it, and Veronica knew it. She watched Gilbert's eyes dart from left to right as he considered what she was telling him.

"Why don't you shut up and pack your things," Tabetha howled at Veronica.

"What were you doing at Marlon's house?" Gilbert asked, feeling threatened.

"Gilbert, what are you talking about?" Tabetha didn't answer his question.

"Were you with Marlon all day? Yes or no?" Gilbert asked.

Tabetha paused for a moment before answering. "Gilbert, we'll talk about that once Veronica is gone," Tabetha stated.

"Huh. Sounds to me like she was rekindling an old flame." Veronica added fuel to the fire.

"You know what, Veronica, worry about your own business and where you're going to sleep tonight. Start packing your shit."

"My brother loves me," Veronica blurted out. "He is not going to put me out on the street just because you said so." Veronica believed that. She believed that—no matter how much drama she caused or how much dirt she did. One thing she always depended on was the fact that Gilbert would never turn his back on her. He would never break the promise he'd made to always be there for her no matter what.

"Veronica, pack your bag," Gilbert said. "I'm not playing with you. I've been trying to help you, but you don't want to help yourself. You have to leave my house." He didn't anticipate how much his own words would cut into his heart. He loved his sister, and he wanted so much for her. Gilbert wanted his sister to live a good life and have a loving family, but his dream of what her life should be like and her dream of life were completely opposite.

"So you're going to choose that whore over me? Your own sister? Blood is thicker than water, Gilbert. Hell, she won't even mix blood with you and give you a son or daughter. The bitch is on a page, Gilbert. She's playing you. I don't know why you can't see that."

"That's it. You're not going to call me a whore in my own damn house." Tabetha leaped toward Veronica, but Gilbert grabbed her from behind and pulled her away. As Gilbert moved her away, Tabetha kicked Veronica, hitting her on the thigh.

"Come on," Gilbert said as he stood her on her feet and pushed her up the stairs. "I want to know what the hell you were doing at Marlon's house all day."

"Do you really want me to pack my things?" Veronica asked as Gilbert headed up the stairs.

"Yes, Veronica. Pack your things," Gilbert answered.

25

Veronica

Veronica was pissed off when Gilbert dropped her off at a motel. He paid the room for one week and placed her luggage inside her room.

"I'm sorry things didn't work out, Veronica," Gilbert said, feeling sad and awful about having to make this choice.

"I can't believe you're doing this to me," Veronica said, feeling hurt and bruised by Gilbert's course of action. "I saved your life, Gilbert. Remember?" Veronica felt her heart swell with pain. "I saved you from Mama's boyfriend. You owe me," Veronica reminded him.

"Veronica, this hurts me much more than it hurts you," Gilbert stated, feeling as if a blade had pierced his heart. "This isn't what I wanted." Gilbert paused in thought. "You know, Mama used to always say, 'God bless the child that's got his own.' I never knew what she meant by it until recently. All she was saying was to make your own way in life and acquire the things that you need in order to make it in this world. I know that she took the words from a Billie Holiday song, but it's true. You need to come into your own, Veronica, and I can't help you. Believe me. I want to, but you're sucking the life out of me. You're draining me. You're dead weight."

Gilbert's words cut Veronica deeply, and for the first time, her sadness gave way to pure anger.

"Mama always did like you better than she liked me," Veronica said. "You were her favorite. You could never do wrong in her eyes." Veronica snarled at Gilbert and at the memory of their mother. "You hold Mama up to be so damn saintly." Veronica laughed angrily. "She wasn't as saintly as you're making her out to be."

"She did what she could, Veronica," Gilbert said, sensing that Veronica was about to destroy something he held dear to his heart.

"Do you even know how I got into doing all the shit that I do?" Veronica asked. "Did you ever wonder how or why I fell into the business so easily?"

"You got involved with the wrong crowd, Veronica," Gilbert answered her with absolute certainty.

"Damn, Gilbert. Tabetha is right about one thing. You walk around with blinders on. Shit goes on all around you, but you don't see it."

"What are you talking about, Veronica?"

"Our precious mother." Veronica had both venom and sorrow in her voice. "She was a thief, Gilbert," Veronica told him. "She and that boyfriend of hers sold diverted merchandise." Veronica laughed at how naive her brother was. "One of the reasons she made you keep a close eye on me was because I'd found out, and she didn't want me going down that same path. But I wanted to." Veronica began to give critical thought to her reflections of the past. "It seemed like so much fun. You could get all kinds of stuff and not pay full price. Only the idiots went to a retail store and paid full price."

"Veronica, I think you've flipped out. Now you've resorted to lying about our dead mother. I don't want you around my family or me anymore. Don't call or visit me. I'm dead to you."

Gilbert's words to his sister hurt him. Veronica purposefully trapped his gaze before he could turn and leave.

"So what does this mean, Gilbert?" she asked. Veronica paused. "You're turning your back on me?"

Gilbert studied the hurt in her eyes. He could tell that her wound was deep and that she was trying to contain an outburst of uncontrolled emotion.

"Good-bye, Veronica." Gilbert said his final good-bye and left.

Veronica watched him as he got into his sedan and drove away.

"This isn't over, Gilbert," Veronica mumbled. She went and plopped down on the bed and picked up the hotel telephone and called Big Money Chuck.

"Hey, Chuck, it's me, Veronica," she said into the phone.

"Girl, where have you been? I've been trying to reach you," Chuck said. "I sold that fur coat you got for me along with some other merchandise that I got top dollar for. I'm in business again, baby." Chuck had a jovial sound in his voice.

"Listen, what's up with the crew you were putting together?" Veronica asked. "I've got an easy job that can produce a few thousand dollars' worth of merchandise for us."

"They're ready," Chuck said.

"Get a truck," Veronica instructed him. "We'll need to move shit quickly."

"What have you set up? Are we hitting a delivery truck? Warehouse? What?"

"We're hitting a home, Chuck. A home with some very nice items."

26

Tabetha

Tabetha was still very upset when Gilbert arrived back home from wherever he'd taken Veronica. The fact that she had to literally get into a fight before Gilbert realized that the woman was no good didn't sit well with her at all. On top of that, Rick was going through some type of emotional outburst about Veronica leaving. At first she was going to allow him to remain at home since Veronica was gone. However, after reconsidering, she concluded that it would be best overall if he got away from some of the drama going on to cool off. Tabetha heard Gilbert place his car keys on the countertop in the kitchen; then she heard the sound of his footsteps coming up to the bedroom.

"I've been doing some thinking about what my sister told me, Tabetha," Gilbert said as he sat down on the edge of the bed, which was filled with clothing from the closet. Gilbert was about to ask why all of the clothes were out of the closet but then realized that Tabetha was still searching for her fur coat. Gilbert began taking off his shoes.

"Were you really with Marlon again all day today?" Gilbert asked.

"You've got some nerve asking me that," Tabetha said, feeling emotionally on edge.

"Answer me, Tabetha," Gilbert said more forcefully.

Tabetha knew right then that he'd once again allowed his insecurities to work him up emotionally to the point that he'd run his blood pressure sky-high thinking about it.

"Yes, I was with him," Tabetha answered not caring about his high blood pressure at that moment. *For all I care, you can pop a blood vessel,* Tabetha thought as she came to accept that Veronica actually did steal her coat.

"Did you get my coat back from her?" Tabetha blurted out angrily. "I paid good money for my coat."

"No, Marlon paid for it. So, technically, you didn't spend anything," Gilbert lashed back at Tabetha. His mind was chewing on what she was doing with Marlon all day. The images that were coming to him were all sexual.

"Maybe Veronica was right. Maybe you did leave it over there and just came back into this house claiming she stole it so I'd put her out."

"Gilbert, that is the dumbest thing I've ever heard." Tabetha's frustration with Gilbert had reached its peak.

"I don't see why," Gilbert lashed back. He didn't like the idea of his wife being with her ex-husband at all. The two reasons being Marlon's wealth, which he tossed around, and their sexual history. Even though Marlon and Tabetha hadn't been together in years, the idea that a past sexual partner still lingered around didn't sit well with him.

"Are you fucking him?" Gilbert asked, feeling his wild thoughts get the best of him.

"What!" Tabetha barked back at him.

"You heard me. Are you fucking him?"

Tabetha didn't answer his questions. She remained silent and began putting clothes back in the closet. Her feelings were so hurt by Gilbert's question that she couldn't find the right words to answer him. She felt tears welling up inside of her.

"Answer me, Tabetha," Gilbert insisted, not fully realizing that his words were just as strong as a punch. "Why were you sneaking around with him?"

Tabetha swallowed hard and allowed some of her anger and frustration to speak on her behalf. "Rick is going to stay with him for a while, Gilbert."

Gilbert could hear her anger floating beneath the tone in her voice.

"What? Why? And what for? We're a family here, and we stick together."

"It would be best for now," Tabetha continued, still speaking with a soft and yet very angry voice. "Veronica somehow, in a short amount of time, influenced Rick to the point that he's upset and wants to hurt you about her being gone. It's best that he stays with his father for a while until this entire thing blows over."

"He's trying to get you guys back into the house with him, isn't he?" Gilbert said, suddenly feeling a strange vibe.

Tabetha glared at him with a strange look that Gilbert instantly picked up on.

"That's it, isn't it?" Gilbert said as he read into the meaning of her gaze.

"Gilbert, I want you to hear me," Tabetha said. "We have problems in this marriage. There is a large lack of respect going on between us. You moved a known thief and otherwise treacherous woman into our home. You gave more validation to the comments of that lunatic sister of yours than you gave to mine. That hurt me, Gilbert. You don't know how badly that hurt me. You're accusing me of having an affair, but I've been nothing but a faithful woman to you, and you can't see that. The only thing you see is someone trying to take your perfect life away from you. Well it isn't perfect, Gilbert. It's fucked up," Tabetha said as a tear ran down her cheek.

"What do you want me to do, Tabetha? I turned my back on

my own sister," Gilbert said, feeling the pain of giving Veronica some tough love. "I did that for you."

"After a big fight, Gilbert. Besides, you shouldn't have done it for me. You should have been able to see that she wasn't worth wasting your time on."

"She's my sister, Tabetha. My flesh and blood," Gilbert added, giving more validation to the idea of family bloodlines than to how she was feeling.

"Gilbert," Tabetha said, seeing an entirely new side of her husband, "you need help. You have some sort of fixed position about this family bloodline thing that you can't see past. Did you have sex with your sister or something?" Tabetha asked, although she really didn't want to know the answer to that question.

"Hell no," Gilbert quickly squashed her claim.

"Well, you act like you have," Tabetha added. There was a long moment of silence between them; the tension in the room was unmistakable.

Finally, Tabetha spoke again. "I'm not certain that you've fully recovered from having to put your sister out," Tabetha said calmly. "I still have fears, Gilbert. I fear that she will call you back with some type of drama and you'll allow her to come right back in here. Until I know that you're over this and can stand up to her, I can't allow my son to stay here and make a dumb and appalling mistake, like getting Veronica pregnant or some other inexcusable act."

"You have problems, too, Tabetha." Gilbert was also speaking under the tension in the room. "Do you know how much it hurts me that you won't have a baby with me? You don't understand how much I want to be a father. I have been a good, decent, and faithful husband to you. I could be out on the street having babies from pillar to post, but I don't because I'm hopeful that you'll give in."

"I don't want you out on the street having a baby with some

strange woman, Gilbert. But us having a baby at this point is no longer on the table for consideration."

"So where does that leave us? What are you saying?" Gilbert asked, feeling defeated.

"I'm telling you the truth, Gilbert. I'm telling you the way it is," Tabetha answered him.

27

Veronica

Veronica, Big Money Chuck, and a small three-man crew returned to Gilbert's home when Veronica knew he and Tabetha would be at work.

"I just love the suburbs," Chuck said. "Everything is so nice and orderly. People have a false sense of security, and it's easy pickings. Especially when people get up to work a nine-to-five."

"It's the house right there. The one on the corner," Veronica said.

"Now, what about the police, Veronica?" asked one of the young crew members. "I can't get arrested again."

"Shut the hell up," Chuck barked at the chubby young man. "Veronica knows what she's doing. If she set it up, it's going to be a smooth operation because she knows how to stay out of jail."

"Stop the van right here," said Veronica. "All right, listen up. I'm going to walk over there and ring the doorbell to make sure they're not home. I'm going to let myself in with the key and then turn off the alarm. I'll open the garage door so that you can back the truck inside. We'll close the garage door and be able to move around the house with ease. Everybody understand?"

"Yeah," said the chubby crew member. "I got the stereo," he said, placing a claim on an item.

"You don't have shit, motherfucker." Chuck quickly put the man in his place. "I'm paying you to do a job. There are no extra perks in this for you."

"When you see the garage door open, back the truck inside," Veronica stated again.

"I got this," answered Big Money Chuck.

Veronica hopped out of the truck, shuffled across the street, and up to the front door. She rang the doorbell but didn't get an answer. She used the door key to let herself inside and then prayed that they hadn't changed the alarm code. When she opened the door, she heard a few short beeps from the home security system, which indicated that she had a short amount of time to enter the code into the panel on the wall. Veronica shut the door behind her and then entered the code that Rick had given her. To her happiness, the code still worked. Veronica sighed, feeling the buzz and excitement of being in the home illegally. She entered the dining room and looked at Tabetha's chinaware, which was decoratively displayed.

"That's such a nice set." Veronica smiled. She was so excited about what she was doing that she suddenly felt the urge to pee. "Shit," she hissed as she rushed to the bathroom.

Veronica made it to the garage and opened the door. She waved for Big Money Chuck to pull the truck inside. Once they backed the truck inside, she pushed the button and lowered the garage door.

"What took you so long?" Chuck asked.

"I had to pee," Veronica answered him sharply.

"I didn't know what the hell was going on. I was about to pull off," Chuck said, but then took his statement back. "I'm just playing. You know that I wouldn't leave you in a jam." Chuck laughed, but Veronica didn't fully believe him anyway.

"Come on inside. I'll show you where everything is," said Veronica.

"Whoa, that's a nice plasma screen television," said the chubby crew member.

"You and you." Chuck popped his fingers at the two other crew members. "Start taking it apart."

"What else do you have in here, Veronica?" asked Chuck.

"The stereo is in the basement. It's a nice system by Sony."

"This is a nice place that your brother has here," Chuck said to Veronica as she led him up the stairs. "What the hell did he do to piss you off?" asked Chuck.

"Don't worry about it," Veronica said.

"No, I need to worry about it, because if you'll rip off your own brother, you're not loyal to anyone."

"I'm loyal to you, Chuck. You know that," Veronica said.

"We'll see," Chuck said, nodding his head. "I'm going to ask you to prove your loyalty, Veronica. You'd better pass the test. Your life depends on it."

"Are you done talking shit now?" Veronica asked.

"Yeah," Chuck answered. "For now."

"Good," Veronica said, opening a door. "That's the son's room in there. He has a very nice computer system. Worth at least two thousand big ones."

"Well all right." Chuck rubbed his greedy hands together as he went inside to take down Rick's computer. While they worked, Veronica entered the master bedroom and began going through a file cabinet that was situated at the rear of one of the large walk-in closets. She laughed to herself as she pried open the cabinet and searched for the important documents she wanted to nab. She'd gotten more information from Rick than she'd planned on. She was playing him so well that he mentioned a bank account that had several thousand dollars in it for his college education. He showed her the bank statement that was under Tabetha's name.

"Bingo." Veronica smiled when she located the folder with

all of the information she was searching for. She was about to close the file cabinet drawer when she saw another financial folder that caught her eye. It was from a retirement plan. She pulled it out, opened it up, and discovered that Tabetha's 401K plan had nearly eighty thousand dollars in it.

"Oh yeah." Veronica smiled with delight. She was mapping out in her mind how she was going to steal Tabetha's identity and snatch her money.

"What the hell are you doing in here?" Big Money Chuck startled Veronica. "They have a safe or something hidden in here?"

"Damn, Chuck, you scared the shit out of me," Veronica said. "No, they don't have a safe in here. I thought they did but they don't," Veronica lied to him. The last thing she wanted him to know was the money she'd discovered. In her mind, her debt to him was now paid in full. She was going to take Tabetha's money, relocate to another city of her choice, and set up her own operation. Once she pulled down the cash, she'd be up and running in no time flat.

"Come on out of there. We're just about done loading stuff up." Chuck turned his back and walked out of the closet. Veronica folded the files and shoved them into her large pockets.

"Does she have jewelry that's worth anything?" Chuck asked as he began pulling out dresser drawers filled with clothes in search of more valuables.

"If she does, I never saw it."

"What about silverware?" Chuck inquired as he moved to another dresser drawer. "Well, just found her sex toy." Chuck laughed as he held it up. "What's going on? She doesn't like the real thing or something?"

"I don't think she does." Veronica laughed. "Lord knows that woman is too tightly wound to enjoy it," Veronica said, not caring that she was speaking unkindly of not only her sister-in-law, but her brother as well.

"Shit, Veronica. You're cold. But I like that about you."

"Whatever, Chuck. After this, you can consider our debt paid in full," Veronica said as she was about to leave the room.

"Hold on." Chuck rushed over to the bedroom door and slammed it shut. "There is one other matter."

"What?" Veronica didn't like the look that Chuck was giving her.

"I need to know something. I need to know how and why you weren't arrested during the raid on my shop. I want to know why they didn't have your name on the arrest list."

"The hell if I know, Chuck! Why are you bringing up old shit?"

"Well, it didn't occur to me until recently how low-down you are. If you'll screw over your own brother, you're not going to think twice about screwing me over."

"Chuck, you know I'd never do that. Now stop playing and let's get out of here."

"Hold on a minute, Veronica!" Chuck grabbed her arm and threw her down on the bed.

"I spent a lot of damn time in that jail cell."

"What? You want to have sex now?"

"No. I want to know if you were working with the police."

"Chuck. Baby. Now is not the time to have this conversation."

"So you were working with the police, weren't you?"

"Of course I was," Veronica answered him truthfully. "They offered me a bargain, and I took it!" Veronica boldly stood up to Big Money Chuck. She didn't care about him at that point, because she was thinking about her life after she stole the money from the accounts. She wanted to get the hell out of the house and be on her way. She really didn't have any intentions of telling Chuck about the deal she cut with investigators to shut him down.

"Thank you for being honest," Chuck said. "But you know you've just screwed up, right?"

"Chuck, if you want to kick my ass, you can do it later. Right now we should get the hell out of here."

"Well, the boys and I are going to leave. But I think you're going to end up dying in a house fire."

"What?" Veronica wasn't sure if she'd heard Chuck correctly.

"You heard me," Chuck said. Before Veronica could react or dodge his vicious right hook, Big Money Chuck hit her so hard she saw a flash of white light before she went unconscious.

When Veronica came to, she had a massive headache, and her ear had a loud ringing sound in it. She slowly opened her eyes, trying to clear out the fog in her mind, but began coughing violently. She organized her thoughts and her situation as quickly as she could and realized that heavy black smoke was billowing under the door.

"Oh my God." Veronica began to panic. "Chuck has set the house on fire!"

28

Tabetha

Tabetha and Gilbert stood in the center of the street, staring in shock at the charred remains of their home. Tabetha was sobbing uncontrollably as the fire chief came out of the house and approached them.

"I'm afraid that I have to declare the house a structural hazard. Don't go in there trying do find sentimental valuables. The entire structure could collapse on you."

"How?" Gilbert uttered the word. The fire chief couldn't hear him because of the hum of a nearby fire engine.

"How?" Gilbert asked again, speaking louder this time.

"Look. I'm not the investigator, but this fire is very suspicious. Had we arrived here sooner, we could have contained the fire a bit better, but we didn't receive a call until the house was fully engulfed in flames."

"We have a home monitoring system. They should've called you."

"That's the funny thing about this fire," said the fire chief. "I can't figure out why the alarm didn't sound. But we'll deal with that later. Do you folks have a place that you can stay until all of this gets sorted out? If not, I can get the folks from Red Cross out here for you."

"We—" Gilbert's words got trapped in his throat. He couldn't get them to come up as he studied his ruined home.

"Do you want me to get them out here?" asked the fire chief again.

Gilbert shook his head no. "We can stay with friends until we contact our insurance company," Gilbert finally said.

"Okay," said the fire chief, and left them to console each other.

"How did this happen, Gilbert?" Tabetha asked as she smeared away her tears. "Did you leave something on?"

"No." Gilbert answered.

"I got up this morning, got dressed, and left. I didn't make coffee or anything," Gilbert said as he hugged Tabetha and walked her over to his car. A few close neighbors offered them a place to stay for the evening along with any additional help that they needed. Tabetha and Gilbert acknowledged their neighbors' kindness as best they could as they continued on toward Gilbert's sedan. Everything felt surreal to the both of them. Neither one could believe that this happened to them.

"Excuse me, Mr. Murphy," a young voice called to him. It was Rick's friend Kevin. "I don't know if this is important or not, but I think I should tell you."

"Tell me what?" Gilbert asked.

"I called the fire department as soon as I realized that the house was on fire."

"Thank you," said Tabetha.

"There is more," said the young man. "I was home sick from school, and I saw a red truck pull into your garage this morning."

"A red truck." Both Tabetha and Gilbert stopped and looked at him.

"Yes, sir. I remember the license plate as well. It was BMC 1863. I remembered it because we're studying the Civil War in history and 1863 was the year the war began. Anyway, I guess the truck looked very strange to me, but I didn't think anything of it. I thought that perhaps you were having furniture delivered or something."

"I don't know anyone who owns a red truck," said Gilbert as he looked at Tabetha.

"Neither do I."

"Son, have you mentioned this to the police yet?"

"No sir."

Gilbert quickly looked around for the squad car that was blocking the street so the fire department could extinguish the flames. He caught the gaze of a police officer and waved him toward them. As the officer approached, Kevin continued sharing what he saw.

"I did see something else too," said Kevin. "I kept smelling something burning, and I thought that I'd left something on in the kitchen, so I went down to make sure. When I came downstairs, I glanced out the dining room window and saw a woman rushing out of your burning house."

"What?" asked Tabetha, who was trying to figure out what Kevin had seen.

"A woman. Her face and clothes were all black with smoke. She ran away from the house, but she didn't look like she was going to make it, so I quickly opened the door and yelled, 'Hey are you okay?' She looked over at me for a brief moment but then rushed away on foot. I saw a lot of heavy smoke coming from your house, so I rushed back inside and called the fire department."

"Could you tell who the woman was?" asked Tabetha.

"I think it was the lady who was staying with you. Rick was always talking about her. If I had to guess, I'd say it was her, even though I've never met her before. I've only seen her from far away."

Both Tabetha and Gilbert looked as if a bolt of lightning had just struck them.

"Can I help you folks out?" asked the officer.

Gilbert suddenly felt weak and lowered himself to the ground.

"No. She wouldn't do me like this," Gilbert said, not wanting to believe that Veronica was this evil.

"Sir? Are you okay?" The officer kneeled down to assist Gilbert.

"Do you see now, Gilbert?" Tabetha howled at him.

As the reality of the situation wrapped itself around Gilbert's mind, he felt as if he'd been kicked in the chest by a mule.

"Do you finally see now?" Tabetha asked again as she turned her back on him and walked away.

29

Gilbert

Gilbert and Tabetha's homeowner's insurance company moved swiftly to assist them. They issued them a very large check to pay for food, clothing, and other necessities, and they set them up with temporary housing while their claim was being processed. Tabetha only stayed with Gilbert for a short time before asking Lynise to allow her to stay with her for a little while. Tabetha was so angry with Gilbert that she couldn't handle being near him during this period of homelessness. Contempt for him had settled into her heart, and she didn't know if it would ever leave.

Gilbert pleaded with Tabetha to stay so that they could work through their problems, but his requests were of no use. When Tabetha left for Lynise's house, Gilbert was left with only his thoughts and the burning question of why. Why did Veronica do this to him? After the fire marshal concluded that the fire was indeed the work of an arsonist, the police issued a warrant on Veronica so that she could be questioned about the fire. Since Gilbert resided in the suburbs, he figured that it would take investigators time to locate Veronica. He knew that he could locate her much quicker. The first place he started was

Lenny Gray's house. They sat at her kitchen table where it was comfortable to speak about tough subjects.

"Baby, I'm so sorry to hear that your sister did you like this," Lenny Gray offered her words of sympathy. "Now, you know that if you need to stay here until things get sorted out, you're welcome to."

"Thanks, Lenny, but I'm okay. I'm hurt and upset, but I'm going to pull through this."

"What about your wife?" Lenny had a sad look in her eyes. "How is she taking all of this mess?"

Gilbert sighed and tried to search for the right words to describe his crumpled marriage. "We're just not getting along right now," Gilbert answered truthfully. "I'm not sure that we're going to bounce back from this one."

"Now don't go talking like that," Lenny said. "You love that woman. Don't let this thing here come between you. Remember, you took a vow that said for better or for worse. Don't lose this fight, Gilbert." Lenny offered more words of wisdom to him. Gilbert nodded his head in the affirmative.

"I won't give up," he said.

"Good. That's what I want to hear," Lenny said as she placed her hand on top of his. She stood up, shuffled over to the dish rack, and removed an old black cast-iron skillet from the cupboard. She washed the skillet and then placed it on the stove. She opened her refrigerator and removed some breakfast sausage. She had a red coffee can filled with cooking grease sitting on the stove. She placed some in the skillet.

"I know that it's not exactly breakfast time, but do you want some sausage and eggs?" Lenny asked.

"No, thanks. I'm fine," Gilbert said.

"Good. That leaves more for me," Lenny said, trying to be humorous. Gilbert didn't laugh because he wasn't in the mood for any type of merriment.

"You're not going to kill her, are you?" Lenny became serious.

"I don't know," Gilbert answered. "I just want to look her in the eye and ask her why."

"What if you don't get an answer?" Lenny asked. Gilbert was silent because he didn't have a response for her.

"Gilbert, listen to me for a minute. If you find that girl before the police do, don't do something that's going to land you in jail. You're over here acting real calm right now, and that's scaring me because it makes me think you're about to flip out."

"Lenny, I'm not going to flip out. I just want to see her."

"Baby, that's why they call it 'flipping out'—you don't expect to lose your mind. It just happens. Just remember that when you find her."

"Do you know where she is, Lenny?" Gilbert asked again, this time with a little more forcefulness in his voice. Lenny placed her sausage in the hot skillet and listened to them sizzle for a moment.

"She came by here a couple days ago," Lenny admitted. "She didn't look good at all. She looked like she'd been up in a chimney or something. She tried to get in here, but I wouldn't let her in. I didn't want any part of whatever kind of trouble she'd gotten herself mixed up in. Do you understand what I'm saying?" Lenny asked.

"I understand, Lenny. I don't blame you for not wanting to let her back in." Gilbert felt his jaws getting tight as the thought of seriously hurting Veronica crossed his mind.

"Good, because I didn't. I may be old, but I nobody's fool."

"So what did she do?" Gilbert asked.

"Oh, she kicked on the door for a while and tried to force me to let her in. She acted like a fool out there. Showed just how much of an ass she can be. I told her that I was going to call the police if she didn't leave. Then she calmed down some and just flat out started begging me to let her in. In my heart, Gilbert, I wanted to help the child, but my mind wouldn't let me. I told her that maybe her girlfriend Bonnie would let her back in because I wasn't going to. I turned my back on her,

Gilbert. It was a hard thing to do, but I couldn't let her get up in here and do something crazy. She might be staying at Bonnie's house. Do you know where Bonnie lives?" Lenny asked.

"Yeah," Gilbert answered. "I know where she stays."

Gilbert spent a little more time with Lenny, who kept speaking to him about not killing Veronica graveyard dead and about working on his marriage. Gilbert eventually left and found himself ringing Bonnie's doorbell. It took several rings before she finally answered through the intercom system of her apartment building.

"Who is it?"

"Yeah, I'm looking for Bonnie Calloway."

"This is she. Who is this?" Bonnie asked.

"Hey, Bonnie, this is Gilbert Murphy, Veronica's brother. I'm trying to find her and was wondering if you knew where she was."

There was a short pause before Bonnie spoke again. "Come up to the second floor, Gilbert," Bonnie said, and then buzzed him inside. Gilbert rushed upstairs to the second floor where he found Bonnie standing in her house robe waiting for him.

"You'll have to excuse the place," Bonnie said as she started picking up some of the toys that her kids had left in the middle of the floor. "My cleaning lady didn't like the pay, so she quit," Bonnie said, attempting to find some humor.

"Don't worry about it, Bonnie," Gilbert said. "It's been a long time."

"Yes, it has," Bonnie answered. "Come on in. Just walk down the hall and into the dining room and have yourself a seat."

Gilbert walked down the corridor and took a seat at the dinette table, which was covered with mail. Bonnie joined him at the table.

"I know that I look like a mess, but I work at night and sleep during the day," Bonnie explained.

"How have you been, Bonnie?" Gilbert asked.

"You know, I've been making it the best way I can. It's not easy, but I'm handling it. My kids keep me going. I've changed my entire lifestyle for them."

"Good for you," Gilbert complimented her. "I wish that I was dropping by under better circumstances," he admitted.

"I see it," Bonnie said. "I see the pain in your eyes. I knew that she'd done something when she came by here. I didn't know what, and frankly I didn't want to know what she'd done. But I will tell you this. She didn't look too good."

"Did you let her in?" Gilbert asked.

"I felt bad for her," Bonnie said. "After all she's done to me, I should feel nothing but contempt for her, but I don't. I don't want to carry hate around with me. Anyway, she looked very dirty. Like she'd been living on the street for a while. I let her in to shower and have some fresh clothes. I gave her a deli sandwich that she couldn't keep down; as soon as she ate it, she went into the bathroom to vomit. To me she looked like she was on something. You know she experimented with hard drugs from time to time."

"No," Gilbert answered, "I had no idea."

"Well, people who use are good at hiding it. Anyway, I thought she'd developed a habit she couldn't control. She wanted to stay with me. In fact, she begged me to let her stay but I couldn't. I made her leave."

"I understand, Bonnie," Gilbert said. "You're a good person for doing what you did for her."

"I pray for her, you know. Sometimes I fear that the police are going to find her dead in some back alley."

Gilbert closed his eyes, held his head down, and slumped his shoulders forward. He didn't understand why he'd been so blind.

"Gilbert?" Bonnie leaned forward, resting her elbows on her thighs. "What did she do?"

"She burned down my house," Gilbert said as he looked into Bonnie's eyes.

"Oh my God," Bonnie said, not wanting to believe that

Veronica had gone that far. "I am so sorry, Gilbert. I am so very sorry."

"I just want to know why she did it," Gilbert said.

"You know, Veronica may never give you a reason. Sometimes that girl just does shit for the sake of doing it. She gets a high off of doing crazy stuff. There have been plenty of times and situations where she's done stuff like that."

"Did she say where she was going?" Gilbert asked.

"No, she didn't," Bonnie said.

"Any idea of where she'd go?"

"If I had to guess, I'd say that she'd probably be heading to see BMC."

"BMC?" Gilbert asked, puzzled.

"Big Money Chuck," Bonnie answered.

"Son of a bitch," Gilbert blurted out as he made the connection to the license plate and red truck that Kevin saw at his home.

"Gilbert? Are you okay? You don't look so good. You look as if you're seeing your life flash before your eyes."

"Bonnie, you have no idea of how clearly I see now."

Bonnie sat up straight and rubbed the palms of her hands on her thighs. "Big Money Chuck has started his business up again. He's running it out of a storefront on Laramie Street. Do you know where I'm talking about?"

"Yeah, I know the area."

"Be careful, Gilbert." Bonnie warned. "Veronica and Big Money Chuck are dangerous people."

"Don't worry. I'm not going to put myself in harm's way. I'm going to share what I've learned with the police. I'm going to let them handle it."

30

Tabetha

"Tabetha, are you sure that you know what you're doing?" Lynise asked her as Tabetha unpacked a multitude of items from the shopping mall and repacked them in a suitcase.

"I've never been more certain in my life," Tabetha answered as she placed three different bathing suits she'd purchased into a side compartment of her suitcase.

"I'm worried about you, Tabetha," Lynise said as she sat down in a chair in the room. "You have so much going on. This is a very confusing time for you. You've lost your house and precious items in a house fire set by your sister-in-law. You've separated yourself from your husband, and your ex-husband wants you back in his life so that he can chase his dream of becoming a politician that may or may not work out. Baby, you need to slow down."

"Lynise, I appreciate your concern for me. I really do. But right now I think that getting away for a little while is the best thing that I can do for my sanity."

"Fine. Get away for a while. I don't have an issue with that.

But going to Marlon's home in the Florida Keys is a bit much, don't you think?"

"No, I don't think it's a bit much. He's offered to pay for everything and has even offered me money for expenses to get back on my feet. Although the insurance company cut us a large check, it was the fact that he thought about it that made the difference," Tabetha argued.

"Tabetha, I understand. I'm just"—Lynise paused in thought—"if that's what you want to do, then you go and have yourself a good time."

"Well, I'm glad that you're supporting me instead of trying to talk me out of this," Tabetha said as she closed her suitcase. "I need this time away. I know that there are a million things going on right now, but I just don't want to deal with that drama. Gilbert created this madness, and he's going to just have to lie in the bed he's made."

"Speaking of Gilbert. What should I tell him when he calls here looking for you?"

"Tell him the truth. Tell him that I'm in the Florida Keys with Rick and Marlon."

"He's not going to like that answer," Lynise said.

"I don't really care what Gilbert likes or doesn't like right now," Tabetha said.

"When will you be back?" Lynise asked.

"In about a week. I've let them know at work that I needed additional time off, and Rick will just have to deal with catching up on his homework when he returns."

"Well, send me a postcard," Lynise said. "And you know that you're welcome to stay with me for as long as you need to."

"Thank you, Lynise. Thank you for being there for me and for being my friend."

"You're welcome." Lynise embraced Tabetha. "You just make sure to enjoy yourself and come back in one piece. Do you hear me?" Lynise said playfully.

"I hear you," Tabetha answered with a smile. At that moment, the sound of a car horn interrupted their conversation. Lynise went to the bedroom window and peeped out. "I suppose that this white limousine sitting in my driveway is for you," Lynise concluded.

"Yes. Marlon sent a car for me."

"I have to give it to the brother. He's got style."

"And money," Tabetha joked as she grabbed her suitcase from the bed and headed down to the car.

Before she left for the airport, Tabetha pulled Rick over to the side for a quick one-on-one chat. "I want you to understand something, Rick," Tabetha said to him. "Gilbert and I separated for a little while to give each other time to cool off."

"I know that, Mom. You told me this already," Rick answered.

"I just want you to know that I'm only coming down here to think about things, okay? This doesn't mean that Marlon and I are getting back together by any measure."

"Okay," Rick answered as if he really didn't want to have this type of conversation with his mother.

"Rick, you're so young. There are so many things about love, commitment, and marriage that you don't understand. Hell, I don't even understand it myself."

"Mom, we're going to Florida. Have a good time and forget all that we've been through. In case I haven't said it, I'm sorry for what I did with Veronica. I'm sorry if I hurt or disappointed you."

Tabetha smiled and embraced her son. "Thank you, I needed to hear that," Tabetha said, and let their conversation rest.

During the flight to Florida, Marlon and Rick spent time talking about football and their thoughts on what the Chicago Bears needed to do in order to have another championship season. Tabetha didn't engage them in conversation. Instead she caught a nap.

When the plane landed, they went down to baggage claim

where a man was standing with a sign with Marlon's name on it. The man escorted them to a waiting car and handled their luggage for them. As they drove out to Marlon's home, Tabetha fell in love with the beauty and calmness of the ocean.

"That looks so peaceful," Tabetha said.

"Yes, I love it down here," Marlon admitted. "Look. I'm really glad that you came. I'm not going to put any pressure on you," he said.

"Good, because that's the last thing I need right now," Tabetha informed him.

"You got it," Marlon said, backing off a bit.

"I hope that you will like the house. I spent a lot of money on it, but I think it's money well spent."

"You probably just have a shack on the beach," Tabetha teased him.

"How did you guess?" Marlon played along with her. "My beach shack doesn't even have indoor plumbing."

"Now that's going to be a problem," Tabetha continued to joke with Marlon.

When the driver pulled up to Marlon's bamboo estate gate, Tabetha's jaw fell open with awe.

"Wow, Dad. Your place is the bomb!" Rick said excitedly.

"The gate really isn't bamboo, it's actually made of long-lasting corrosion-resistant metal. The house does have a bamboo theme throughout," Marlon offered as additional information. He opened his home so that Rick and Tabetha could walk around freely while he took care of tipping the driver. When Tabetha entered the double front doors, she immediately fell in love with the bamboo staircase that spiraled to the second level of the home. She loved the open and spacious floor plan and the furniture Marlon had selected.

"How do you like it so far?" Marlon came into the house.

"This is beautiful," Tabetha admitted.

"Can you see yourself in it?" Marlon asked, testing her even though he said that he wouldn't.

"I know you didn't select this furniture," Tabetha said, purposely avoiding answering his question. "You don't have a good eye that can coordinate like this."

"You're right. I had an interior designer come in and do it for me. Where did Rick go?" Marlon asked.

"As soon as we came in, he rushed upstairs to see what it looked like."

"Come on. I'll show you around the place."

Tabetha followed Marlon through the home as he showed her the living room and dining room, which were furnished in good taste.

"Here is the kitchen," Marlon said.

"I love the floors," Tabetha said. "And the countertops." She stood in the center of the large kitchen and studied the cabinets, the faucet handles, and the appliances.

"My goodness. This is like the kitchen of my dreams," Tabetha said.

"Can you see yourself cooking in it?" Marlon asked.

"Stop that," Tabetha said. "Don't do that to me."

Marlon smiled and once again agreed to back down.

"Come on. Let me show you one of my favorite rooms," Marlon said.

"What? Your theater room?"

"No." Marlon chuckled. "The room I want to show you will blow you away."

Tabetha trailed behind Marlon up the staircase and into a bedroom.

"This is where you'll be sleeping," Marlon said as he opened the door for her to step inside.

"Oh my God." Tabetha was thunderstruck by a sunset scene painted on the ceiling. The scene was so well done that it was difficult to differentiate where the real sunset ended and the painted one began. The blues, yellows, and oranges were spectacular.

"Do you like it?" Marlon asked.

"Oh, I could just stay here forever," Tabetha said as she stepped out onto the balcony and took in the ocean view. She rested her hands on the white iron railing and allowed the warm breeze to kiss her skin.

"Come on. You haven't seen the other side of the house or the backyard yet."

"There's more?" Tabetha asked, feeling as if she'd already seen enough to make her want to stay forever.

"Yes, there is more."

"How in the hell do you keep this place clean?" Tabetha asked.

Marlon laughed. "I use a cleaning service. If you give serious consideration to my offer, you wouldn't have to worry about housecleaning ever again."

Before Tabetha could warn him again, Marlon hustled down the bamboo staircase.

"Come on. Don't be slow," he said.

Tabetha followed Marlon out to the backyard, where they found Rick.

"Mom, look at all of this," Rick said. "Look at this swimming pool! It goes on for days." Rick continued taking his unguided tour of the house.

"It's a free-form swimming pool," Marlon began explaining. "There is a bridge crossing"—Marlon pointed to it—"a whirlpool, a gazebo that has a kitchen, and bath facilities. Walk around this way with me," he said. "Over there is the beach. As you can see, you can just walk up from the beach to my backyard. And over here is one of my favorite parts. It's a huge grotto with a waterfall."

"Marlon, I thought your home back in Chicago was fabulous. But this one here. Wow. It really takes the cake. I don't know what to say." Tabetha began considering the lifestyle that Marlon was offering her. She began fantasizing about being in the house and hosting parties.

"Come on," Marlon said.

Tabetha didn't want Marlon to sense that she was giving serious consideration to getting back together with him, but based on the look in his eyes, she could tell that he was enjoying showing her all that he could do for her.

"You wouldn't have to be burdened with having more children," Marlon said as he walked her back through the house. "It may take a little time, but we could work on rekindling the romance we once had."

"Marlon," Tabetha warned again.

"Okay." Marlon gestured with his hand and remained silent until he opened another door. "This room here is the theater room."

"Wow," Tabetha said.

"Dad, this is tight!" Rick said, and he leaned back in one of the reclining chairs. "How do you turn it on?" he asked.

"Hand me that remote on the table," Marlon said. Rick handed it to him and Marlon pressed a few buttons. The one-hundred-inch screen and home theater audio system came alive.

"How come every time I come in the kitchen, you're in the kitchen eating up all the food." Comedian Johnny Winterspoon was eating grapes and talking to his son Craig.

"I love this movie," Marlon said, laughing.

"You like the movie *Friday*?" Tabetha asked, stunned.

"Yeah. This shit is funny as hell," Marlon said. "Come on, we can all watch it together and get a good laugh." Marlon sat down in one of the leather seats.

"Have a seat, girl," Marlon played with Tabetha. "It will get your mind off things."

Tabetha smiled, took a seat, and watched the film.

Tabetha had to admit to herself that she enjoyed the time she was spending down in Florida with Marlon. She was lodging in a dream house with a man who was much more self-assured and confident than Gilbert. Although she knew that Marlon had an agenda, it seemed to be overshadowed by the fantasy she was experiencing.

"This is like being on Fantasy Island," Tabetha said to herself as she stood at the kitchen countertop and scaled a pineapple. Marlon worked during the day from his home office, and Tabetha rather enjoyed bringing him refreshments from time to time. She couldn't help but think that he would enjoy slices of some sweet pineapple. She placed the slices on a tray and entered his office. Marlon was having a phone conversation but waved her in. Tabetha walked toward him, feeling herself getting hot. She found his chocolate bald head to be sexy. She placed the fruit before him and was about to leave.

"Hold on a second, Charles," Marlon said, and covered the receiver with his hand. "Thank you, Tabetha," Marlon said.

Tabetha suddenly felt herself buzzing with sensual energy. She looked at Marlon a certain way that caused him to raise an eyebrow in curiosity. Tabetha couldn't stop herself. Even if she could at that moment, she didn't think she'd allow herself to. She approached Marlon, walked around his desk, and placed a soft moist kiss on top of his chocolate head. She massaged his smooth bald head and enjoyed watching him get caught up in the blissful feeling that she was offering.

"Charles, let me call you back."

"No," Tabetha quickly whispered and stopped. "Do what you have to do. I'm going out to the pool with Rick," Tabetha said, and made a quick exit.

Late in the evening, Tabetha woke up because her womanhood was on fire and demanding attention. She wished that there was some way she could enter into Marlon's room, fuck his brains out, and come back to her room without him knowing that it was her. Tabetha decided to step out onto the balcony and allow the breeze to blow through her silk pajamas and help cool her off. She looked at the moonlight illuminating the secluded beach and suddenly thought it would be nice to go out to the shoreline, stand under the moonlight, and allow her feet to sink into the sand. Tabetha opened up the linen closet, grabbed a large beach towel, and left the house. When she arrived at the beach, she spread the towel out and sat down. For the first time in days, thoughts of Gilbert crept into her mind. She hadn't even called him and had purposely turned off her cell phone so that he couldn't reach her. She began to feel bad about doing him like that, but her feelings changed when she heard Marlon's voice from behind.

"You can't sleep either, huh?" Marlon asked.

Tabetha glanced over her shoulder in the direction of his voice. "Don't just stand back there. Come sit next to me," Tabetha welcomed him.

"I made a martini for you," Marlon said as he handed it to her.

"Thank you," Tabetha said.

Marlon sat down next to her, and they were both silent for a moment as they listened to the sound of the waves washing ashore.

"What was that about in my office today?" Marlon asked.

"It was nothing," Tabetha said.

"Well, that little nothing certainly felt good," Marlon admitted. "Are you enjoying yourself?"

"Yes. This is such a wonderful departure from my crazy life back at home," Tabetha said as she took a drink of her martini. "Oooh. That's kind of strong. What are you trying to do? Get me into bed or something?" Tabetha joked.

"Well, we were good together," Marlon reminded her.

"Yes, we were," Tabetha confirmed his statement.

"Tabetha—"

"Don't say a word, Marlon," Tabetha insisted. "Just let me enjoy this moment."

Marlon honored Tabetha's wish and sat silently with her. He scooted closer to her so that their hips and thighs were touching. Tabetha welcomed the contact. She finished off her martini and set the glass down next to her. Feeling blissfully relaxed,

Tabetha let her guard down. She wanted to ride Marlon, she couldn't deny that.

"Lie down," she told him. Marlon complied with her request. Tabetha had always wanted to fuck on the beach beneath the moonlight. She took off her pajama pants and then pulled Marlon's shorts down. Tabetha straddled him and was about to insert him inside of her.

"Wait," Marlon said, "we don't have a condom."

"I know. Just let me feel it for a minute," Tabetha whispered as her passion took hold of her. "I just want it inside of me," she said, only caring about satisfying her passion. "Oh, damn, you feel so good," Tabetha cooed as she eased herself slowly down on him. Tabetha ground her hips and allowed his manhood to sweep the walls of her sugar basin. "Oh, I like the way you feel inside of me," Tabetha said.

"About to cum," Marlon admitted.

"No. Not yet. It's too soon," Tabetha said, but it was too late. Marlon released.

31

Gilbert

"What do you mean she's in Florida with Marlon?" Gilbert wanted Lynise to explain to him why Tabetha decided to take off on a vacation to Florida without so much as asking him, inviting him, or even leaving contact information. Gilbert placed his face in his hands as Lynise offered him a slice of coffee cake and an espresso. Gilbert didn't want to accept that his marriage and relationship with Tabetha had sunk to a level so low.

"Gilbert, I know you're upset," Lynise validated his feelings. "But that's what she wanted to do. She said that she just needed a little time to get away."

"That I can understand. I don't understand why she's with Marlon, though," Gilbert said truthfully. "Lynise, you're her girlfriend. I want you to be straight with me. I want you to tell me the truth. No matter how awful it is. I can take it." Gilbert gestured with his hand. "Just tell me if she's having an affair with him."

"Gilbert, sweetie, I can't comment on that. I don't even know. I can't even speculate on it," Lynise said.

"Then why do you think she's with him?"

"Gilbert." Lynise sighed. "I hate to see you like this. You're under so much stress and pressure. There is so much going on in your life. You need to slow down a little."

"Answer my damn question, Lynise!" Gilbert suddenly exploded at her.

"Whoa! Okay," Lynise said cautiously now. "Gilbert, I think you should go home now."

"Lynise, I didn't mean to bark at you like that. This just isn't easy. I love her."

"Then you need to let her know that, Gilbert. Right now she's very vulnerable and so are you. You guys really need to work it out. And if you can't, perhaps a marriage counselor could help."

"I'll do anything to keep her, Lynise." Gilbert felt tears of regret welling up in his eyes.

"Then fight him for her, Gilbert. Don't allow his wealth to blind her from a good man who loves her unconditionally."

"When is she due back?" Gilbert asked.

"In two days," Lynise said. "I'm expecting her to return here on Sunday."

Gilbert sat silently as he ate his coffee cake and drank his espresso. When he finished, he thanked Lynise for her time.

"I'll be back on Sunday," Gilbert said.

"I'll see you then," said Lynise, and escorted him to her front door.

32

Veronica

Veronica was lying in the bed next to Big Money Chuck, who was still asleep. She was, for the first time in her life, forced to take a hard look at the lifestyle she was leading. She'd always believed that she could depend on her friends and family to bail her out whenever she got into a jam. She always believed that if she stayed away from them for a little while after she'd messed up, they'd eventually forgive her and allow her back into their lives. Never in her darkest dreams did she ever believe that they'd all turn their backs on her the way they did. Never in her wildest dreams did she ever consider that one day she may not have a place to turn to. It wasn't easy for her to come crawling back to Big Money Chuck after what he'd done to her. *He literally wanted to kill me,* Veronica mentally said to herself. Having to crawl back to Big Money Chuck lowered her pride and self-worth. Veronica felt worthless. She felt like trash, and Chuck treated her accordingly; but for some reason she felt as if she deserved what she was getting. Veronica was, for the first time in her life, feeling lost, dazed, and confused. Chuck turned over in his sleep and turned his back to her. For some reason when he did that, she began to cry. She tried to cry silently, but her emotions were getting the best of her. Veronica didn't like feeling this way and wanted the pain in her heart to stop. She began crying uncontrollably again as she thought about how Big Money Chuck treated her when she came to the door of his apartment and asked for help. Even though he'd tried to kill her, she had no other place to turn.

"Look who's back from the dead, boys. It's the ghost of Christmas past. You look like shit," Chuck snarled at her.

"I need a place to stay, baby," Veronica pleaded with him.

"Do you see this, boys?" Chuck said to the crew he'd put together to rob Gilbert's house. They appeared to be playing a card game.

"I literally tried to take this wench out of this world, and like a stray dog she comes crawling back to me with her head held down and her tail tucked between her legs. You're not so big and bad now, are you?" Chuck laughed at her.

"Baby, I made a mistake. That's all. I won't do it again. Please let me stay with you for a minute. It's cold out on the streets," Veronica said. "Plus, I haven't eaten anything. And the homeless shelter is overrun with men. They only give priority housing to women with children. I'm afraid to stay there."

"Plus you look sick as hell," Chuck said.

"I still have smoke in my lungs, Chuck. I've been coughing up black shit for the past few days."

"So now you want me to have mercy on you? Is that it?"

"Just let me stay here for a few days. I'll do anything. I just need to get off the street." Veronica hated herself for saying that. She remembered the sinister grin that formed on Chuck's face when she said she'd do anything. She knew that she'd just given him a license to treat her any damn way he felt.

She turned her back to him to muffle her tears of pain. She thought about getting high. *It would help to ease my pain,* she thought. Veronica sat up in the bed and then went into the bathroom. She closed the door behind her and slid down to the floor.

"I'm so sorry, Gilbert," she said to herself. "I'm so sorry."

At that moment, Veronica heard several loud crashing sounds and voices yelling.

"Get out of the bed now!"

Veronica stood up, opened the bathroom door slightly, and saw the police in full armor pointing their weapons at Big Money Chuck.

"Oh God." Veronica began to panic as she tried to remain as quiet as she could.

"Check the bathroom," she heard one of the officers yell. Veronica closed her eyes tightly and awaited her fate.

33

Tabetha

"Do you want to know what happened?" Gilbert asked softly. He and Tabetha were sitting inside his sedan, which was parked in Lynise's driveway. Tabetha couldn't look Gilbert in the eyes, so she focused on an airplane that was floating across the sky. She wondered whether the people on board were going or coming.

"Do you want to talk at all?" Gilbert asked as calmly as he could. It was very difficult for him to restrain his outrage, but he was managing it well.

"Yes," Tabetha answered him. She'd decided to let him speak first before she told him that she wanted a divorce. She concluded that it would be easier to let him speak first while she searched for the words he needed to hear.

"I turned her in," Gilbert said. "I found a person who knew where Veronica was and gave that information to the police. She and the crew she was working with were captured."

"That's good to know," Tabetha said as she tried to control her tears from spilling over.

"They, uh, found our computers and some other valuables as

well. Veronica"—Gilbert paused and then swallowed hard—"she was going to clean us out," Gilbert admitted. "She'd stolen financial information from our home and was going to clean out your 401K and Rick's college fund."

Tabetha huffed as she swiveled her head disapprovingly. She felt her nose beginning to run, so she opened up her purse and removed a tissue to prevent it from happening.

"I'm sorry, Tabetha. I made a major mistake. I should have listened to you. I should of—" Gilbert paused.

"If I, could I, would I, should I," Tabetha remarked as she thought about an old tune. "What is she being charged with?" Tabetha asked.

"Criminal trespassing, burglary, and arson," Gilbert answered.

"Have you spoken to her? Did you ask her why?" Tabetha glared at Gilbert.

"I went to see her to ask that same question. But she refused to visit with me. She sent a note back through the guard that read, 'Go away.' " Gilbert held his head down for a moment before he began speaking again. "I've been doing a lot of thinking, Tabetha. I've been thinking about how I've been walking around with blinders on. And about how I didn't want to really see things the way they were. I'm the blame for all of this," Gilbert said. "Had I not moved Veronica in, none of this would have happened."

"Gilbert, I have a question that I've always wanted to know the answer to," Tabetha said.

"What?"

"What was going on between you two? I've always sensed that there was something very unusual about your relationship. Why were you always on her side even when you knew that she was wrong?"

"I felt as if I owed her my life, Tabetha," Gilbert answered truthfully. "Years ago, we came home from school and our mother's boyfriend was beating the shit out of her. I mean, he was really whipping her ass. I jumped in the fight to prevent him from hurting her more. He got the best of me and was literally killing me with his bare hands. Veronica was brave enough to hit him with a skillet. She almost killed him with one swift blow." Gilbert was silent for a moment before speaking again. "Afterward I made a promise to her that I'd always be there for her the way she was for me. And I meant every word that I said. My word is gold, Tabetha. In my heart, I knew that Veronica had issues, but I honestly thought that I could save her. I wanted to save her," Gilbert said.

"You couldn't save her, Gilbert," Tabetha said. "The woman didn't even want to help herself."

"I know," Gilbert admitted. "But I still had to try. Just like now. I'm trying to salvage our relationship. I'll do whatever it takes."

Gilbert's words sliced right through Tabetha's heart. The renegade emotions that she was keeping at bay had gotten loose, and her tears began to flow. Gilbert put his arm around her in an effort to comfort her.

"No, stop." Tabetha pushed him away from her.

"We're not going to make it, Gilbert," Tabetha said. "I want a divorce."

"It's Marlon, isn't it?" Gilbert answered his own question. "I'm not going to let him win, Tabetha," Gilbert said with absolute conviction. "I'm going to fight for you. Because I know that in your heart you love me the way that I love you," Gilbert said as he held his insecurities at bay. "Look. Here's an example of how much I love you." Gilbert forced Tabetha to look at him. He trapped her gaze and spoke truthfully.

"I don't care what you did with him down in Florida, and I really don't want to know. I forgive you, Tabetha. I will never mention it again."

"Gilbert—" Tabetha tried to speak.

"No, you listen to me." Gilbert wouldn't allow her to interrupt him. He swallowed hard. "I'm not granting you a divorce.

When I took the vow and said 'For better or for worse,' I meant it."

"Gilbert. I hear you. I really do. But—"

"Shhh," Gilbert said. "We can work through this."

Tabetha held her comment for the moment. She'd concluded that it would be better at that point to convey her decision through action rather than words.

34

Gilbert

Gilbert determined that the key to proving to Tabetha that his commitment to her was golden was to start romancing her. He wanted to remind her that being with him was fun and worthwhile. He wanted to make her feel special, appreciated, and loved. He returned to Lynise's house the following week after work with reservations for dinner at Gibson's Steak House and tickets to a Tyler Perry stage play. When Lynise opened the door, she greeted him with a hug.

"How is it going, Lynise?" Gilbert asked.

"Good," she answered.

"Is my lady here?" Gilbert asked.

"Yeah, she's in there," Lynise said, studying Gilbert.

"I have plans for that woman in there," Gilbert said as he entered the house.

"Well, personally, I'm glad you do. She needs to be saved from herself," Lynise whispered just as Tabetha entered the room. Gilbert wanted to ask Lynise exactly what she meant by the comment but decided he'd ask her for clarification at a later time.

Tabetha and Gilbert went to dinner and enjoyed their meal,

then headed over to the Arie Crown Theater, which was situated inside the McCormick Place Convention Center on Lake Shore Drive. They enjoyed the humorous entertainment of the stage play, which featured crazy-like-a-fox family members with personal agendas. Tabetha and Gilbert related with the larger-than-life characters on many levels. After the play, Tabetha and Gilbert walked back through the convention center toward the underground parking garage. Tabetha's mind drifted for a moment as they walked, because her thoughts were on Marlon. She hadn't been in contact with him much since they'd returned. His schedule was hectic and didn't allow much time for her. She accepted that for the moment, concluding that he was doing what he needed to do in order to be successful. She didn't like having to take a backseat to his work, but she figured that soon there would be a small window of time that he could devote to working on their relationship. However, in the back of her mind, uncertainty and suspicion were lurking about.

"Did you enjoy yourself?" Gilbert asked.

"Yes, it was nice, Gilbert," Tabetha admitted.

"Good. Because I like spending time with you," Gilbert said. "I know that lately things have been a little crazy, but I want you to know just how I feel about being with you."

Tabetha didn't respond to Gilbert, because she was trying to not build up his hopes of getting back together. She'd only agreed to spend time with him to keep her thoughts from focusing on Marlon and what he was doing without her there. Her mind played tricks on her sometimes, because it told her that he was gallivanting around with other women. But she nixed the notion several times, especially after his poor initial performance in Florida. She couldn't believe that Marlon, after all this time, had turned out to be a minute man in the bedroom. *I'll just have to work with that,* she thought.

"Can I take you by the house?" Gilbert asked. "The construction company has completed its repairs, and I've moved back in. The place looks like new," Gilbert said.

"Sure," Tabetha agreed. She was interested in seeing how well they put the place back together. In her mind, she wanted to either sell it or let Gilbert buy her out.

When Tabetha walked into her old home, she was pleased with the job the contractor had done.

"I had them redo all of the kitchen countertops, cabinets, and floors for you," Gilbert said. "I know that you've been wanting to update this kitchen for some time and thought you'd appreciate having it done."

"It looks nice," Tabetha said as she touched the surface of the countertop. Tabetha thought that she'd emotionally detached herself from the house, but as she walked through it, her feelings changed.

"The basement has been redone nicely as well," Gilbert said. "I paid a little extra for the contractor to make some custom bookshelves. I know how much you like to read. Hell, let me just be honest. I pretty much had them rebuild the house with you in mind. I wanted to update everything that you wanted."

Tabetha's words got trapped in her throat. She couldn't speak, so she just nodded her head approvingly.

"Come on upstairs," Gilbert said. "I want to show you something."

Tabetha trailed behind Gilbert and followed him into their redesigned and refurnished bedroom.

"You got the bedroom set that I wanted," Tabetha said. "Oh, this looks just the way I pictured it."

Gilbert smiled, feeling that he'd satisfied her.

"Here, come into the bathroom." Gilbert showed her the new whirlpool bath he had had installed.

"Nice." Tabetha smiled. "Very nice," she said, suddenly feeling different about Gilbert. She walked back out into the bedroom and looked at the new furniture.

"The rest of the house isn't furnished yet. I did spend some of the money on something extra special for you," Gilbert said as he went into the closet. Tabetha was now feeling awful about having to tell Gilbert that his efforts were in vain.

"I picked this up for you." Gilbert placed a new black full-length mink coat on the bed for her.

"Gilbert!" Tabetha couldn't believe it. Her heart began to beat at a fast pace.

"Try it on," he insisted. "I know it's the right size because it's the same size as the one I was supposed to get for Christmas."

Tabetha tried on the coat, which fit her excellently.

"Oh, you do look stunning in that," Gilbert said.

Tabetha walked into the bathroom to look at herself in the mirror.

"I did all of this for you, baby," Gilbert said. He approached her from behind and began kissing her on the neck. Tabetha's heart and body betrayed her by giving in easily to Gilbert's soft lips on her neck. She exposed a little more flesh on her neck and allowed herself to enjoy what she was feeling.

"Gilbert wait," Tabetha said, stopping him. "Give me a moment, okay? All of this is overwhelming to me right now. Just give me a moment in here alone, okay?"

"Okay," Gilbert said, not putting any pressure on her. He exited the bathroom, and Tabetha shut the door. She was at a crossroads. Her heart and body wanted to be with Gilbert, but her mind was focused on another man. She didn't understand why things were so complicated with her. She looked at herself in the mirror and exhaled. She was aching to be made love to. That much she knew. And she wanted to make love to Gilbert. She wanted him. Without further ado, Tabetha removed the fur coat and got undressed. She took a shower, toweled herself off, and then put on only the fur coat. She entered the bedroom where Gilbert was resting on the bed.

"Wow," Gilbert said.

"I've always wanted to make love to you with my fur coat on," Tabetha said.

"And I've always wanted you to have a fur coat," Gilbert said.

"Get undressed, Gilbert," Tabetha ordered him. "Go take a shower and then come back in here."

Gilbert followed Tabetha's instructions and then returned to the bedroom where she was waiting for him. Gilbert dimmed the lights and walked over to Tabetha, who was lying on her back. Gilbert positioned himself above her, gazed into her eyes lovingly, and began kissing her. Their tongues hungrily chased each other. Tabetha opened her legs as she pulled him down on top of her.

"Hold me," she requested as she held on to him as if her life depended on his strong embrace. After a long moment of hugging, Tabetha felt desire and wanted to be gratified. She situated Gilbert onto his back and then straddled him. She took his manhood and stroked it up and down a few times to be certain of his readiness. She swept the head of his manhood up and down the entrance of her paradise. She was on edge with anticipation. Finally, she lowered herself down on him gently. Gilbert knew her body well, and she adored the way he caressed her breasts.

"Oh, baby," Gilbert cooed as passion rushed through him. "It's been so long."

Tabetha rode his shaft slowly and sensually. She was stirring up an orgasm that was long overdue.

"Rub my ass, Gilbert," Tabetha requested. His strong hands grabbed and massaged her ass, and she loved the feel of his touch. She looked down at Gilbert and gazed into his eyes.

"I've missed you so much," Gilbert whispered to her. His words were comforting and sweet.

"Hit it, baby," Tabetha said. "Hit it."

Gilbert knew exactly what she meant by that and thrust himself deeper inside of her. Tabetha climaxed instantaneously. Her orgasm was so strong it placed her in a euphoric state of mind.

"Come on, baby," Tabetha said. "I want you to get yours."

Tabetha was so wet. Every time she had an orgasm, he could feel her sweet nectar ooze down the head of his manhood.

"Oh, how I love the way you feel inside of me," Tabetha said as another wave of passion consumed her. "Oh, you feel so good, Gilbert," she said.

"I love you, Tabetha. I love you more than you'll ever know," he said, then used more powerful thrusts to show her physically the level of passion he held for her.

"Baby, I'm going to get it," Gilbert said.

"Right there, Gilbert," Tabetha responded. "We'll get there together." She matched his powerful thrusts with her own. Finally, they both reached the point of no return together.

35

Tabetha

"I'm late," Tabetha told Lynise when she arrived at her place after work.

"What? On a bill?" Lynise asked, missing Tabetha's point.

"No, girl. I'm late," Tabetha said with a tone that Lynise understood.

"You're bullshitting," Lynise stated, not believing her.

"Girl, I wish I was," Tabetha said. "I stopped at the pharmacy and got a pregnancy test."

"Did you take it?" Lynise asked.

"I'm afraid to," Tabetha admitted as she sat down on the sofa.

"Well, you have to take it to find out," Lynise said. "Don't go getting yourself all worked up. You could be late because of all the drama going on in your life. Stress will throw your cycle way off," Lynise said.

"I know that," Tabetha said. "I just didn't want to be alone when I took it."

"Go do what you have to do," said Lynise. "I'm here for you no matter what."

Tabetha went into the bathroom and followed the instructions

on the home pregnancy test box. She waited for the results, which
came back positive. Tabetha came out of the bathroom and entered the family room where Lynise was.

"Oh shit," Lynise said. She knew the answer based solely on
the look etched on Tabetha's face.

"I don't believe this shit," Tabetha uttered. "This shit isn't
right. What is this, some kind of fucking joke? Some freakish
act of nature?" Tabetha was very uspet.

"Calm down, Tabetha. Let's deal with one thing at a time.
Does Gilbert know yet?"

"I don't think it's Gilbert's," Tabetha said, looking Lynise directly in the eyes. Tabetha noticed how Lynise's face seemed to
lose color.

"You think it's Marlon's?"

Tabetha nodded her head in the affirmative.

"Oh, Jesus, Tabetha."

"Don't say that." Tabatha didn't like the tone in her friend's
voice.

"What are you going to do?"

"How in the hell should I know? I just found out," Tabetha
snapped. "Why did this happen now? Why? Why? Why?" She
repeated her question as if some heavenly being was going to respond with an answer.

Marlon had been avoiding Tabetha, claiming that he was
working and just didn't have the time to speak with her about
his plans for their relationship. Tabetha decided that he'd pushed
her to the side long enough, and it was time that they had a serious face-to-face meeting. She drove to his home during evening
hours to visit with Rick and him. When she arrived at the gate,
Rick allowed her access onto the premises. As she drove down
Marlon's long winding driveway, she spotted Rick standing at
the door waiting for her.

"Hey, Mom." Rick came out to the car to greet her. He gave
her a strong hug, and then they both went inside.

"Where is your father?" Tabetha asked.

"He's on the other side of the house somewhere. I'm not allowed over there while he's working." Rick mocked his father's words.

"Well, take me over to where he is. He and I need to have a serious conversation," Tabetha said.

"Is that a good thing or a bad thing?" Rick asked.

"I don't know yet," Tabetha said.

Rick escorted his mother to the other side of the estate, where Marlon claimed to be working. They entered his office and were both thunderstruck when they found Marlon embraced in a passionate kiss with another woman.

"Hey!" Marlon barked at Rick. "What the hell are you doing coming up in here without knocking first?"

"Hey, I didn't know. My bad, man," Rick answered.

"Rick." Tabetha swallowed hard as she gazed into his eyes. "Go back to the other side of the house. Your father and I have some unfinished business to discuss."

Rick left the room but didn't go over to the other side of the house like he was instructed to.

"I was wondering when the real Marlon would show up," Tabetha said. To her surprise, she was calm about discovering that Marlon had another woman.

"Marlon, who is she?" asked the woman, who was very young.

"Robbing the cradle, are we, Marlon?" Tabetha criticized him. "Don't worry, missy. Apparently I'm nothing to him."

"Sit down for minute while I handle this," Marlon said to the woman.

"Tabetha, let's talk in the other room," Marlon requested.

"No." Tabetha denied his request. "What I have to say can be heard by her. That way she'll know what type of low-down slimy son of a bitch you are."

"Tabetha, don't you go there with me or I swear I'll knock your ass out."

Tabetha saw the murderous look in his eyes.

"You'd better not place a single hand on her," Tabetha heard Rick's voice behind her.

"Marlon, if you hit me, you'll be placing your hand on me and your unborn child."

"Unborn child?" Marlon glared at Tabetha with an ugly expression. "What the fuck are you talking about?"

"I'm pregnant, Marlon."

"Oh, come off it, Tabetha. You're too old to be pulling that high school bullshit."

Tabetha noticed that Marlon's chest was heaving with contempt. He swiftly invaded her personal space and glared down at her. "If this is about trying to extort money from me, I will go through hell before I give you one red cent."

"Hey, Dad." Rick came over. "You need to calm down, man," Rick said, pulling his mother out of harm's way.

"Why did you even bother me, Marlon?" Tabetha's emotions suddenly got the best of her. "Why did you even act like you wanted to get back together? Huh? What was that all about?"

"The deal is off, Tabetha! I thought you'd get the hint when I kept blowing you off." Marlon's words were as cold as an arctic wind.

"What?" Tabetha asked, not fully comprehending what he was saying.

"Look, I offered you a way out of your miserable life with the bus driver in order to pursue my political goals. That deal didn't go through. So that makes our deal null and void. You knew what I wanted you back for. So don't bring your ass in here acting like you're fucking shocked. I know I said you'd be stuck with me if I lost my campaign. That was a lie. I don't want you any more than hell wants heat."

"You can't toy with me like that!" Tabetha was outraged.

"I just did. Now get the hell out of my house."

"Hey, you don't have to talk to her like that!" Rick got upset with his father and his use of language.

"And take Rick with you," Marlon said, showing just how cold and heartless he was toward both of them. Tabetha and Rick stared at Marlon in shock. "What are you two standing there for? Do I need to get a security team up here to drag your sorry asses out of here?"

"Let's go, Rick." Tabetha began walking backward out of the room. "There's nothing here for us. We don't need him at all," she said as she and Rick left.

"He can't do us like this!" Rick shouted. "I should go back and kick his ass!"

"Rick, calm down," Tabetha said. "I want to kick his ass too but that's not going to change or solve this situation. Believe me. It's taking every ounce of strength that I have to restrain myself," Tabetha admitted as she and Rick got in her sedan and drove off.

36

Gilbert

Gilbert took a seat in the court room at the Cook County Criminal Court building on the corner of Twenty-Sixth and California streets. He wanted to get one last look at Veronica as the charges against her were read. The section of the courtroom where the defendants, plaintiffs, judge, jury, and sheriff's deputy were situated was enclosed by bulletproof glass so that no one could take justice into their own hands.

"All rise." Gilbert heard a voice come over the speaker system. The judge entered the chamber, followed by the prosecution team, Veronica's attorney, and finally Veronica, who was wearing a bright yellow jumpsuit. Gilbert captured her gaze for a brief moment but that was it. She refused to look at him anymore. After the charges against her were read, a court date was set. Veronica was then escorted back to jail. Gilbert left the courtroom feeling a sense of closure. Veronica was going to pay her debt to society, and whether or not he was there for her didn't matter to her. He saw that now and knew that he'd never get an answer to why she did what she did.

* * *

Gilbert had just finished his shift and pulled his bus up to a designated spot and left it there for the next driver. As he walked toward his car, he heard someone call out his name.

"Hey, Gilbert, wait up." Gilbert turned in the direction of the voice and saw Rick approaching him.

"Hey, Rick," Gilbert said, surprised to see him. "What are you doing here?"

"I came to see you," Rick said.

"Oh yeah?" Gilbert said, a bit surprised.

"I want to talk to you about something."

"All right," Gilbert said. "Hey, do you want to grab a bite at Al's Italian beef?"

"Ah, man." Rick smiled. "That sounds like a plan to me."

During the drive to the restaurant, Rick began talking. "I owe you a big apology," Rick admitted. "Man, this is hard."

Gilbert was surprised to hear an apology coming from Rick. "Apology for what?" Gilbert asked, wanting Rick to open up more.

"Man." Rick paused as he got his words in order. "For being such an idiot. I mean, it's like I was putting you down because you weren't like my real dad. You didn't have a lot of money, and you couldn't get me stuff. But what you were offering me was much more valuable. I never understood what people meant when they said that there was a difference between a daddy and a father."

Gilbert listened as Rick swallowed hard.

"You're a good guy," Rick said. "You were always there, and you cared about me. My daddy, on the other hand, is a cold-hearted son of a bitch."

"I was wondering when you'd see that," Gilbert said, suddenly filled with pride. "I'm so glad that you've learned this lesson. I know that I don't say it as often as I should, but I love you, Rick. I'll always be there for you."

"Yeah, I know," Rick said. "I heard that the house is finished."

"Yes, it is," Gilbert said, turning into the parking lot of the restaurant.

"Are you ready to come home?" Gilbert asked.

"Yeah." Rick nodded his head. "I'm so ready. I can't deal with staying at Lynise's house or sleeping on the lumpy sofa."

"You know we still have to get one more family member back into the house with us," Gilbert said.

"I know," Rick answered. "Did she tell you what happened?"

"Yeah. I know about the pregnancy," Gilbert said.

37

Tabetha

"I was so stupid, Gilbert," Tabetha said to him. "I'm just some old foolish and shallow woman." Tabetha was beating herself up. "Here I was being so critical about you walking around with blinders on, and I had on my own set."

Gilbert listened to Tabetha, who was reflecting on her faults and behavior.

"I was going to get rid of it. But I thought about it long and hard and decided that I can't do that. If it's meant for me to have this child, then that's what I'm going to do," Tabetha said. "If you want to divorce me, I won't fight you. I'm strong and can handle your decision." Tabetha tried not to cry. "God, I can't believe how dumb I was."

"Tabetha, stop beating yourself up. You're not dumb."

"Oh no, Gilbert, I was very dumb. I had a man who loved me with all of his heart. And I wanted to trade him in for a man who only loved his money and what it could buy."

"That's the flip side of money, I suppose," Gilbert said. "You can't buy real love with it. I once told you that when I married you and took the vow that said for better or for worse, I meant every word. And I'm going to tell you that again. Tabetha, I'm with you always. I promise not to take you for granted anymore. I promise to stay with you through thick and thin. But most of all, when push comes to shove, I'll be by your side. Come home, baby," Gilbert said. "If that baby is a part of you, it's a part of me."

"But you might change your mind, Gilbert. You may hate me in the long run. You may hate the baby too."

"I don't hate anyone, Tabetha. I don't hate you, I don't hate Rick. Hell, I don't even hate Veronica. I'm not that type of man."

"Do you really mean that?" Tabetha asked as she looked into his eyes and searched for his true feelings.

"Damn right I mean it," Gilbert answered.

Tabetha began crying and hugged him tightly to release all of the emotions that she was holding in.

38

Gilbert

"Come on, baby, push!" Gilbert encouraged Tabetha.

"I'm too old to push this baby out!" Tabetha screamed out.

"Come on, Tabetha. You can do it." Gilbert was excited.

"This baby is breaking my bones!" Tabetha complained as she gave another hard push.

"I can see the head, baby," Gilbert said. "The baby has curly hair."

"One more push should do it," said the doctor.

"This had better be the last one!" Tabetha snarled at the doctor as she gave one final push.

"There we go," said the doctor as he and the nurse quickly took care of cleaning up the healthy newborn, who began crying.

"It's a girl, Tabetha," Gilbert said excitedly.

"Okay, Dad," said the doctor. "Let's cut the cord."

Gilbert took pride in cutting the umbilical cord of his new daughter. The nurse put the baby in a receiving blanket and gave her to Tabetha so that she could bond with her daughter.

* * *

The following morning, Tabetha was sitting up in her bed bottle-feeding her daughter while Gilbert took photos.

"Enough with the pictures, Gilbert. I look horrible."

"No, you don't. You look beautiful."

Tabetha ignored Gilbert as she studied their daughter's features.

"Trina doesn't look anything like Rick did as a baby," Tabetha said.

"No, she doesn't." Gilbert's voice was full of pride. He pulled a photo out of his jersey pocket. "She looks just like the baby in this photo." Gilbert gave Tabetha the picture. The photo was of Gilbert as a baby. He had a head full of black curly hair just like Trina.

"Trina is without question my baby girl," Gilbert said. "We'll get a test to confirm it, but I really don't care one way or the other, because I am going to love and spoil this baby."

At that moment, Rick and the nurse entered the room.

"Excuse me," Gilbert said to the nurse, "would you please take a picture of the four of us together?"

"Sure," said the nurse.

Gilbert, Tabetha, Rick, and Trina all posed for the photo.

"Oh, you guys look like such a happy family," the nurse commented as she clicked the photo.

Rip and Burn
on the computer.